*As lines,*
*Themse[...]*
*But [...]*
*Though [...]*

"Is that the definition of love?" Julie asked, wiping away tears with her fingers. "Two parallel lines that can never meet?"

"Not necessarily," Lord Canfield said with a smile, taking note of how the sun was haloing her hair.

"I think there may be much truth in it," she said, sighing sadly and lowering her head.

"Come now, my dear," he said gently. He reached out and lifted her chin again. "The parallel lines will bend for you, I promise."

Something about her—liquid eyes, the parted lips, the sun-tipped hair . . . he would never know what—aroused in him an irresistible impulse. Almost without thought, he leaned toward her and kissed her mouth. It was a gentle kiss, so soft she did not jump or pull away; she merely made a little sound in her throat, and her hand came up to his cheek.

The touch aroused him even more. Before he quite realized what he was doing, there in the mote-filled sunshine, he lifted himself up on his knees and pulled her into a tight embrace, his mouth never leaving hers . . .

# Matched Pairs

## Elizabeth Mansfield

JOVE BOOKS, NEW YORK

MATCHED PAIRS

A Jove Book / published by arrangement with
the author

PRINTING HISTORY
Jove edition / January 1996

ISBN: 0-515-11785-4

A JOVE BOOK®
Jove Books are published by the Berkley Publishing Group,
200 Madison Avenue, New York, New York 10016.
JOVE and the "J" design are trademarks
belonging to Jove Publications, Inc.

PRINTED IN THE UNITED STATES OF AMERICA

10  9  8  7  6  5  4  3  2  1

Every couple is not a pair.

—*Old English Adage*

# Matched Pairs

# 1

TRIS DID NOT ANTICIPATE A QUARREL WITH JULIE about his plans to wed another girl. If there was one thing about which he and Julie were in complete agreement, it was that they would never wed each other. Nevertheless, he felt uneasy as he paced round the summerhouse, the capes of his greatcoat flapping in the chilly March wind. *Not that there's any reason for unease,* he told himself. *We've always sworn that we would never marry, no matter what our mothers said.*

This interview would not have been necessary at all if, nineteen years ago when Juliet Branscombe was born and he, Tristram Enders, was merely three years old, their mothers had not officially betrothed them. But they had. The two mothers, with wicked premeditation, had had the banns read at church and had even sent an announcement to the *Times.* Later, when the two victims were old enough to understand what their mothers had done, they had quite understandably rebelled. Since they were more like squabbling siblings than lovers, marriage between them was out of the question. "We don't have to comply with a compact in which we had no part," Tris would often declare.

"Just because our mothers arranged it," Julie would agree, "it doesn't have to follow that we must accept it."

Tris truly believed that arranging a betrothal between children was ridiculous. "No one makes birth-matches anymore," he'd said more than once.

"Royalty, perhaps," Julie would add, "but no one else."

"It's been out of fashion for centuries."

1

"Leg-shackling children at birth! Medieval, that's what it is!"

Thus they'd made a pact that, when the time was right, they would join forces and reject their mothers' plan. That was the one matter on which they'd been in agreement for years. So there was no reason for Tris to feel so deucedly uncomfortable now. No reason at all.

He turned and peered out past the hedges that separated Enders Hall's north field from Larchwood, the Branscombes' property. A stile that provided an opening between the hedges gave him a view of the grounds leading to the rear lawns of Larchwood, but there was no sign of human movement anywhere. What was keeping the girl?

He'd sent her a note asking her to meet him at the Enders' summerhouse, but he hadn't told her why. He'd chosen the summerhouse for the meeting because it was a place he knew would be safe from prying eyes. It stood at the far corner of the Enders' northernmost field, where the slope of the land kept it from being seen from either house. In summer the structure was beautiful; graceful and delicate, it was a cool retreat, with its open sides shaded by flowering vines that covered its latticed balustrades and its carved posts holding up a sloping hexagonal roof. But in other seasons it looked bare, as it did now. Today—on a day so chill and gray it was more like February than March—the place was depressing. The ornamental trees and shrubs that shaded it in summer were still bare of leaves, and there was not yet a sign of flowering on the vines. There was not a touch of color anywhere. Tris shivered as the winds, still wintry-sharp, blew a swarm of dead leaves about his legs.

Expelling an impatient breath, he leaned against a post and looked about him. The rolling lawns of his family home were just beginning to shed their winter dullness. Bits of green sprouts could be faintly seen pushing up beneath the frost-dimmed grass and glimmering along the edges of the shubbery. *I shall be in London when spring comes,* he thought with a momentary twinge of sadness. *I'll miss seeing the colors burst forth.*

The thought brought his primary problem right back to his consciousness. Why was he so reluctant to tell Julie what was on his mind? There was no reason to believe that she would not be in complete sympathy with his intentions. She'd always felt as he did on the subject of their mothers' oddities.

Tris recalled a conversation he'd had with Julie after his mother had ordered him to give the girl a heart-shaped locket on her seventeenth birthday. Julie accepted the gift without comment, but she'd known perfectly well that the gesture had been forced on him. Later, when they were alone, they laughed about it. "How dreadfully sentimental our mothers are," Julie said, carelessly swinging the silver bauble by its chain. "Did they really believe I'd be so moved by a trinket that I'd fall in love with you?"

"They're sentimental fools," he said, "both swooning over courtly love and chivalric behavior. I can't convince them that I'm not a white knight."

"Nor am I Elaine of Astolat. As if a heart-shaped bauble could inspire love! I sometimes think they actually *believe* in nonsense like charms and amulets and talismans. The trouble is that they're both too fond of literary romance."

"Fond? They're positively looney!" Tris declared. "One can see it in the names they gave us. Tristram, indeed. What sensible mother would name a son Tristram? I'm surprised your mother didn't name you Isolde."

"Heaven forbid!" Julie gasped. "Juliet is bad enough. What would you have done if your mama had named you Romeo!"

Tris shuddered at the very thought. "Romeo! I'd have been laughed out of school!"

Conversations like those did not mean that Juliet Branscombe and Tristram Enders were close friends. In truth, they often wondered if they really liked each other. Having been brought up together on adjoining estates and encouraged to do everything together—play together, study together, attend church services together, celebrate birthdays and holidays together—each claimed the other was often not only uninteresting but positively irritating. The one matter on which they agreed was that they could never have been, were not now, and could never be, lovers.

"We know each other too well," Tris would often remark.

"Much too well," Julie would second. "There's no excitment."

"No suspense."

"No mystery. Not the slightest tinge of mystery."

Thus they were in complete agreement that a match between them was not to be thought of. So there was no reason for him to feel like a scoundrel for having fallen in love with someone else. Julie would not care. She didn't want him anyway. He was quite certain of th—

"Tris?"

He turned in time to see Julie climbing over the top of the stile. The girl was her usual disheveled self. Her yellow bonnet had blown from her head and was hanging against her back by its green ribbons, thus allowing long strands of hair to blow wildly about her face. Her cheeks were ruddy from the cold wind, and the shabby old dull-green shawl, which she was clutching to her throat with one gloved hand, blended perfectly with the dead grass of the lawn behind her.

Julie jumped down from the stile with a clumsy thump of her muddy boots and waved his note at him. "What's amiss?" she asked as she hurried toward the wide wooden steps of the summerhouse. "I had to tell Mama a fib about where I was going."

"Nothing's amiss." Tris frowned down at her uplifted face in disapproval. She was a pretty little thing, with that silky auburn hair and those light hazel eyes that always seemed to be seeing something in another world. Any man would find her lovely if she had the least idea of how to show herself off. But he would not say that aloud; he rarely said anything kind to her. "Put that bonnet back on your head," he growled in disgust. "You've let the wind make a fair hodgepodge of your hair. We may have to disentangle the strands from your eyelashes."

"Thank you, sir, you flatter me as usual," she responded dryly. "You, on the other hand, look very fine. You haven't dressed that way just for me, I'd wager."

"You'd win that wager. But never mind my clothes. What dreadful fib did you tell your mother?"

"I said I was going to call at the vicarage. Mrs. Weekes is, fortunately for us, ailing."

"Mrs. Weekes is always ailing. Call on her before you go home, and then you'll not have fibbed."

"That, Tris Enders, is a liar's reasoning," she retorted. "A fib's a fib." Then she looked up at him inquiringly. "If nothing's amiss, why did you send me this cryptic note?"

"I wanted to speak to you before I left."

She blinked. "Oh? Are you going away?"

"I'm going back to London this afternoon."

"Again?"

He nodded. The uneasy feeling, suddenly returning, caused him to look down at his boots.

"To see *her,* I suppose," Julie said, peering at him suspiciously.

"Her?" His eyes shot up to hers, his brows lifted in amazement.

"Your Miss Smallwood."

"Good God! You *guessed?*"

Julie shrugged. "Well, your one and only letter from town was so full of her . . ."

"Oh."

The girl studied him with interest. She'd known him all her life but she'd never known him to care for a girl. Had he actually fallen in love at last? "Since you've been home less than a fortnight," she ventured carefully, not wishing to sound as if she were prying, "I must assume you are so impatient to return to town because you have a real *tendre* for your Miss Smallwood."

"I wish I *could* call her mine," Tris said ruefully. "Cleo has yet to accept me."

Julie's eyes widened. "You've already *asked* her?" The matter must have progressed farther than she thought!

"No, not yet. That's what I intend to do, however, when I get back to town. Ask her."

"Oh. I see."

Though this response was given in one brief, quiet exhalation of breath, Julie was finding Tris's news staggering. Tris was truly in love! And intending to wed! Astounding!

Julie hadn't ever given thought to what such a development might mean to *her.* She'd always found Tris irritatingly high-handed, argumentative and critical, but though they were longtime adversaries, she had no good reason not to wish him happy. *Good-bye, good luck and God bless,* she ought to say to him. Why not?

But of course it was not that simple. There would be consequences that were certain to be unpleasant, not the least of which would be to face their mothers at last about the birth-betrothal. Facing their mothers would be far from easy. Tris's mother, Lady Phyllis, was soft-voiced and sweet, but she wore an iron determination inside her velvet glove. And her own mother, loud and overbearing, would surely make a scene. Julie hated scenes. The prospect of this one was so dreadful to contemplate that it tightened her chest.

Trying to catch her breath, she sat back against the balustrade and studied Tris with a furrowed brow. He was changing right before her eyes. He seemed to have suddenly become older than his twenty-two years. His face seemed leaner and less irritatingly mischievous than it had been just yesterday, when they'd been forced to dine with their mothers at the Branscombes' table. She couldn't even detect that annoying dimple that always appeared in his left cheek when he smiled. Today he looked . . . well, different. He was only of average height, but today he looked almost tall. It wasn't merely that he'd dressed for town, his usually tousled dark hair brushed into a modish Brutus and his new beaver hat with its stylishly curled brim set on his head at an especially rakish angle. Nor was it that that his shoulders looked broader than usual in the caped greatcoat he'd thrown over them. It was just that he seemed, all at once, more knowing, more purposeful, and more . . . more manly. Was it love that had done it? she wondered. Did love have the power to make one more mature?

"It's too cold to stand about," Tris was saying. "Let's walk."

He offered his arm, but she shook her head. In silence, they set off together along the gravel path that edged the woods shared by the two estates. Julie gathered her thick wool shawl more closely about her shoulders but let the wind blow her long auburn tresses freely about her face. "Tell me about her," she requested suddenly, feeling both fascinated and repelled.

"About Cleo?" He gave a careless shrug. "Not much to tell. Cleo's beautiful, of course, but in a different sort of way from the usual beauties."

"In what way different?"

Tris considered the question with a furrowed brow. "Her hair, for one thing. She cuts it short, little curls close to her head."

"Like Caro Lamb," Julie offered with a knowing nod.

"Yes. I find it charming. And she moves with the most enchanting swing of her limbs." His eyes shone with a reminiscent glow. "Her gestures are all like that, sort of . . . loose and . . . and wide. They're all of a piece with her character."

"Her *character* is loose and wide?" Julie asked, amused.

He threw her a quick glare, the kind he habitually tossed at her. "Of course not, you goose. What I meant was that her gestures are, in a manner of speaking, spontaneous."

"Spontaneous?"

"Yes. You might call them uninhibited. And . . . and self-assured. They seem to reveal her inner nature. She thinks well of herself, you see."

"Does she really?" Julie could not help being impressed by his description.

"Oh, yes. She's very sure of herself. Not simpering and missish like other girls."

Julie's step slowed. "That's a swipe at me, isn't it?" she asked ruefully. "I suppose you think that *I'm* simpering and missish."

"You?" He looked down at her in sincere surprise. "No, I didn't mean that at all. You're not missish. Not with me, at any rate. However," he added, reconsidering, "you may be so with other fellows. They all say you're too shy."

"Shy? *Me?*"

"I don't know why you're surprised. You know how you are when you're in your mother's shadow."

Julie winced. "Yes, I know."

"It's your own fault. You shouldn't let her overwhelm you as she does. I don't believe shyness to be an asset to a girl, Julie. Even being missish and simpering would probably be an improvement. At least you'd giggle and flicker your lashes at a fellow, instead of just . . . just hiding."

She stiffened. "Hiding?"

"Yes, hiding." Tris, ignoring her obvious dismay, barged on. "That's what you do in society, you know. You hide. Behind your dowdy shawls, behind your mother, behind your fan."

"Really, Tris," she said, her voice rich with sarcasm, "you shouldn't flatter me so."

"If you want flattery, my girl, ask someone else. You should be grateful for the truth."

"You're quite right. I'll write you a note of thanks as soon as I get home."

He laughed. "That's the spirit. That was saucy. Don't you see, Julie? That's how you *should* behave in society."

"You want me to be *saucy?* I could never—"

Disgusted, he shrugged and walked on. She followed, not speaking. But after a while, she caught up with him. "I'm not surprised that you love your Miss Smallwood," she remarked thoughtfully. "Someone who thinks well of herself . . . that must be rare."

"She is rare," Tris said. "I think you'd like her."

"I only hope—*Oooh!*" The gasp came from deep in her chest, and her whole body froze in horror. There in the path ahead of them lay a small, furry little animal, quite dead.

"Dash it, Julie, you needn't carry on so," Tris scolded. "It's only a dead rabbit." He stepped over it and put out his hand to help her follow.

But Julie hung back, staring down at the lifeless bit of fur. "Shouldn't we do something? Bury it or something?"

"Bury it? Good God, girl, one would think it was your pet! Must you always be so deuced squeamish? We'll leave it where it is. The groundskeeper or some passerby will find it and think himself lucky for coming upon a good dinner without having to waste a bullet."

Julie swallowed her distaste at the thought of the poor creature being turned into rarebit and surrendered to Tris's good sense. She took his hand, stepped over the body and proceeded down the path.

Tris, dismissing the incident from his mind, returned to the subject of their meeting. "So you see, I wanted to warn you. The next time you see me, when I've won Cleo's hand, we're going to have to face our mothers."

"We?" This time it was Julie who looked scornful. "In the first place, I don't see why this is any concern of mine. In the second place, what makes you so sure your Miss Smallwood'll have you?"

He stopped in his tracks. "Well, she seemed to encourage . . ." His eyes narrowed, and he peered at Julie through knit brows. "Do you think she won't?"

"I'm sure I couldn't say. I don't know the lady. But if it were me, I wouldn't."

"You only say that because you know I won't ever ask you. I'll have you know that Cleo hinted she considers me a catch."

"A *catch?*" Julie gave a disdainful little laugh. "Really, Tris, you can't be serious."

"Why not? I've a title, haven't I? And an estate that's not inconsiderable. And a certain confidence in address.

And I'm told that my appearance is pleasing. So why am I not a catch?"

"Because you're a peacocky, bumptious *ass* is why!" She stalked off down the path, tossing some of her long tresses over her shoulder contemptuously.

"Ass?" he echoed angrily, striding quickly after her, grasping her shoulders and pulling her round. "How dare you call me an ass?"

"I dare because you *are* one. Do you think you're *worth* your wealth just because you *have* it? Anyone who believes that a title and an income will win him a lady's heart *has* to be an ass. If the lady in question is half the creature you described, she'll be looking for more than mere superficialities in the man she weds."

"So that's what you think of me, eh? Merely superficial?"

"It doesn't matter what I think, does it?"

"No," he snapped back, "it doesn't matter one bit."

"Then why ask me?"

"I don't know why I did." He loosed his grip on her and threw up his hands. "It was a moment of weakness."

Julie relented. "You needn't look so murderous. Your lady may not find you as superficial as I do."

"Thank you, ma'am, for that encouragement. You are saying, therefore, that in order to succeed, I need only hope that my lady remains ignorant of the shallow nature of my character."

"Don't let my words worry you," Julie assured him with a sudden, unexpected smile. "She'll probably have you. Most girls would."

"Good God, ma'am, have I heard you alright? Did you actually say something kind?"

She laughed. "It was a moment of weakness." But then her eyes abruptly clouded. *"You'll* have to tell our mamas."

"Yes, soon or late." Tris, his expression darkening also, kicked at the pebbles in the path. "But not quite yet."

Julie threw a quick glance up at him. "Why not yet?"

"I haven't even made Cleo an offer. It's best to wait until the matter is a fait accompli, isn't it?"

"Is it? Or are you just being cowardly?"

Tris glowered at her. "Is that what you think? That I lack courage? That I'm a deuced muckworm?"

"My, my, you are quick to take offense today. I don't look on you as a muckworm, you gudgeon. I just don't see why you can't tell them now. Straightaway."

"Would you, if you were in my place?"

"Of course I would," she answered promptly.

"Ha! What a hum! You of all people."

She lifted her chin in offense. "Why not me?"

"You shudder at the sight of a dead rabbit!"

Her eyes fell. "I'm not saying it would be easy . . ."

"Easy!" He gave a mirthless laugh. "*Impossible* is more like it. I can just imagine the scene—my mother weeping copious tears, and your mother shouting the roof down."

Julie sighed in agreement. "I know, Tris. But you'll have to face it, as you said, soon or late."

"Better late. When I'm already wed, their tears and shouts won't have any effect."

"Tris! You're *not*—!" She stared at him in horror. "You can't mean you're planning to wed before telling your mother!"

"I'm not planning anything," Tris responded tersely, striding off angrily down the path away from her. "I told you before. Cleo hasn't even accepted me yet."

"Well, you needn't snap at me," she called after him. "It isn't my fault that she hasn't."

He paused and turned slowly back. "I'm sorry. I tend to lose my temper when I think of the fix our mothers put us in." He grinned sheepishly, the dimple in his left cheek making an appearance. "In a way, all this *is* your fault, you know. If you hadn't been born, our mothers couldn't have leg-shackled us."

"Yes," she said with a sneer, "that would have been nice for you."

"Nice? It would have been bliss."

"You wouldn't have had me to contend with."

"True. No discord. No wrangles. No bickering. Oh, the peace and quiet!"

"No two-family dinners. No shared birthdays. No being pushed to go to the assembly together . . ."

"A veritable heaven on earth!"

"Yes, heaven," she agreed, "but may I point out that it would have been just as heavenly if it were *you* who hadn't been born?"

"You have me there." He sighed in mock surrender. "I suppose we'll have to accept what is."

"Yes." She too expelled a sigh, but hers was real.

He studied her face with sudden, unexpected compassion. He was on the verge of escaping this life, but she was still mired in it. "Don't look so glum, Julie," he said cheerfully. "My betrothal to Cleo will change everything. Our mothers will have to admit defeat."

Heads lowered in thought, they slowly returned to the summerhouse. There they said their good-byes. "As soon as Cleo says she'll have me, I'll come back and deal with our mothers," he promised. "And after they accept the fact that they've lost this battle, things will change. Life is suddenly full of interesting possibilities."

"Yes, for you," she muttered glumly.

"For you too. Just wait. You'll see." He tipped his hat and started toward home, adding, "As soon as I'm betrothed, you'll be perfectly free to find yourself a fellow of your own."

"That *is* an interesting possibility," Julie said, throwing him a last wave.

She climbed the stile, but before dropping down on the other side, she looked back at his retreating figure. He looked almost tall in his fine beaver, with the capes of his greatcoat flapping in the wind. As the distance grew between them, she reviewed the one hopeful note that had been sounded in all that had been exchanged between them this afternoon. *You'll be perfectly free to find a fellow of your own,* her mind echoed as she watched him walk away. *A fellow of my own. Yes!*

But . . . who?

# 2

WITH HER CHAIR PUSHED BEHIND HER MOTHER'S, A mere six inches back from the line of seats placed along the edge of the dance floor, Julie sat quite literally in her mother's shadow. *But there's nothing remarkable about that,* she told herself ruefully as she watched the dancers swirling round the dance floor in a lively "Horatio's Fancy." Everyone at this small Derbyshire Biweekly Assembly knew she was always in her mother's shadow, figuratively as well as literally. Even Tris had said so.

Julie cast a glance over at her mother. It was no wonder she was overshadowed by the woman. The dowager Lady Branscombe was a formidable presence. In her stockinged feet Mama would have towered over all the other women in the room, but tonight she seemed even taller because her imposing head of carefully coiffed hair was topped by a jeweled turban with plumes. And she was not only noble in height but in breadth. With wide hips and an ample bosom, Julie's mother did indeed make an impressive picture.

The tall feathers of Lady Branscombe's turban were bobbing gently as she chatted with her best friend, Lady Phyllis Enders, who was seated on her other side. But after a moment, as if she felt Julie's eyes on her, Lady Branscombe turned and cast her daughter a look of disapproval. "Hiding yourself again, I see," she scolded. "Juliet Branscombe, you promised me when we set out this evening that you would try to have a pleasurable time. I would have no objection to your circulating about the room. Or even if you danced one or two of the country dances."

"Yes, Mama," Julie mumbled, coloring, "but—"

"You know very well why our dear girl is not dancing," Lady Phyllis intervened gently. "All the young men in the neighborhood are aware that you disapprove of them. She'd be dancing often enough if my Tris were here."

"Under duress on both our parts," Julie muttered under her breath.

"What did you say?" her mother asked suspiciously.

"Nothing, Mama."

"Hummmph!" was Lady Branscombe's only reply. She knew that Lady Phyllis had spoken nothing but the truth: all the young men who attended this weekly assembly (which drew its constituency from the fewer than fifty families comprising the entire society of the town of Amberford and its environs) were well aware of Lady Branscombe's intentions for her daughter. They knew there was no point in dancing with the girl, for as soon as they showed her the least interest, the mother would not permit them any further association—not even a second dance. Everyone understood the rules: Juliet Branscombe was spoken for.

Meanwhile, Lady Phyllis's underlip was quivering. "I'll never understand why Tris had to run off to town so suddenly."

"No need to shed tears," Lady Branscombe said brusquely. "What's done is done."

Lady Phyllis shrugged in defeat, and all three ladies turned their faces toward the dancers and watched in silence.

*Tris, again!* Julie said to herself in disgust as she settled back into her chair. It was always Tris. Since childhood, her mother had thrown Lady Phyllis's son at her head. How her mother and Lady Phyllis could have decided, the moment she was born, that she and Tristram Enders were meant for each other was more than she or Tris would ever understand. That deuced birth-alliance! In all the years since, the two mothers had never troubled themselves to wonder what the *subjects* of the agreement, Julie and Tris themselves, felt about the matter. Nor did the mothers acknowledge what their offspring repeatedly tried to tell them: that the whole idea was positively *medieval*!

Someone who did not know them would surmise that the ladies had made the arrangement for financial reasons. If Tris and Julie should wed, the estates would be unified, and the Branscombe lands would not be lost to the distant cousin who was the next male in the line. But Julie and Tris knew better. Julie's mother had a quite sufficient competence of her own, so holding on to Larchwood was not essential to her happiness. And as for Lady Enders, there was no need ever for her to be concerned about finances; the Enders family could only be described as wealthy.

The real reason for the ladies' stubborn insistance on the betrothal was more sentimental than financial. Lady Phyllis and Lady Branscombe had been best friends since childhood and, in their affection for each other, had decided that their offspring should marry and cement the friendship for all eternity. It was a silly conceit, but they had fancied it for so long they could no longer be made to see the foolishness of it. Neither mother could admit—or even *see*—that Juliet and Tristram were being made to suffer for their mothers' mawkishness.

Julie, her eyes fixed on the back of her mother's head, felt with renewed force the astonishment she always experienced when she thought about the close friendship of these two very different women. Lady Phyllis, Tris's mother, was small of stature, so delicate of feature that she still retained a youthful beauty despite her thick gray hair, and as gentle and soft-spoken in manner as she'd been as a girl; while Juliet's mother had grown in strength and size over the years until she'd become not only a large, imposing figure physically but strong and purposeful in character as well. *Too strong and too purposeful,* Julie thought with a sigh.

It was her mother's fault that she sat hiding in the

shadow. She was no longer asked to dance, even by the bumpkins attending this dowdy provincial assembly. Knowing they would never get Lady Branscombe's permission to court her, they'd all given up trying. Juliet Branscombe was always a wallflower these days. Even if a miracle should occur, and a stranger should happen to attend this modest country gathering, and *if* he should happen to notice a shy but passably pretty girl sitting in the shadows, and *if* he should happen to ask her to dance, and *if* she should have the courage to accept him, and *if* she should show the least enjoyment in the encounter (a great many *ifs* to have to become *whens),* her mother would frown at him so coldly and drag her daughter away so abruptly that he would never have the courage to approach her again.

Of course these suppositions were nothing but foolish imaginings. Tris's last words to her before he left had inspired these ludicrous fancies. In the first place, what stranger would possibly find his way to this backwater assembly?

At that moment, there was a stir at the doorway, and she looked up to see that the plump, officious Sir William Kenting, who always acted as master of ceremonies at these assemblies, was ushering in a tall gentleman Juliet had never laid eyes on. A stranger had *indeed* found his way to this backwater assembly!

And what a stranger! The mere sight of him caused Juliet's breath to catch in her throat. He seemed a creature who'd materialized from her dream of masculine perfection. His height and the breadth of his shoulders filled the doorway; his hair was dark except for one streak of gray highlighting a center lock that fell over a high forehead; his eyes were light and piercing, his nose as perfect as a Grecian statue's, and his lips full and curved into a thrillingly sardonic smile. And his clothes! No Derbyshire tailor could have fashioned that marvelously fitting evening coat, nor had any provincial valet tied that pristine neckcloth into such intricate folds. *Heavens!* she thought, a clench of excitement tightening her chest. *Have my silly imaginings become real?*

Her pulse seemed to stop beating as she watched the man's eyes roam over the room. Wouldn't it be wonderful, she asked herself, if this dazzling creature noticed her? And—absurd thought!—what if he actually asked her to dance?

Meanwhile, everyone else in the room was staring at him too. "Who *is* that?" Lady Branscombe asked, raising her pince-nez.

Lady Phyllis blinked at the gentleman in the doorway for a moment. "It must be the fellow who bought Wycklands. Canfield's the name, I believe. Lord Canfield."

"Oh, yes." Lady Branscombe nodded knowingly. "Canfield. I've heard of him. The eldest of the Granard brood. They say he's a toplofty libertine. Not a welcome addition to our assemblies, I fear. Well, we needn't take any notice of him." And she lowered her spectacles, dismissing him from her sight and her mind.

But her daughter continued to watch him with racing pulse. The fellow's gaze was encompassing the entire room, but he did not seem to take particular note of anyone, much less an inconspicuous young woman in the shadows. After a moment, in response to a request from Sir William, the stranger looked about once more, shrugged his beautifully clad shoulders in obvious dismissal of the entire company and followed his host into the card room.

Julie spent the next hour keeping watch on the card room door for his reappearance, but there was no sign of him. By that time Lady Branscombe had had enough of watching the dancing. She turned from her friend to her daughter. "Let us get our cloaks, my love," she said. "I think it's time we took our leave."

Julie, who for the first time in months was finding the assembly interesting, suppressed a sigh, obediently rose and followed her mother and Phyllis out of the ballroom. As they waited in the hallway while a footman ran to the cloakroom for their apparel, they saw Sir William leading the stranger toward the cloakroom. "Ladies," he chortled heartily as he came abreast of them, "how fortunate to have met you here. You must let me make you known to our new arrival. Lady Phyllis Enders, Lady Branscombe and Miss Juliet Branscombe, may I present Peter Granard, Lord Canfield, newly of Wycklands?"

They all murmured how-de-dos and made their bows. Then Lord Canfield took his host aside and whispered something in his ear. Just as the footman reappeared with their cloaks, Sir William, his plump cheeks quivering, hurried back to them. "Lady Branscombe, I beg you not to run off so early. Lord Canfield is interested in asking your Juliet to stand up with him." Lowering his voice and beaming, he added, "Let me assure you that he's truly interested. He says your daughter is the prettiest creature here."

Her ladyship frowned at the fellow coldly. "It's much too late, I'm afraid," she responded, so loudly that Lord Canfield had no choice but to overhear. "We already have our cloaks. Furthermore, Sir William, please inform his lordship that my daughter does not need to have buttersauce poured over her."

Sir William colored to the ears. "Buttersauce, ma'am? Let me assure you he never meant to—"

Lady Branscombe, noting that the footman had draped all three ladies with their cloaks, cut the master of ceremonies short with wave of her hand. She then bid him a brusque good night and pushed her daughter toward the stairs, Lady Phyllis scurrying behind.

Julie, humiliated beyond words, threw a glance over her shoulder to see how his lordship had taken the slight. But Lord Canfield had already turned away; she could not see his face. If she *could* have seen it, she was certain that his expression would have revealed either utter disgust or, at best, nothing more than cool indifference.

She felt her heart sink. *I suppose,* she said to herself glumly, *that that's the last I'll ever see of him.* After her mother's foolish snub, who could blame the man if he never attended another of these dowdy, dull assemblies?

But later, as she climbed into the carriage after her mother and Lady Phyllis, it occurred to her that she might very well see the gentleman again. He had purchased Wycklands, which made him a permanent resident. In so narrow a society, they were bound to be invited to the same dinner party someday. Or she might, when making an afternoon call, find herself in the same drawing room as he. Or they might even attend one of Mr. Weekes's Sunday services at the same time. Unless the man was a recluse (and obviously he was not, for hadn't her mother called him a libertine?), they were bound to meet one day. Tris had said that life was full of promising possibilities. She'd doubted him at first, but at this moment she was quite eager to believe him.

# 3

LORD CANFIELD, WHO'D BEEN ON THE VERGE OF leaving the assembly before he'd succumbed to the temptation to ask the shy little chit in the hallway to dance with him, turned at once toward the cloakroom again.

Sir William followed at his heels. "I hope you've taken no personal offense, my lord," the master of ceremonies muttered worriedly. "Lady Branscombe is brusque to everyone, let me assure you. She is quite the dragon."

"Is she indeed?" Lord Canfield smiled down comfortingly at the red-faced fellow. "But I'm not in the least offended. In fact I rather admired her brusqueness. The lady didn't like me and indicated her dislike quite honestly. I much prefer brusque honesty to hypocritical politeness."

"But no, my lord, it wasn't dislike, let me assure you. She puts off anyone who tries to pursue her daughter."

"Oh?" Canfield threw the plump little fellow an inquiring look as he threw his evening cloak over his shoulders. "Is there something wrong with her pretty, dreamy-eyed daughter?"

"Oh, no, nothing at all. Juliet's a fine young woman, let me assure you, very fine. But her ladyship has planned for the girl to wed her friend's son—Lady Phyllis's boy, you know—and she becomes . . . er . . . uneasy if any other fellow shows the girl attention."

"Ah, I see." Lord Canfield, who was already moving purposefully toward the stairs, paused in his rapid progress along the hall and peered down at the master of ceremonies with brows raised in mild disapproval. "But, Sir William, if the girl is betrothed, do you think it was proper of you to encourage me to request her hand for the dance? In London, a young lady who is betrothed dances only with her intended or with friends who know her situation. She is not encouraged to dance with strangers."

"Let me assure you that is our way also. We are not such a backwater that we don't know how things are done in town. But in this case the matter is rather muddled. You see, the girl in question is *not* betrothed. At least not as yet." The master of ceremonies shook his head and sighed unhappily. "Her mother escorts her to these assemblies just as any mother of a marriagable daughter would do, seemingly expecting the girl to dance. Yet as soon as a young man shows the slightest interest, the mother snatches the girl away."

"How very curious," his lordship murmured.

"Curious it is," Sir William agreed glumly. "It certainly puts *me* in a strange position, let me assure you. I am enjoined to present partners to all the unmarried young ladies who attend our assemblies, but when I try to do so in this case, you see how I am abused."

"You certainly have my sympathy," Canfield said with a kindly smile, "but I feel even more for the girl."

"For the girl?" Sir William echoed in surprise.

"Yes, of course. She's in a more difficult situation than you are if she's forced to attend and then must sit out all the dances. How very awkward for her, pretty as she is, to be always a wallflower."

"Yes, it must be. Julie Branscombe, a wallflower! That, let me assure you, is a most ridiculous epithet for that sweet young girl."

"So it seems to me too," his lordship agreed. "She has the most amazing eyes. As if she were gazing at us from some other world." Then, realizing he was thinking aloud, he blinked and shook his head. A bit embarrassed, he quickly waved his good-bye to his host and started down the stairs. "If I ever come face-to-face with that pair again in similar circumstances," he said over his shoulder with a laugh, "I shan't let the dragon put me off so easily. I'll get that young lady on the dance floor yet. Let me assure you."

# 4

As the Branscombe carriage rocked over the unpaved road from Amberford to Enders Hall, Lady Phyllis gazed at the dozing Juliet with a look of such fond affection it could only be called doting. "Madge, my dear, you're much too hard on the girl," she whispered to her friend.

"I can't help it," Lady Branscombe muttered in an undervoice. "I am irked beyond words that she did so little to keep Tris from dashing back to London."

"It is more Tris's fault than hers," Tris's mother said in the girl's defense. "He'd set his mind quite firmly on going back to town. I don't believe *anyone* could have changed his mind. I very much fear . . ." Here her soft voice faltered.

Madge Branscome fixed a wary eye on her friend's face. "Fear what?"

Lady Phyllis's eyelids flickered nervously as she pulled a large, lacy handkerchief from the bosom of her dress. "I very much fear the boy has set his heart on some female in London."

"'Twould serve Julie right if he has!" Madge Branscombe's full bosom heaved in distress. "During Tris's entire visit, did she once wear any of the new gowns I had made for her? No! Did she do up her hair, blacken her lashes or behave in any way like a girl trying to attract a man? Of course not! All she did during the entire fortnight was bicker with him. Honestly, their perpetual wrangling makes me wild. Sometimes I want to wring the girl's neck!"

"I know. They do seem to be always squabbling." Phyllis's eyes filled with tears. "Do you think," she asked with a pitiful tremor, "that they will not marry after all?"

Lady Branscombe winced. "If he's given his heart to another, I suppose not."

"I know he seems to be behaving like a deuced coxcomb," Phyllis admitted, "but he can't actually have come to love someone else! He just *can't*! Perhaps he's only gone off to . . . to keep an assignation with a . . . a . . ."

"If you're trying to say the word *paramour*, Phyllis Enders, then just say it! This is no time to be mealymouthed."

"Well, I don't like to believe my son has a paramour, but I suppose that would be preferable to his falling in love with someone suitable. If he affianced himself to a proper sort of female, what could we do then?"

Madge dropped her head in her hand. "I have no idea," she mumbled in discouragement.

Lady Phyllis dabbed at her eyes with one corner of her huge handkerchief. "You don't think, do you, that it's time to admit that the matter is hopeless?"

Madge Branscombe threw her friend an angry glare. "I refuse to give up. We must not admit defeat. So long as the boy remains unmarried, there's still a chance—"

The smaller woman shook her head sadly while unwittingly twisting the handkerchief into a tight coil. "But, my dear, it may already be too late. During this past fortnight, I too looked in vain to discern a sign of a romantic spark between them, but there was never anything remotely affectionate. It's our fault, you know. We raised them too closely. They've become utterly uninteresting to each other."

"It *is* our fault." That was a difficult admission for Lady Branscombe to make; her whole body seemed to sag. "We should have kept them apart. If we'd forbidden them to associate, they would *then* have been delighted to defy us."

"Yes. I should have played Montague to your Capulet.

But that chance is quite lost. By this time, Tris is so accustomed to the sight of your beautiful Juliet that he doesn't even notice how lovely she is."

They both sighed together with the same hopelessness and fell silent with the same rapt concentration. The two women often showed this sort of similar reaction to the circumstances of life. Though their looks were very different, their tastes were very much alike. They'd become friends in girlhood, when they'd attended the same school. Phyllis, though she was the daughter of an earl, had from the first fallen under the spell of Madge Selwin, who, though her family had no titles, was the most clever and strong-willed girl in the school. Phyllis's delicate reticence was a perfect match for Madge's robust decisiveness.

The friendship grew even stronger with time. One month after Phyllis married Sir Charles Enders, Madge wed his cousin, Edward Lord Branscombe. (It was often remarked by people who knew them well that Madge Branscombe had chosen for her husband a man whose character was very like her friend's: a reticent, wistful fellow who permitted himself to be led round by the nose by his overbearing wife.) After their wedding, Madge convinced her husband to purchase Larchwood, an estate within walking distance of Enders Hall. From that time onward, there was rarely a day during which they did not spend some time together.

Each woman had one child, Lady Phyllis first with Tris, and three years later Lady Branscome with Juliet. Both ladies were widowed a few years later. Each declared with perfect sincerity that she could not have borne her loss without the support of the other. Through all the vicissitudes of their lives, they had remained fast friends. They could not have been closer if they'd been sisters.

But having similar tastes does not imply having similar characters. Not at all. Phyllis was as different from Madge as sugar from pepper. In the rains of life, one would dissolve in tears and the other explode in temper. This evening's conversation was a perfect example. In the matter of the betrothal between Tris and Julie, Phyllis was quite ready to surrender to fate, but Madge Branscombe was made of sterner stuff. "I shall never say die. I'll not give up," she said loudly.

"Shush!" Phyllis hissed. "You'll wake the girl."

"What if I do? Honestly, Phyllis, you mollycoddle her too much. Not that I blame you. Delicate flower that she is, she sometimes seems more your daughter than mine."

Phyllis sighed. "I hoped she *would* be my daughter. What did you mean when you said you won't give up? I don't wish to give up either, but I don't see what we can do."

"We can go to London," Madge declared with sudden decision. "We can take Julie and go down for the season. We didn't believe a come-out was necessary for a girl who was already betrothed, but since matters are not proceeding as planned, we'll give her one."

Phyllis blinked her misted eyes. "But, Madge, I don't quite see—"

"Don't you? It's simple. Giving her a season in town will make it possible to thrust the girl in Tris's path. Just leave it to me. He'll find her in his line of vision everywhere he goes."

"Yes! Oh, yes!" Phyllis clasped her hands to her breast, causing her handkerchief to flutter through the air like a pennant. Hope, that beam of sunshine, dissipated the clouds that had shrouded her eyes. "Madge, you're a genius! What a positively wonderful idea! When Tris comes upon her in those surroundings—in those London ballrooms, dressed in the most beautiful town finery we can contrive, prettier than any of those London chits and being pursued by hordes of swains—why, he'll see our Julie in a whole new light!"

Madge threw her a look of scorn. "I wouldn't count on hordes of swains, my dear. Julie hasn't any of that flirtatiousness necessary to attract hordes. But I certainly hope the rest of what you envisioned will come to pass."

The words had scarcely passed her lips when the carriage drew up at Enders Hall. Lady Phyllis glanced at the

sleeping girl. "Tell her good night for me," she whispered
to her friend before climbing down. "I'll see you tomorrow, and we shall make our plans."

But Julie was not asleep. She'd heard every word. She
knew that eavesdropping was a wicked misdeed, but since
she herself had been the subject of the conversation, she
hadn't been able to resist listening. She soon discovered
that the maxim *eavesdroppers never hear good of themselves* was quite true. Everything she'd heard during the
endless ride had filled her with disgust.

The most troubling part was her mother's plan to take
her off to London. She'd never wished to have a London
come-out. She had no love for the whirlwind that consti-
tuted the "season" in town. Too shy to enjoy the noisy
routs and fetes and balls of London's social life, she knew
that the experience of a London debut would be nothing
but torture to her. Furthermore, her mother's timing
could not have been worse. When an interesting gentleman had finally moved into the Amberford environs
and offered the promise of some excitement, that was the
time when her mother decided on London! What an
irony!

As if all this was not bad enough, there was Tris to
consider. He was in love! How would he feel if both
mamas descended on him in town? He didn't need med-
dlesome mothers interfering with his courtship.

As the carriage continued to rattle its way toward
home, Julie's mind raced about trying to concoct schemes
to avoid the horrid future her mother was devising for
her. There had to be a way to prevent the interfering pair
from dragging her to town. There had to be.

But she could think of only one thing to do. That night,
before going to bed, she sat down at her writing desk, cut
herself a fresh nib, and dashed off a note. *Dear Tris,* she
wrote. *Something very dreadful is occurring. This matter is
most urgent. Come, if only for your own sake. Please do not
fail me, or we shall both be in dire straits. Hurry! Julie.*

# 5

THE NEXT MORNING, DESPITE A HEAVY SKY AND A light rain, Julie took out her horse. She loved her morning rides. She often rode with Tris, but she was just as content to ride alone. With Tris, she had to keep up a flow of conversation or worry about the condition of her hair. He always teased her about looking unruly. Alone, she could think her own thoughts, go at her own pace, and allow her hair to blow about as it willed, or, as now, to hang about her face in flat, dripping strands. This was just the sort of ride she liked, for she could go wherever she wished without a care for how she looked. Today she hadn't even bothered to put on her riding habit. She'd worn an old, dark skirt of heavy broadcloth, cut so full she could ride astride instead of sidesaddle, and she'd thrown her faded green wool shawl over her shoulders to keep off the rain. And of course she hadn't bothered to wear a hat. It didn't matter. No one would see her; no one else in town would be out riding on a day like this.

This morning she let her horse meander along the bank of what the Amberford natives called their river. It was, in reality, nothing but a stream that flowed from the north highlands down past the property line of Wycklands, through the town itself and on to the south, past the western boundary of Enders Hall. In a dry summer it dwindled to a mere trickle, revealing the rocks and rubble that made its bed, but in spring, when the winter runoff swelled its flow, it became a gurgling, rushing torrent, overspreading its banks and rampaging down the spills, as it did now. She loved to watch the water come bubbling over the stones, splashing and burbling along in a kind of happy hysteria. It was a sight to bring one joy, despite the rain.

In many places the water's overflow covered the banks, and she had to ride unusually close to the tree line. Occasionally a low-hanging branch grazed her face and had to be brushed aside. One such branch, much larger than the others, had to be bent and held firmly down to permit her to pass. When she passed and let it go, however, it caught the hem of her skirt on its tip and sprang up with vigor, pulling the garment up with it and revealing Julie's legs, bare except for a pair of brief pantaloons and her boots. The horse, feeling a tug, stopped. Julie pulled at the skirt, but it would not come loose. She lifted herself to a standing position on the stirrups but couldn't reach the skirt's hem. Even when she bent the branch, the tip remained out of her reach.

At that moment, to her horror, she heard the sound of hoofbeats squelching on wet ground. "Good morning, ma'am," came a pleasant male voice. "You seem to be in difficulty. May I be of assistance?"

She looked round to discover that the rider was the very man who'd taken her breath away the night before. Of all the men in the world, Lord Canfield was the last one she wanted to encounter at this moment. He looked, of course, as marvelous as he'd seemed last night. He was wearing chamois breeches, a tweed riding coat and a tall beaver which he was tipping politely. She wanted to die! She knew she looked a sight, with her dripping hair, her skirt lifted up above her knees, and her legs—bare!— hanging from the horse *astride!*

"Let me help you," he said, urging his horse between hers and the tree.

"No, please," she said, choked, turning away her head. "Just . . . go away!"

He laughed, stood on his stirrups, reached up and released the skirt. "There," he said, tipping his hat again. "No trouble at all."

She pulled down the offending garment, swung a leg

over the horse so that she sat sidesaddle and lowered her head. "Th-thank you, my lord," she mumbled miserably.

"Why, it's Miss . . . Miss Branscombe, is it not?" he asked, peering at her through the raindrops and the strands of hair that fell over her face. "We met last night, I believe."

"Yes, I believe we d-did," she managed.

"This is good luck," he said cheerfully. "I'd hoped to encounter you again."

"That is k-kind of you to say," she said, pushing tendrils of hair back from her eyes and throwing a quick glance at his face, "but I would have preferred a less humiliating encounter."

"Why humiliating? Anyone might have gotten caught in these deuced brambles."

"Perhaps," she said ruefully, "but not many would have revealed such . . . such bare legs."

"True," he agreed with a chuckle, "but not many would have such pretty legs to reveal."

Though she knew he'd meant the remark as a compliment, she couldn't take it so. It was too intimate for so brief an acquaintance. "I would have preferred," she said as proudly as her overwhelming embarrassment permitted, "that you hadn't seen them at all, even if they'd been covered with stockings and petticoats. Which, to my everlasting shame, they weren't."

He held up a gloved hand. "Were they not? I swear I never noticed."

A laugh hiccoughed out of her. "You lie, my lord, but like a gentleman."

"What makes you think I lie?"

"Because you say you didn't notice the legs were bare but noticed they were pretty."

"I'm a gentleman, my dear, but also a man. As a gentleman, I do not take notice of ladies' undergarments . . . or the lack of them. But as a man, how can I be expected not to notice such pretty legs as yours?"

She blushed. "Then, as a lady, I hope you will permit

me to thank you for your gentlemanly discretion and to
ignore the . . . the rest."

"Done," he said, and offered his hand.

She took it. "Thank you." She smiled up at him timidly
for a moment before removing her hand and picking up
the reins. "And now I think it time we went our separate
ways. You are becoming soaked."

"And so are you. May I not see you home?"

"No, thank you, my lord," she said, turning her mount
about and starting off at a gallop. "You've seen quite
enough of me for one day."

# 6

LORD SMALLWOOD PEERED OVER THE TOP OF HIS newspaper with a frown of disapproval. His daughter, who was sitting opposite him at the breakfast table nonchalantly buttering a hot raisin muffin, was, as usual, raising his hackles. Everything about her this morning, from her posture to her dress, was not what he liked. Although Lord Smallwood truly adored his daughter, he didn't quite approve of her. Widowed when the girl was only thirteen, he was responsible for her upbringing, but he'd often secretly admitted to himself that it was *she* who'd raised *him.*

Smallwood was a small-boned, short, soft-spoken man of sixty-two years who'd won the respect of his peers merely by the dignity of his bearing. He had fine features, a head of white hair, a retiring nature that made him avoid confrontation, and a somewhat pedantic, precise habit of mind. Yet his daughter, the twenty-one-year old beauty Miss Cleo Smallwood, had inherited none of his ways. That was the trouble.

He shook his head at her hopelessly. She was casually leaning one elbow on the table as she attended her buttering. *That girl,* he said to himself, *has no sense of decorum.* Not only was her posture rude and her hair unkempt, but her clothes were inappropriate. There she sat, brazenly swathed in a frilly morning robe meant only for the bedroom, with, undoubtedly, nothing underneath but her nightclothes. "Isn't it time you were dressed?" he asked plaintively.

"I'm in no hurry," the girl responded without a trace of

embarrassment. "I don't expect my caller until two this afternoon."

"Hummmph" was her father's only comment as he barricaded himself behind the *Times*. He knew the identity of his daughter's "caller," and he had no intention of entering into another argument over the fellow. If Cleo wanted to attach herself to a country bumpkin, it was her own affair. He was not the sort of father to lay down the law. And even if he were, it would do him no good. Cleo had a very decided mind of her own.

He rattled the newspaper, trying to concentrate on the news of the opening of a new bridge across the Thames, which was named Waterloo in honor of Wellington's triumph. But he could not concentrate on it; thoughts of his obstinate daughter kept intruding themselves on his consciousness. The girl was a charmer, that much was true. Any gentleman of the ton would agree. Tall and lithe, she had her mother's laughing eyes, a taunting smile, dimples that would come and go at unexpected times and a head of short, curly hair that set her apart from all the other girls with their loose curls or thick chignons. Her hand had been sought by at least three of the most desirable men in society, one a duke. Several others with lesser qualifications would have liked to ask, but they knew they would be refused. Why this most desirable creature should show a preference for the undistinguished newcomer Sir Tristram Enders was more than her father could see. "I don't understand you, Cleo," he muttered, unable to prevent himself. "Your mother, if she were alive to say it, would call you a fool."

"No, she wouldn't," Cleo declared firmly. "Mama understood a woman's nature. She knew what love is."

Lord Smallwood sighed. "Yes, she did, bless her soul. She would have known as well as I that what you feel is mere puppy love."

Cleo, completely unperturbed, continued to smooth the butter on her muffin. "If it *is* mere puppy love, my dear," she said complacently, "then it will fade in time. So why don't we just wait and see?"

"But if you go ahead and wed him and *then* learn it was only puppy love, it will be too late."

"I'm not marrying the fellow tomorrow, you know," his daughter laughed. "Besides, he hasn't asked me yet."

"But he will," Lord Smallwood muttered. "They all do, as soon as you give them the least encouragement."

Cleo smiled with only her green eyes, like a cat in the cream. "Yes, they do, don't they?"

Lord Smallwood was accustomed to her immodesty and took no note of it. "If you must be infatuated with someone, why did you choose Enders? The fellow is nothing more than a baron. You could have a duke for the asking."

Cleo nibbled at the edge of her well-buttered muffin. "The duke did not have Tris's charm. Nor his dimple. Nor his thick black hair. Nor his interesting blue eyes that show everything he feels. Nor his—"

"Enough!" Lord Smallwood retreated behind his paper. "Dimples, indeed. A good reason *that* is for choosing a mate."

"It's as good as any other," Cleo murmured absently, her mind already dwelling on the ride through the park she would soon be taking in Tris's ancient phaeton. Her father, taking another glance at her from above his newspaper, noted that she'd already left her muffin discarded and forgotton. After liberally covering it with butter, she was leaving it uneaten. It was typical of her. She would cover a vegetable with hollandaise or a cutlet with sauce and then push it aside after only a bite. He would never understand her.

But Cleo, if she'd been asked, would have explained that she could not keep her mind on food when life was so full of more interesting experiences. Who cared about something so mundane as breakfast? It was a lovely day— warm and pleasant, with a light wind from the south—and she would be spending it with the only suitor who'd ever truly captured her heart. Tristram Enders. Even the name was lovely. She smiled to herself in joyful anticipation.

Today, she was certain, would be the day he offered for her.

As her father watched her abstracted face, trying to read her thoughts, she sat staring with unseeing eyes at the discarded muffin on her plate. *For this special day,* she was thinking, *I must choose my costume carefully.* After long and serious consideration, she decided on her new rose-and-gold walking dress; it had a full skirt that would flutter enticingly in the breeze. With her wide-brimmed straw bonnet, yellow slippers and pale yellow gloves, she'd be top-of-the-trees. And she'd carry her ruffled parasol. From beneath it, she would gaze at Tris coquettishly from the corner of her eyes, eyes that many men had told her were spellbinding. Tris would not be able to resist. The circumstances were ideal. He would surely declare himself this afternoon. She could hardly wait.

Her father, of course, could not read her thoughts. But the cat-in-the-cream look in her green eyes told him as much as he wanted to know. *Poor Tris Enders,* he thought with a mixture of alarm and amusement, *your goose is cooked.*

# 7

LATER THAT AFTERNOON, WHEN CLEO RETURNED from that eagerly anticipated ride and strode in, alone, to the drawing room, her red-and-gold skirts swished and her mouth was tight with anger. Her father deduced at once that things had not gone as planned. "Aha," he chortled, looking up from the chessboard on which he was engaged in playing a game against himself, "so the fellow did not come up to snuff after all, did he?"

"No, he did not," Cleo said, handing her parasol to the butler who'd hurried into the room behind her.

"Good for him. Perhaps he's not such a bumpkin as I thought."

"Of course he's not a bumpkin," she said in disgust, dismissing the butler with a wave of her hand and dropping down upon the sofa. "But I can't imagine what's tying his tongue."

"Good sense, perhaps," her father ventured mildly.

She threw him a scornful look but let the quip pass. Instead, she began to review the details of the afternoon in her mind. But she could think of nothing that had gone awry. It was a mystery. She knew the fellow cared for her; she'd had too many admirers in the past not to know the symptoms. But something had kept him from making an offer. Perhaps there was a simple detail . . . some small thing that had gone askew . . . that would explain his default. "Is there something wrong with how I look?" she asked, rising and posing for her father. "Is my hat brim too wide? My lash-blacking smudged? My gown too gaudy?"

"You are perfect," Lord Smallwood assured her. "Absolutely lovely."

"That's what I thought. Then where can I have gone amiss?"

"Perhaps you overwhelmed the fellow. He's just a country bumpkin, after all."

"I wish you'd stop calling him that, Papa. He's as self-confident as any London native. And he was not the least shy during our ride. He joked and teased and was in every way perfectly comfortable with me."

"Then I see no reason for you to be in such a taking." He returned his attention to the chessboard and moved a pawn. "He probably merely decided to make his offer at another time and place," he added absently.

Cleo blinked at her father in sudden apprehension. *"Yes,"* she breathed, "I think you may be right! When he set me down, he did ask if I would be at home tonight. I was tempted to tell the idiot my evenings were engaged for the rest of the month, but . . ."

"But—?" her father asked, looking round at her curiously.

She smiled ruefully. "But his eyes looked so hopeful, I couldn't hurt him. I told him to call at nine." She sank back against the sofa cushions, her mood having swung from irritation to eager anticipation. "Do you suppose he plans to do it *tonight?*"

Lord Smallwood did not look up from his game. "I haven't the slightest idea."

But she didn't need her father's agreement. "Of *course* he does. How foolish of me not to have seen it! A shabby old phaeton in broad daylight would not seem a romantic setting to a man like Tris. He means to ask me tonight! Here in a proper drawing room. In candlelight!"

Her father turned about on his chair. "But you don't intend to accept him, do you?" he asked, suddenly worried. "You said this morning that you would wait and see."

"That was this morning. Now I'm absolutely certain of

my feelings. I love him, Papa. I truly do. When he asks me, I shall leap into his arms."

"Good God!" Lord Smallwood winced and put a hand to his forehead in a gesture of helplessness.

Cleo saw it, and her smile faded. She knew she often behaved with callous selfishness, but she truly loved her father. She hated to see him so upset. Rising again from the sofa, she crossed the room and propped herself on the arm of his chair. "Don't look so alarmed, Papa," she said gently. "You'll learn to love him, just as I did." She leaned down, brushed back a wisp of her father's white hair and kissed his forehead. "He's not as shallow and foolish as my usual swains, you know. He cares a great deal about politics and the state of the world. He spoke to me about the plight of the poor Derbyshire workers, just as you did. He's as sympathetic to their riots as you are. And you mustn't think he's a mere country squire. He has a lovely, large estate in Derbyshire and is delightfully plump in the pocket even though he does drive about in that aged phaeton. After we're wed, you shall spend months at a time in the country with us and dandle your grandchildren on your knee."

"Grandchildren!" Lord Smallwood shuddered. She was moving much too fast for him.

"Yes, grandchildren. You'll come to bless this day, really you will!" With that, she took hold of his chin and made him look up at her. "You *will* make yourself scarce tonight, after he comes, won't you, dearest Papa? To give us some time alone?"

The poor old fellow was, as always, putty in her hands. "You are a shocking minx," he muttered in a last-ditch struggle. "Do you think I can permit you to visit with a man without chaperonage?"

"Don't be so medieval. We've a houseful of servants at my beck and call should I need them. And I assure you, I won't need them. Tris is every inch the gentleman."

The white-haired man sighed in surrender. "Very well. I'll spend the evening at my club."

She threw her arms about him and planted another kiss

on the top of his head. Then she ran to the door. "I think
I'll wear the ivory satin tonight," she said over her shoulder as she flew down the hall. "It has a shocking décolletage. I was saving it for the Harrington's ball, but tonight
is more important. Yes, the ivory satin. It will drive him
wild!"

A few hours later, when Tris was admitted to the can-
dle-lit drawing room, he was indeed driven wild by the
sight of her in the ivory satin. He actually gaped when he
caught his first glimpse of her. She was standing before
the fireplace, her slim body profiled in the firelight, her
elbow resting on the mantel and her head turned toward
him over her shoulder, her chin high. The firelight gave
the room, her hair, the side of her face and the curves of
her breast a golden glow. "You are a *vision*," he whispered
in a kind of breathless agony. "I never want to take my
eyes from you."

She smiled. "Well, then, you needn't. Not for a while,
anyway." This was the sort of greeting she'd hoped for.
The evening was getting off to a very promising start.
"You are free to gaze at me all evening long," she murmured, her voice a purr.

The young man's eyes dropped. "No, my dear, I'm
afraid I can't."

*"What?"* She felt herself stiffen, as if something inside
her—a basic female instinct—were warning her, before
she actually knew why, that things were not going to proceed as she'd expected. "What on earth do you mean?"

"I've just had a message from home. An urgent message. I must leave."

She stared at him in disbelief. "Leave? Surely you don't
mean . . . *now?*"

"I'm afraid so. My carriage is waiting. I just stopped in
to explain . . ."

"Explain?" Her arm slipped from the mantel, and as a
wave of fury swept over her, her fingers clenched into
fists. "Yes, *do* explain. What is so dreadfully urgent that
you must go dashing off tonight?"

"I don't know the details. She didn't say. But it's urgent,

right enough. It must be. Julie has never sent for me this way before."

"Julie?"

"Yes. Julie Branscombe. My . . . my closest neighbor. Her mother and mine are bosom bows, you see, and Julie and I were brought up together. Like brother and sister."

"Indeed." Cleo's voice was like ice. "Like brother and sister. How interesting."

"I wouldn't call it interesting," Tris said with boyish innocence, having no inkling of the storm to come. "Troublesome would be a better word. But something dreadful must be brewing or she wouldn't have written the way she did. Please forgive me, Cleo, for this abrupt departure, but I must go." With a quick bow and a rueful grin, he started toward the door.

"Just one moment, my good sir!" Cleo strode angrily across the room and blocked the door. "Let me be certain that I understand all this. You are breaking off an appointment with *me*—an appointment which you yourself requested and to which I *generously* agreed, despite having to cancel *several* others—to dash off to Derbyshire on the *whim* of a young woman named *Julie?*"

Tris blinked, suddenly recognizing the anger in her tone. "Yes," he said, puzzled and defensive, "but I don't think it's a whim—"

"A young woman who is *no* relation—not even a *sister?*"

"Yes, that's right, but—"

"And for an emergency the details of which you do not even *know?*"

Tris felt not only helpless but decidedly foolish. "Yes," he admitted. "That's more or less the gist of it."

"You don't know the details, but you deem the matter *more important* than an evening with *me?*"

"Well, I wouldn't put it that way, exactly . . ."

"No? Then how would you put it?"

"It isn't a matter of relative importance. Damnation, Cleo, don't look at it that way. You must know how important you are to me." He took a step toward her and grinned at her sheepishly, hoping she'd find it charmingly reassuring. "I'll return as soon as I possibly can, I promise. And then we can pick up right where we left off tonight."

"Is *that* what you think?" She stared at him for a moment in furious disbelief. Then, brushing by him, she swept across to the fireplace, her back to him. "No, my dear sir, you will *not* return," she said with ominous distinctness, "not to this house. Once you cross that threshold, you will never cross it again, not as long as I can take a breath."

"Cleo!" He stared at her, aghast. "You can't mean—!"

"I *do* mean it!" She turned her head to him, her eyes glittering with rage. "Take a *good* look, Tris Enders, for once you leave this house, this is the last you'll see of me."

"B-But—" he stammered, completely nonplussed.

"If you are going, then go!"

"You don't understand," he said desperately. "It isn't that I *want* to go. It's just something I must do."

"Then go and *do* it! No one's holding you."

He hesitated for a moment, wondering if he should forget Julie's note and stay where he was. Cleo was heartbreakingly beautiful at this moment, and she evidently wanted him to remain, while on the other hand, Julie's summons was vague. Couldn't he at least wait for tomorrow? He was torn, like a classic hero, between love and duty. But, like a hero, he chose the harder road. He turned away from temptation and threw open the door. "I *shall* go," he declared as firmly as his choked throat permitted, "but I'll be back. I'll be back, will you or nill you!" With that, he stalked out to the corridor, ran past the astonished butler and flung himself out of the house.

When Lord Smallwood returned home an hour later, he found his daughter lying prone on the sofa in complete disregard of the condition of her new gown, sobbing as if her heart would break. "Cleo!" he cried in alarm, kneeling down beside her. "What on earth has happened here?"

"Oh, Papa!" She raised herself up and flung herself into

his arms. "He doesn't l-love me! He doesn't care for m-me one whit!"

"Who? The bumpkin?"

Cleo could only nod.

"There, there," her astonished father murmured, patting her back helplessly. "You mustn't let yourself become upset over him. The fellow is a fool. A country bumpkin. What can he know of quality?"

But even as he said those words, Lord Smallwood's respect for Tristram Enders grew by leaps and bounds. Not one other suitor for his daughter's hand, not even the most sophisticated of city dwellers, had ever shown himself remotely capable of reducing his remarkable daughter to such bitter tears. He shook his head in grudging admiration. That deuced bumpkin must have depths of character . . . depths that he, Smallwood, had never suspected.

# 8

ALL THROUGH THE LONG NIGHT'S RIDE HOME, TRIS relived the scene in the Smallwood drawing room. Over and over he questioned his own sanity. Had he made a foolish choice? Had he ruined his chances with the magnificent Cleo Smallwood? Had he sacrificed the one great love of his life (for he would surely never again find a woman as lovely, as charming, as perfect as Cleo) for what she'd called a whim? What on earth had made him feel so obligated to answer Julie's summons? Why had he taken her note so seriously? And why had she written to him in the first place? If it turned out that it *was* a whim, he would wring Julie's neck!

It was almost dawn when he arrived at Larchwood. He stopped his carriage at the foot of the Branscombes' drive, tethered the horses and stole on foot up the drive and round to the south side of the house. A gray light was beginning to pierce the darkness of the sky in the east. Placing himself in the shadow of a clump of shrubs, he threw a handful of dirt up to a curtained window on the second story. It took three more careful tosses before he saw the curtain being drawn. The window opened and Julie leaned out. "Is it you, Tris?" she called in a hissing whisper.

He stepped out into the faint predawn light. "Who did you think it was? Hurry and let me in before the whole household wakes."

"Yes. Go round to the veranda. I'll come down and open the door."

She came to the door wrapped in an old wool robe and

worn slippers, her hair in two plaits, like a child. It was strange, he couldn't help thinking, how careless she was about her appearance. Cleo would never permit herself to be seen looking so pathetically dowdy.

Julie, not at all conscious of how she looked, led him up the stairs to an unused room that had once been her schoolroom, and carefully closed the door. "There!" she sighed in relief. "No one will discover us here."

He perched on the child-sized table that still occupied the center of the room, while she blew out the candle she carried. They could talk in the darkness; she didn't want any servants discovering candlelight seeping out through the crevices of the door frame. Besides, it would soon be light.

"Well, what's amiss?" Tris demanded, his arms crossed over his chest. "This had better be serious . . . at least serious enough to warrant my traveling all night without sleep."

"It's serious enough. Our mamas have decided to give me a London come-out."

*"What?"* He gaped in astonishment at her shadowed shape looming over him. That she could have such a ridiculous reason for summoning him had never occurred to him. He wanted to murder her! "A *come-out?*" he ranted. "You summoned me here about a come-out? Are you *mad?* I thought that someone was deathly ill! Or that one of our houses had burned to the ground! Or—at the very least—that one of our mothers had lost a fortune on the 'change."

"Hush, will you?" Julie hissed. "Someone will hear you!" She sat down on the table beside him. "You don't realize how serious—"

"Serious? You call that serious?" He grasped her by the shoulders and gave her an angry shake. "Dash it all, Julie, do you realize what you've done? You made me lose my chance to win the most magnificent woman in London just so that you could tell me you're having a come-out. I ought to wring your blasted neck!"

She flung his hands from her arms. "What do you mean? How could I have affected your suit?"

"Never mind how! The fact is you did." He got up and strode over to the window, where he stood glowering at the slowly brightening landscape, feeling very sorry for himself.

She stared for a moment at his form silhouetted in the light seeping in from the reddening sky. Then she rose, came up behind him and put a hand on his arm. "I'm sorry, Tris. I never meant to cause you harm. I thought I was helping you."

"I know," he said softly, his anger melting away at her gentle touch. "I'm sorry I shook you. But how on earth did you think you'd be helping me by sending for me to talk about your damnable come-out?"

"It's not the come-out that's the problem. It's the ramifications. They are dreadful."

"Ramifications? What ramifications?"

"You'll be expected to play a part in the affair, don't you see?"

"No, I don't see. What has your come-out to do with me?"

"Everything. You see, the trip to London is intended to affect *you,* not me. Our mamas mean to make you escort me everywhere. To every ball, every dinner party, every gala and rout for which I'll require a partner. And furthermore, they'll see that I'm thrust in your way wherever you go. They're determined to make you see me in a new light . . . a London light."

"Good God!" he swore, gaping at her with sudden comprehension.

"Good God, indeed."

"It'd be worse than being betrothed!"

"Yes, just so! That's why I sent for you. It's the very situation we've been trying to avoid all these years."

They eyed each other in silence, each trying to envision being perpetually yoked to the other.

"You were right," Tris admitted at last, crossing back to

the table and sinking down upon it. "Something must be done."

"Yes," Julie agreed. "But what?"

"I don't know." Tris stared down at the floor glumly.

"You know, Tris, I've been giving the matter a great deal of thought ever since I heard them making their blasted plans, and I think the best solution is for you to wed your Miss Smallwood as soon as possible. Once you're wed, as you yourself pointed out to me, our mothers will be forced to give up."

"Yes, that *would* have been a possible solution yesterday," Tris said in disgust, "but didn't you hear what I said a few moments ago? I can't wed Miss Smallwood. I've lost her."

"Oh, Tris, no! Are you absolutely sure?"

"As sure as one can be in such matters. I fully intend to try my luck with her again, but at best I've set my chances back by weeks, or even months. It will take time to win her again. And my cause will not be helped if, while I'm courting her, they drag you to London, and I'm obliged to squire *you* about right under Cleo's nose."

"Yes," Julie sighed, despairing, sitting down beside him, "I see what you mean."

Tris turned to her. The light was now bright enough for him to see her plainly. Despite her plaited hair and shabby robe, she was undoubtedly a lovely girl. "It's *you* who must be wed, Julie," he said, taking her hands. "And quickly too."

She snorted. "Now you're grasping at straws. Who is there to wed me?"

"I don't know. Isn't there anyone in all of Derbyshire who's caught your eye?"

"You know perfectly well there isn't. Except of course . . ." A picture of Lord Canfield astride his horse, with rain pouring from the brim of his beaver, flew into her mind. "No, no," she muttered, shaking her head vigorously, "he wouldn't . . . he couldn't—No . . . it's impossible."

Tris's eyebrows lifted in immediate interest. "There *is* someone? Who?"

"No one. Nobody. Never mind. I was just jabbering. There's no one."

But he could see her cheeks redden. "Come now, my dear, this is no time to be coy. *Tell* me!"

"I'm *not* being coy," she declared, wrenching her hands from his hold and turning away. "It was very silly of me to even *think* of him."

He forced her to face him. "Think of *whom?*" he insisted angrily. "If I agree that it's really a silly thought, I'll drop the subject forever. I won't tease you, I promise."

She lowered her eyes. "A gentleman has bought Wycklands," she murmured. "His name is Canfield. Peter Granard, Viscount Canfield."

"Ah!" Tris grinned a wide, eager grin. "Canfield, eh? And you *like* him, do you?"

"How can I say? I've scarcely met him."

"Then why did you think of him in this connection?"

"Because he's a new face in the neighborhood. And because he asked me to dance. And because he's . . . he's . . ."

"What?" Tris prodded. "Because he's what?"

"Because," she burst out, "he's absolutely the most glorious man I've ever laid eyes on, that's what!"

"Well, well!" Tris chortled. "Will wonders never cease! A glorious man, eh? And he danced with you?"

Julie lowered her head. "He only asked. Mama didn't let him."

"Of course she didn't," Tris muttered. "I should have known."

"So you see, it's all quite hopeless," Julie said.

He lifted her chin and smiled down at her. "No, it isn't. I'm home now. I shall make it my task to meet this fellow and arrange some social events. Then I'll fix you over, dress you properly and teach you to flirt. And then, my shy Miss Branscombe, we shall see what we shall see."

"Oh, Tris, don't be such a fool. You can't mean . . . I couldn't possibly—"

"Yes, you can." He beamed down at her, his eyes shining in eagerness to meet the challenge he'd set himself. "What do you wager I'll make you Lady Canfield? I tell you, Julie, we'll have you wed to him before the month is out."

# 9

WITH A HEAD FULL OF PLANS, TRIS LEFT LARCH-
wood and went home to Enders Hall to inform his
mother that he was back. Though he intended to return to
London sooner or later, he told her, he would remain at
home for an indefinite—in fact an extended—stay. Then,
despite the fact that it was seven in the morning, he kissed
her cheek and went off to bed.

Lady Phyllis was beside herself with delight. She scur-
ried across the fields to Larchwood as soon as she'd break-
fasted. "Perhaps we won't have to subject Julie to a London come-out after all," she chortled to Madge
Branscombe.

Lady Branscombe was skeptical. "Perhaps. But let's see
how the two of them get on this time before we become
too hopeful. What I'd like to know is why the boy has
returned from London so soon. And why he's here for an
'extended' stay."

"Yes," Lady Phyllis agreed, her joyous mood somewhat
dampened, "now that you mention it, so would I."

Tris spent the next six hours catching up on his sleep.
But when he woke later that afternoon, the first thing he
thought of was Julie's revelation. Never before had he
heard her speak about a man in just that way, as if she
were truly enamored of the fellow. If Tris could accomplish what he'd promised—actually get her wedded to this
paragon who'd caught her eye!—all his troubles would be
over. But perhaps he shouldn't have *sworn* he could do it.
After all, he didn't know the man. Perhaps he would have

49

been wiser to wait and see just what sort of person he'd be up against. He'd made a too hasty promise.

There was, therefore, only one thing to do: he had to get a glimpse of the fellow—and at once!

He dressed quickly, mounted his favorite horse, cantered through Amberford and over the two hills that separated the town from Wycklands and, in less than an hour from the moment he'd made the decision, was presenting himself at the viscount's door. "I'm Tris Enders of Enders Hall," he said to the butler, "here to welcome Lord Canfield to the neighborhood."

The butler kept him cooling his heels in the entry hall for what seemed a long while. When he returned, he led the visitor down a long corridor, past a portrait gallery and a series of impressively dignified rooms, until they reached what was obviously a library. But the condition of the room differed markedly from the other rooms Tris had glimpsed along the way. Those others had all been models of shining, well-kept elegance, but this room was a shambles. The long table and chairs which normally would have been placed at the center of the room had been pushed back against the window wall, and the rugs had been rolled up and also shoved aside, all to make room for a great number of wooden boxes which were scattered round the room. Some of them were open, their contents—a great multitude of books—spilling out and piled round them on the floor. And in addition to the disarray of the furnishings and the boxes, there was a general atmosphere of must and dust. A cloud of dust motes danced in the golden rays of the sun that shone in from the huge windows. The entire scene seemed to Tris to be incongruous in this well-appointed mansion.

The glare of the light from those tall, uncurtained windows blinded Tris for a moment. Not until his eyes accustomed themselves to the light did he see, standing among the wooden boxes, a tall, broad-shouldered fellow in his shirtsleeves. His hands were filthy, and his face streaked with dust. He'd evidently been caught in the act of shelving books. "Oh! I'm dreadfully sorry," Tris said awkwardly, trying to back out of the room. But the butler had already withdrawn and shut the door. "I seem to be intruding," he mumbled in embarrassment.

"Not all all," said the viscount, smiling and coming toward him, "not if you don't mind meeting me in all my dirt." He put out his hand. "I'm Canfield," he said.

Tris, noting that beneath the dirt the fellow was as imposing and handsome as Julie had led him to expect, grasped the extended hand. "I've never been afraid of a little dirt," he grinned. "Or a lot of it, for that matter."

Lord Canfield grinned back, his white teeth gleaming in his streaked face. "There's a lot of it here, I admit. It's these blasted books. They do seem to bring an amazing amount of dust with them. I'm trying to organize them, you see, but it's taking long hours of labor."

"I'm surprised you aren't leaving this labor to your servants," Tris remarked frankly.

Some might have found the remark rude, but the viscount did not take offense. "If I did, I'd only have to rearrange them later," he explained. "But let me not keep you standing. Come over here, where the dust is not so thick. I think that chair near the hearth is fairly clean. Shall I send for some tea? Or would you prefer a glass of port?"

Tris sat down. "Nothing, thanks. My mother expects me back for tea in a little while."

Canfield perched on the hearth before him, stretched out his long legs comfortably and peered closely at Tris's face. "So you're Enders," he remarked. "It's very good of you to put yourself out just to come and bid me welcome."

"Not at all. To be frank, I wanted to get a glimpse of you, having heard a great deal about you."

"From your mother? I met her, I believe. Last week at the assembly."

"Yes, I did hear about you from her. And from . . . others."

"Did you indeed?" Canfield's eyes glinted in amusement. "Am I the subject of gossip already?"

"You must realize, your lordship, that you are famous

here. Everyone in Amberford is talking about our new
inhabitant, the viscount who bought Wycklands."

"I'm not surprised," Canfield said pleasantly. "That's to
be expected in a town as small as this. No one's business is
completely his own. I'd already heard about you too. But I
was led to believe you were in London."

"Yes, but I've come back for a bit." He turned and
looked about the room. Even with the confusion of boxes
and the motes of dust revealed by the rays of sunlight, he
could see it was a room of impressive grandeur. The ceil-
ing was at least twenty feet high; wood panels, beautifully
carved, covered three of the four walls and held dozens of
shelves; the windows occupied all of the fourth wall in
both breadth and height; and—the most magnificent touch
of all—a shallow gallery, reached by carved circular stair-
ways, circled the three unwindowed sides of the room.
They contained more bookshelves, but these were already
filled with leather-bound, gold-imprinted volumes. "My
word, your lordship, you certainly have a great many
books!" Tris murmured in awe.

"I've been collecting books all my life," Canfield said.

"And reading them all?"

"As many as possible."

Tris shook his head in disbelief. "How can you be a
sportsman and a libertine and still find time—?" Realizing
what he'd said, his face paled, then reddened in chagrin.
"I'm sorry . . . I didn't mean . . ."

Canfield laughed. "Of course you did. You needn't look
so stricken. I've heard myself described that way many
times. And there's some truth to it, I suppose. I've spent
more years than I care to remember in racing my horses
and betting on boxing matches. And I've had more than
my share of affairs of the heart. The town gossips blame
me for at least three broken troths, for two of which I'm at
least partially at fault. I'm not proud of those facts. That's
why I moved here to Derbyshire."

"To escape from the gossip?"

"No, I don't think there's any escape from that. To
change the way I live my life, I suppose. Since I left school,

I've spent too much time in dissipation, without truly enjoying it. I'm past thirty now, you see, and have become very bored with town life. I want to live quietly, here with my books."

Tris studied the man with some alarm. This did not sound like a fellow who would easily let himself be tempted into wedlock. "Are you saying you've become scholarly? That you're intending to become a . . . a recluse?" he asked, horrified.

"No, no, not at all. I'm not a scholar. Merely a country gentleman, with an estate to manage, a stable of horses to breed, a library to organize, books to read . . . a sort of life that I think will be more agreeable to me than the one I lived in town."

"Then you're not giving up social life entirely?" Tris asked, hope springing up in him again. "Or sporting activities either?"

"Of course I'm not. I have no intention of burying myself away. You seem to be a lively, healthy young fellow, so I assume you ride. If you do, why don't we go riding together one day soon, so that I can prove to you I don't intend to spend all my time dusting off books?"

"I'd be delighted, your lordship," Tris quickly agreed. "Shall we say tomorrow?"

"Yes indeed, if you're willing to ride early. And on the condition that you skip the your-lordships and call me Peter."

They made arrangements for the time and place, and Tris rose to leave. Canfield walked him to the door. "I was almost forgetting why I came," Tris said before departing. "My mother is giving a small dinner party on Saturday. Very informal, with no more than a dozen guests . . . her friend Lady Branscombe and her daughter Juliet, Sir William Kenting and his lady, and a few others from town. We thought it might be a good way for you to meet some of your neighbors in a rather more intimate setting than at one of those deuced assemblies." He looked at his host with an expression that combined hope and doubt. "After what you've told me, I suppose a small country dinner party like that—completely informal, as I said—will seem to you as dull as ditchwater, but if you think you could bear it for one evening, we'd very much like you to come."

"Of course I'll come," Canfield said, his bright smile reappearing. "I'm sure it won't be dull at all. And you have my promise that, even though it's informal, I *will* wash this dirt away before making my appearance."

# 10

LADY PHYLLIS DID NOT HAVE ANY DIFFICULTY IN persuading her son to escort her to the Branscombes for dinner that evening. To her astonishment, he seemed almost eager to join her. Was it possible, she wondered, that the situation between her son and Julie was about to change? Did the dream that she and Madge had shared so fruitlessly for so long suddenly have a hope of coming true?

However, she tried not to let herself climb too high into alt. The shreds of evidence that a *tendre* was developing between her son and Julie were too thin to count on. There were only two: Tris's unexpected return from London, and his willingness to endure an evening meal at the Branscombes'. Hardly enough reason to rejoice. Nevertheless, she could barely restrain her smiles as they set out in their carriage for Larchwood.

Tris could see that his mother was in high spirits. He decided, therefore, that this was a good time to inform her that he'd invited Lord Canfield to a dinner party for the coming Saturday night. When she heard his request, she stared at him blankly. "A dinner party? In less than a week?"

He shrugged. "I hope you won't find it too difficult to arrange the affair at such short notice."

"But you've never done such a thing before . . . invited someone for a party that hasn't even been arranged!"

"Don't look so flabbergasted," Tris laughed, patting her hand soothingly. "You arrange dinner parties so well that

I knew you'd not be overwhelmed by this last-minute request."

Lady Phyllis was indeed flabbergasted, for Tris had
never before invited anyone to the house without giving
her appropriate warning. But since she did not wish to
spoil the good spirits of the evening by giving him a scold,
she muttered an assent. Besides, arranging a dinner party
in four days was *not* an overwhelming task for her. She
had a large staff, after all, and would not have to do more
than give them orders. "I'll send out invitations tomorrow," she said, merely throwing her son a look of mild
annoyance.

The dinner at Larchwood was a pleasant affair, with
Julie and Tris apparently on very good terms. Phyllis and
Madge couldn't help exchanging gleeful smiles when, after dinner, Tris asked that he and Julie be excused to play
a game of billiards. "Go right ahead," Lady Branscombe
said, barely able to conceal her delight. "Don't worry
about us. Phyllis and I always have plenty to talk about."

Once in the billiard room, Tris reported to Julie the
details of his meeting with Canfield that afternoon. "I
liked him," he concluded, "though I don't think snaring
him will be easy."

"I told you that," Julie said sourly.

"Yes, but it's too soon to despair. I've arranged two
social events already, so we may as well be optimistic."

"Two events?"

"Yes. One to go riding tomorrow and another for a
dinner party at Enders Hall on Saturday." He smiled at
her in triumph. "And you'll be present at both!"

Julie shook her head dubiously. "I shall attend the
party, of course," she said, aware of a growing feeling of
absolute terror, "but I don't see how your riding appointment can possibly include me."

"It's quite simple. You'll go out riding by yourself in the
morning—something you've often done anyway—and
you'll 'accidentally' come upon us."

Julie found the suggestion so revolting that it took Tris
almost an hour of firm persuasion before she would agree.

When finally she did, he would not let well enough alone. "One more thing," he ordered, reaching for a billiard cue, "you are *not* to wear your old shabby riding habit. Didn't you say your mother had had a new one made for you?"

"Yes, but it's much too elegant for riding in the country," Julie said, her forehead still creased with worry about the scheme she'd so reluctantly agreed to. "It's fit for a princess to wear when riding about on the grounds of Windsor Castle, not for a country girl to sport when frisking about on the south fields of Larchwood. I'm embarrassed to tell you, Tris, that it actually has *satin lapels!* And sleeves puffed out to *here.* And Mama insisted on buying me one of those silly cocked hats to wear with it, the kind the London ladies wear tilted over one eye when they ride in Hyde Park."

"It sounds just the thing," Tris said, chalking his cue.

"Tris! You can't possibly expect me to bedeck myself in such a ridiculous rig. I won't do it!"

He leaned on the cue, eyeing her in exasperation. "Yes, you will!"

"See here, Tris," she snapped back, equally exasperated, "I've already let you ride roughshod over me by agreeing, despite my best instincts, to take my horse out for this 'accidental' meeting tomorrow. But ordering me to wear that ostentastious, immoderate, silly creation is pushing me too far."

"No, my dear child, *you* see here! If we're to succeed at this enterprise, you must put yourself completely in my hands. Completely. And that means following my orders on *everything!* I refer to such matters as clothes and hairstyles and conversation and flirtation and anything else I deem necessary. And unless you're willing to agree to that *one ruling principle* here and now, I shall drop the entire matter, take myself back to London and leave you to face a London come-out without any assistance from me."

She frowned at him in revulsion. "Indeed! I believe an ultimatum of that sort is called blackmail."

"Call it what you like. But choose now. Yes, or no."

She glared at him a moment more, considering the matter. This scheme of his would never work, she was sure of it. She could never win a man like Viscount Canfield, no matter how Tris dressed her up. He might try to bully her into acting like a flirt of the haute ton, but she was at bottom nothing but a mousy little country girl, and that was all she could ever be. No matter how she was disguised, her real nature would reveal itself before long and thus doom the whole enterprise. But there was one huge advantage in going along with Tris and his ridiculous scheme: it would cancel—or at least postpone—the dreadful prospect of a London come-out. That alone would make giving in to his demands worthwhile. "Oh, very well," she murmured, her shoulders sagging in defeat, "have it your way. There isn't much one can do against blackmail."

"Good. Then be sure to come riding along the south bank of the river tomorrow morning at eight-thirty precisely. Wearing the new habit *and* that hat!" He glanced over to where she was standing, her head lowered and her body drooping, and he felt a momentary twinge of conscience. But he ignored it. He'd been hard on her, he knew, but it was for a greater good. So he merely turned his back on her and said gruffly, "Now, let's stop this bickering and play some billiards."

# 11

TRIS AND LORD CANFIELD MET A LITTLE AFTER
eight the next morning. They'd not been riding
long when Tris heard the bells in the Amberford clock
tower strike the half hour. "Come this way," he said to his
companion. "There's a fine bridle path along the river."
And without waiting for an answer, he guided him over a
rise toward the riverbank. There, precisely as he'd di-
rected her, he saw Julie, a lone horsewoman silhouetted
against the glowing morning sky, riding toward them. He
smiled in self-satisfaction, for everything was going exactly as he'd planned. His clever machinations were apparently going to succeed.

But his pleasure was short-lived, immediately changing
to anger when he saw that Julie was wearing neither her
new riding habit nor the cocked hat. His teeth clenched in
fury. *Damnation* he swore to himself, *I ought to wash my
hands of her!*

But as they drew closer, he saw with a twinge of relief
that she was not wearing her shabby old habit either.
She'd chosen a walking dress of dark blue kerseymere
with a full skirt. It covered an underdress of some sort of
gauzy white material, with long sleeves and a soft collar
that he had to admit was very becoming. She'd also
pinned back her hair in a tight, neat bun so that it couldn't
fly about her face as it usually did when she rode. Of
course she was wearing her time-ravaged riding gloves
(he'd not thought of ordering her to find herself a decent
pair), but by and large, he concluded in relief, she looked
passably presentable. "Look, Peter," he said aloud,

"there's my friend Miss Branscombe. Do you mind if we ride over and greet her?"

"Not at all," Lord Canfield assured him, having already recognized the lone rider as the young woman whose eyes —and legs—he'd so admired.

Tris shouted a loud hello and rode quickly ahead of Canfield to exchange a word with Julie alone. "This makes *once* that you've disobeyed my orders," he muttered sternly, reining in his horse close to hers. "I'll say no more this time, but the next time you do it, I shall consider our bond broken."

She bit her underlip guiltily. "I'm sorry, Tris. I tried, really I did. That habit was just too dreadful . . ."

"All right, never mind it now," he whispered, scarcely moving his lips as he glanced over his shoulder. "You look fine. He's coming, so smile!"

The three horses pulled up together on the riverbank. Tris made the introductions. Julie gave his lordship a shy how-de-do, but, for some reason she could not explain, neither she nor Canfield indicated that they'd met before. Tris, to cover the ensuing silence, asked with sham innocence what she was doing out so early.

Julie, not liking the sense of subterfuge that seemed to permeate his every utterance, threw him a look of reproach. "I often ride before breakfast, as you well know," she said.

"Without escort?" Lord Canfield asked, throwing her a surreptitious glance.

"There's no real need for an escort," Tris explained. "We're only moments from the Larchwood lands. Besides, a young lady can ride safely in these environs. It's very quiet here."

"I see," his lordship said with his slow half smile. "I seem to be habitually thinking like a Londoner. In town, you know, it would not be permitted."

Another long silence followed, during which Tris studied Canfield's face, Canfield studied Julie's, Julie studied her hands, and the horses pawed the ground. "Why don't we follow the river to the Larchwood south fields?" Tris suggested at last. "We can have a good gallop there and then ride over to Enders Hall for refreshment."

The others agreed, and they turned their horses toward the south. As they rode, Tris managed to pull up close enough to Julie to whisper, "Now, listen carefully. I've a plan. Whatever I say this morning, be sure to agree with me."

She had no opportunity to ask what he meant, for his lordship, who'd ridden a bit ahead, was looking at them over his shoulder, his eyebrows raised curiously.

They caught up with him and cantered along the river in silence. When they came to the line of shrubs that bordered Larchwood, they all took the leap over the hedges with ease. As they started across the field at an easy trot, Tris pulled his horse to a sudden stop. "I say, was that your gardener I just saw?" he asked Julie abruptly.

She blinked, startled. "Jenkins? Why, no, I don't think it could've been—"

Tris cut her off with a furious glare. "I want to ask him something," he said, abruptly turning his horse toward the east. "Go on ahead, you two. I'll catch you up." And before either of the others could say a word, he'd spurred his horse and ridden off.

"Well, *he's* getting a good gallop, at any rate," Canfield observed dryly, looking after the rapidly disappearing horse and rider.

"Yes," Julie said awkwardly. "I must apologize for him. That was very rude."

"Not at all. I'm rather glad he's gone, actually."

"Really?" She lifted her eyes to his for the first time in their encounter. "Why?"

"It gives me the chance to talk to you. After all, I was not given that opportunity the last time we met. You rode off so abruptly."

Her eyes fell, and her cheeks reddened. "Yes, I remember. But I wish you would forget all about that encounter."

"It's not very likely. It was a memorable meeting. But I won't speak of it if you prefer that I don't."

"I do prefer it," she said.

"Very well, ma'am. Then let's speak of the *first* time we met. I was not given the opportunity to get acquainted with you that time either."

"I know. I was sorry about that. I would have very much liked . . . er, that is, I'd have enjoyed dancing with you. I'm afraid my mother is . . . is . . ."

"A bit of a dragon?"

His directness caused a laugh to gurgle up from her chest. "Yes, exactly! Did someone describe her that way to you, my lord, or did you come to that conclusion on your own?"

"Both, I think. She did seem to eat me alive that night. But must you call me my lord? Your friend Tris calls me Peter quite easily."

He blush deepened. "I don't think I can be expected to do it quite so easily as he does."

"Why not?"

"Because you two apparently have become . . . acquainted."

"But so have you and I."

"Yes, I suppose . . ." She threw him a quick, shy little glance. "But not very *well* acquainted."

"Ah, I see. And you won't call me Peter until we're well acquainted, is that it?"

She answered only with a small movement of her shoulder that didn't say yes or no. He studied her with interest, wondering how he could penetrate her shyness. It was like a wall she'd erected to keep her safe from the rest of the world, although even in the short time he'd known her, he'd caught glimpses of the charm she kept hidden behind it. "Is there something I might do or say to make us well acquainted?" he asked earnestly.

She did not have the courage to meet his eyes. "I don't think one can rush such things, do you?"

"You're probably right," he said in good-natured agreement. "Close acquaintance is akin to intimacy, is it not?

And in matters of intimacy, one must let nature take its course."

His understanding words were rewarded by a quick glance of approval from her dream-drenched eyes. "Yes," she said softly, "just so."

He gave her a rueful smile. "Though I can't help wishing I could push matters just a bit. At least enough to . . ." Here he had to pause to steady his horse, who was not accustomed to standing about. ". . . to permit you to use my given name."

"Your mount is growing impatient with our chatter," Julie said, thankful to have found a way to change the subject. "He wishes to run. Why don't we take a quick gallop right now? Since Tris was rude enough to leave us so abruptly, I feel no obligation to wait for him, do you?"

"Not in the least. Shall we race to that line of trees?"

She nodded, and they spurred their horses.

A few moments later, windblown and breathless, they reached their destination. Canfield grinned at her admiringly. "I think, ma'am, that you are the best horsewoman I've ridden with in many years."

"Thank you. It's because I'm a country girl. I have more opportunities for riding than the young ladies you ride with in town."

"Perhaps. But whatever the reason, I'd like another race." He looked over the terrain to suggest a destination, but at that moment caught a glimpse of Tris just riding over the horizon toward them. "Dash it," he swore under his breath, "I'd hoped we'd have a little more time."

He hadn't meant to say the words aloud, but she heard him. "Time?" she asked.

"Yes," he said, deciding to be frank. "Time to ourselves. To improve this acquaintance. That little bit of a race didn't deepen the acquaintance enough to make you ready to use my given name, did it?"

"Perhaps not quite enough," she said, softening the words with a small smile, "but the prospect seems less frightening than before."

His half smile reappeared. "That, at least, gives me

hope." His horse shied, and he bent to stroke the animal's neck. When he straightened up again, his eyes swept over her with an appreciative gleam. "The race has loosed your hair," he informed her. "It's blowing about in delighted liberation. This sight of you looking so unceremoniously windblown certainly increases my feeling of close acquaintance."

Her smile faded at once. "Oh, dear!" she murmured, trying desperately to gather the strands together. "Tris will be so annoyed with me."

"Will he?" His lordship peered at her curiously. "Why? What on earth has he to say about it?"

She shook her head. "I don't . . . I . . ." Her voice died away and her eyes fell.

"You have my word that you look quite lovely this way. Does it matter so much what Tris thinks?"

She bit her underlip and held up a hand as if to restrain him from further comment.

He immediately regretted what he'd said. "I'm sorry. It's not my affair. I shouldn't have asked."

"No, please," she murmured in a low voice, "you didn't . . . It's not important."

"I should have remembered what Sir William told me."

Her eyes flew to his. "What was that?"

"That you and Tris are betrothed. Or almost betrothed."

"No, we're not," she said. Her tone was decisive, more decisive than he'd yet heard it.

"Not even almost?"

"Not even that."

Tris was coming close. Whatever else Canfield wanted to say to her would have to be brief. "In that case, Miss Branscombe," he said quickly, "I shall feel free to repeat my request for a dance with you at my very next opportunity."

She paused in the act of pinning back her hair and looked up at him, a smile lighting her eyes. "Despite the dragon?"

He smiled back at her. "Dragons don't frighten me. I'm

quite capable of fighting them. I'm determined to dance with you one day, no matter how carefully you're protected by dragons. Or by not-quite-betrotheds, for that matter. So be warned."

# 12

CLEO SMALLWOOD HAD SPENT THE DAY AFTER Tris's departure closeted in her bedroom, not even emerging for meals. Her father, listening at the door at intervals during the day, heard either sobs, agitated footsteps or fearsome silences. By evening he was becoming distraught. Such behavior was utterly unwarranted, he believed, and utterly self-indulgent. From time to time he pleaded through the shut door for her to be sensible. "Now, listen here," he declared when his patience became exhausted, "if you don't come out at once, I shall . . . I shall do something drastic!"

Her response was to ignore this dire threat and remain in seclusion for the next two days.

The following day, however, she emerged from the room in a completely different mood. Her movements were quick and lively, and her eyes glittered with determined animation. She informed her father that she was going out, and out she went, dashing about madly in a whirl of visiting, riding and shopping (each activity requiring a complete change of clothing), and then topping off the day by attending three routs in one evening. When she returned home at four in the morning—an hour at which no properly reared girl would still be awake—her father, who'd been pacing the floor anxiously, attempted a mild admonishment. "I am forced to have to tell you, my girl," he said as firmly as his mild nature permitted, "that this behavior will not do at all."

She glared him, ready to do battle. "I am not a child," she began belligerently, "a mere child who must be scolded for staying out la—" But all at once her face fell, and she burst into a flood of tears. "Oh, Papa," she wept, falling upon him, "I'm so m-m-miserable!"

"Good God!" he exclaimed, shocked at the vehemence of her emotions. "Cleo, my love, all this rodomontade *can't* be about that bumpkin Enders, can it?"

"Yes, it can," she sobbed, "and it is. He's broken my heart!"

"You poor child, I can see that he has, and I'm very sorry for you," he said, patting her shoulder, "but hearts can be mended, you know."

"Yes, b-but how?"

"I don't know. Time, I suppose. Time will make you forget him. That's what they say. What I *do* know is that you'll do yourself no good by indulging in this sort of emotional display."

"I know. I've been very foolish." She shuddered, gulped down what remained of her tears and sank down on the nearest chair. "But the truth is I don't wish to forget him. I want him back."

"If you wanted him so much," her father pointed out in the foolish way that parents have, "you shouldn't have thrown him out."

"No, I shouldn't have," she agreed glumly. "But what's done can't be undone."

"Quite. So let's end this useless discussion and go up to bed. We'll both feel a good deal better after a proper night's sleep."

"Perhaps you will, but I won't." She stood up and followed slowly after her father, who'd headed to the stairway. "Papa, would you be willing to help me win him back?" she asked from the bottom of the stairs.

He'd reached the first turning, but he paused and looked down at her curiously. "I? What could *I* do?"

"Something difficult. Important but difficult. Would you do it?"

"You know I don't think much of the fellow . . ."

"I know. But you'll change your mind once you know

him better." She climbed a stair and gazed up at him. "So, what do you say?"

"I don't know what to say. What is it you wish me to do?"

She twisted her fingers together uneasily. "I want you to accompany me to Derbyshire," she said in a small voice.

"To *Derbyshire?*" His voice was a loud squeal. "Are you considering *chasing* the fellow? To the *country?* Have you gone *mad?*"

"I think I have, rather. But the idea is not as mad as you make it sound. He did invite me, once."

"What sort of invitation? Did it have a specific date?"

"Well . . . no, but—"

"Then it wasn't a true invitation at all. Besides, even if it were, your quarrel would nullify it."

"I don't care," the girl said with a shrug. "Once we arrive on his doorstep, he'll have to welcome us. He *is* a gentleman, after all."

"Balderdash!" Lord Smallwood was a mild man, but even he could be pushed too far. He drew himself up to his full height and glared down at her. "I've never heard of such a thing! Are you actually suggesting that you wish to engage in a pursuit of a man who is quite beneath you? And that I accompany you all the way to Derbyshire to drop in on someone who isn't even expecting us? You *are* mad! You sound like an immodest, manipulative virago! I won't even discuss such a brazen idea!" And he turned on his heel and marched up out of her sight.

Cleo sank down on the step and leaned her forehead on the bannister, her mind in a whirl. It *was* a brazen idea, she thought, just as her father said it was. But it was also a good one. There was much she could accomplish in a visit to Tris's home. For one thing, he would, as her host, be forced by simple good manners to reconcile with her. She would meet his mother, for another. And she would get a glimpse of the mysterious Julie, the "neighbor" who had such power over him that one crook of her little finger had lifted him from her own arms and sent him rushing home. Cleo wanted more than anything else to get a look at that female.

Yes, it was in Derbyshire, rather than in London, that she, Miss Cleo Smallwood, could learn what she needed to know of the real Tris. And if in the process she appeared to her father—and to the rest of the world—to be a manipulative, immodest virago, so be it. It would be worth it.

Of course, she couldn't make the trip without escort; she wasn't such a virago as all that. But there was no one other than her father who could escort her. He'd refused to do it, and in terms that seemed to brook no argument. But she could change his mind; his refusal did not worry her. Papa would succumb to her blandishments sooner or later, she was sure of that. By the time she was ready to leave, she'd surely have won him over. She could always twist him round her little finger. When Tris had stormed from the house, she'd worried that she'd lost some of her power to charm men. But not her power over Papa. Good God, no! She couldn't have lost as much as *that*.

# 13

AN HOUR BEFORE THE GUESTS WERE DUE TO ARRIVE for the dinner party, Tris decided to look into the dining room to check on the preparations. What he saw struck him like a blow. This was not the small informal dinner he'd envisioned. The table had been expanded to its fullest length—seating twenty-four!—and was set with the finest china and plate. At least five goblets were lined up at each place, and two footmen were busily setting up floral centerpieces at three-foot intervals on the table, having already adorned the sideboards with an alarming number of decanters, silver servers, chafing dishes, candelabra, epergnes and trays. The room glowed as if in preparation for the regent himself.

Turning quite pale in chagrin, Tris immediately turned about and stormed up to his mother's bedroom. "Mama!" he shouted, bursting in on her with no more warning than an angry knock. "What have you done?"

She was sitting at her dressing table in an enormous dressing gown, her abigail doing up her hair. "Done about what?" she asked calmly, turning about in her chair to face her son.

"About tonight's dinner! It was supposed to be *small.* And *informal!*

"Smaller than twenty-four was not possible," Lady Phyllis explained, signaling the abigail to leave them. "If, for example, I'd invited the Frobishers without asking the Severns, the Severns would have been dreadfully offended. And the Kentings have two houseguests who had to be included. And the Harroway daughters are back from London, which of course I didn't know, for if I did I'd never have sent the Harroways a card. Those Harroway girls, you know, are the two most irritating chatterboxes in the world, and why they're called girls I never will understand, for they are thirty-five if they're a day! And I couldn't omit Lady Stythe and her sister—"

"Enough!" Tris said, holding his ears. "I see your point; you needn't go over the entire guest list. But didn't you hear me say it was to be informal?"

"Of course I did. The cards all said it would be informal. 'An informal dinner and musicale' are the very words I used."

"Then why are there five glasses at each place, for heaven's sake?"

Lady Phyllis raised her eyebrows. "Of course there are five glasses. Good heavens, Tris, it *is* a dinner party, after all. You don't expect the table to be set as for a picnic, do you?"

Tris groaned. "So anything less than five goblets makes a picnic setting, does it? And I suppose everyone will appear in all their formal finery too. Satins and jewels and such?"

"They will be dressed for a dinner party, which is exactly as they should. And if you don't stop berating me and take yourself off, I shall not be ready to greet the first guests."

Tris shook his head helplessly. "This is *not* the sort of evening I wished for. I thought it would be like an ordinary family dinner. That was how I described it to our guest of honor—a small, intimate affair, I said. What if he makes his appearance in his riding coat? How will you feel then?"

"He will do no such thing. He is a gentleman, is he not? He knows enough, I'm sure, to dress for dinner." She turned back to her dressing table, picked up a little bell and rang for her abigail to return. "Now, stop all this nonsense and go along and dress yourself."

Despite his mother's serene dismissal of his concerns, Tris remained worried all the while he dressed. He'd given

Julie complete instructions on how to behave toward Canfield this evening ("Let yourself be saucy instead of shy," he'd advised her, "and laugh at anything he says that smacks even remotely of wit."), but he'd been counting on a small group. Now that the group had become a crowd, there would probably be little chance for the guest of honor to converse with Julie with any degree of intimacy. And if Canfield should clothe himself in too informal a manner, the fellow would be embarrassed into awkward silence and would probably cut out as soon as politely possible. All Tris's efforts to set up this affair would have been for naught. The evening was bound to be a complete failure.

But Tris soon learned that he needn't have worried. Just as his mother had predicted, Canfield did indeed know enough to dress for dinner. In fact, when Tris went down to welcome him at the door, he found him quite resplendent in a superbly cut dinner coat and elegantly tied neckerchief. "Peter, you coxcomb," Tris greeted him as he led him up to the already crowded drawing room, "how did you know to wear such finery when I said we'd be informal?"

"I did tell you, didn't I, that I intended to wash before I came?" his lordship laughed. "Did you think I'd show up in shirtsleeves and breeches?"

"Well, I didn't think you'd come looking fit to meet Prinny. Though everyone else has dressed to the nines to meet *you.*"

"I thought they might, but not because of me. It's because of the cards your mother sent."

"The cards?"

"I'm not such a greenhead that I don't know what a hostess means when she cordially invites one to an 'informal dinner party and *musicale.*' That word *musicale* is a clear signal that one had better wear the proper evening clothes."

"Ah, so that's it!" Tris exclaimed, chuckling at his own ignorance. "I see I have much to learn of social conventions, even in my own circle."

Tris led his honored guest into the drawing room and introduced him to all the assembled crowd. His lordship seemed not at all discomfited by their large number and put everyone at ease by exchanging pleasantries with admirable unaffectedness. Meanwhile, Tris's eyes roamed the room, searching for Julie.

He discovered that she was seated, as was her wont, unobtrusively in a far corner. *I should have warned her against that,* he thought in annoyance. The girl was never able to think for herself about how to put herself forward. However, all was not lost, for Sir William's son, Ronny Kenting, was leaning over her shoulder, trying as always to make some headway with her. Tris usually found his persistent attentions to Julie as annoying as Julie did herself, but today he was pleased. It would be good for Peter to see other young men hanging about her. "I say, Peter, there's Miss Branscombe," he said to his guest. "Let me take you over to her. You remember her, don't you? We rode together a few days ago."

"Of course I remember her, you gudgeon," his lordship said, bluntly, "so there's not the least need for you to escort me. With your permission, I'll make my how-de-dos to her on my own." With that he gave his host a quick nod and crossed the room to Julie's chair.

Tris watched intently as the viscount approached her. He saw with real satisfaction that Julie smiled up at the fellow with what seemed to be real pleasure. Furthermore, she responded with a gurgling laugh to whatever it was that Peter said to her. It was such a warm, sincere laugh that Ronny Kenting withdrew with a glower. Could it be that Julie was actually doing what he, Tris, had told her to do? Not only that, but she'd managed for once to look just as she ought. Her hair was neatly but softly drawn back into a bun at the nape of her neck, her eyes had a most becoming glow, and her gown—a full-skirted, rose-colored silk concoction—seemed to radiate its color to her cheeks. *Good girl!* he chortled to himself. *Perhaps I can allow myself to believe that this evening might not turn out to be such a disaster after all.*

He could not know, however, that disaster was rapidly approaching—that a carriage bearing the Smallwood crest had pulled into the courtyard of the Peacock Inn in Amberford, and that, at that very moment, the coachman was jumping off the box to inquire of the ostler the direction to Enders Hall.

# 14

WHAT PETER HAD SAID TO MAKE JULIE LAUGH WAS "I've lived the last few days in the hope that tonight's 'musicale' will include dancing, Miss Branscombe. I've come prepared either to fight the dragon and stand up with you, or to perish on my sword."

Julie's gurgling laugh in response had nothing to do with Tris's orders to "laugh at anything he says that smacks even remotely of wit." She was truly charmed. But she had to tell him that his hope would be dashed. "Your encounter with the dragon will not occur tonight, my lord," she said, holding out her hand in greeting, "for the musicale will *not* include dancing, I'm afraid."

He took the proffered hand and held it for a long moment before making his bow over it. "And I see that my other hope—that you will call me Peter—is also to be dashed," he said as he made the requisite genuflection. "I am crushed."

"Oh, dear," she said with a mock sigh, "we mustn't have our guest of honor crushed. What if I promise to *try* to bring your given name to my tongue at some time during this evening? Will that possibility revive your second hope?"

"Oh, more than that," he assured her, his appealing half smile reappearing. "You've completely reanimated my spirits!"

At this point she laughed again, causing the disheartened Ronny Kenting to stalk away in chagrin and Tris, across the room, to beam in triumph.

Someone else heard Julie's laugh, but the sound

brought no sense of pleasure to that listener. It brought dismay. Lady Branscombe did not approve of Lord Canfield's flirting with her daughter. Worse, she could not bear the sight of her daughter flirting with Lord Canfield. Any man who received a favorable gleam from Julie's eye caused her mother to have palpitations of the heart, and this time her dismay was greater than ever before, because Lord Canfield was a more formidable threat than most. She stiffened at once, ready to do battle. She had not planned all these years for her daughter to wed her best friend's son only to have the girl snatched away by the first truly attractive man to come along.

As soon as Lord Canfield's tête-à-tête with Julie was interrupted (as it was bound to be in such a crowded room, in which everyone present wanted a word with the guest of honor), Lady Branscombe inched her way toward him, watching for an opportunity to catch his eye. It did not take long. "I've been wishing most eagerly to speak to you, Lord Canfield," she said when she was near enough to grasp his arm.

"And I to you, ma'am," Canfield said smoothly. "I have wanted to speak to you ever since the night at the assembly when you expressed some disapproval of me."

If Lady Branscombe was surprised at his frankness, she did not show it. "Did I express disapproval? I *do* regret having given that impression. I promise that it was unintentional."

"I'm glad to hear it, ma'am, for I understand that your approval will serve me in good stead in this neighborhood."

"You overestimate my importance, my lord. Nevertheless, the reason I wish to communicate with you *is* in the hope of doing you some good here." She used her tight grasp on his arm to propel him to a secluded corner. "You are a bachelor, I understand."

"Yes, I am."

"And I suspect that your mother is deceased, is that not so?"

His eyebrows rose curiously. "Yes, for more than a decade now. Why do you ask?"

"Because if she were alive, she would not have permitted you remain a bachelor for so long. You are, what, thirty? Thirty-two? She would have advised you that bachelorhood is not a desirable state, and that it is time for you to settle down."

"I suppose she would have felt so," he murmured, somewhat at a loss. "And I would completely agree."

"Good. Then you won't object to my acting in a motherly role and pointing out to you all the very desirable, marriageable young ladies who are here tonight?"

"No, I won't object at all." He suddenly guessed what her purpose was, and he realized with some amusement that his first joust with the dragon was about to begin.

"Then, first," she began, her tone seductively sincere, "there is Elinor Severn, over there at the window. She is a charming girl, barely twenty-one, with a fine education in all the arts. She paints very well—one of her canvases is hanging in this very house, in the hallway near the door—and she has a lovely voice. You will hear her sing later tonight."

"How very enchanting. I look forward to it."

"And over there, standing with Tris Enders, is Sally Halloway. She is past her first bloom, I admit, but her appearance is very youthful, is it not? And her conversation is so lively one never has to strain to find something to say to her. And just there, to your left, the girl in the pink brocaded gown, is Emmaline Frob—"

"Yes, I've met her," Canfield interrupted. Fully aware of the approaching dangers, he decided to waste no more time but throw himself into the fray. "But surely your ladyship realizes that the loveliest girl in the room is your own daughter."

He could feel her arm stiffen. "Thank you, your lordship," she said coldly, "but that is quite beside the point. We are speaking of eligible girls, those who are suitable for you to pursue. I must inform you that my daughter is not eligible."

"Oh, is she not? Why?"

"She is promised to another."

Canfield looked down at her with eyebrows raised. In this first tilt with the dragon, it was time to make a jab. "Is she indeed? I take it you are referring to Tris Enders. But Miss Branscombe told me quite explicitly that she was *not* betrothed."

The dragon barely flinched. "It has not been announced, but the betrothal has been in effect for years."

He kept jabbing. "If that is so, then why hasn't it been announced?"

"When the agreement was reached, they were too young to make an official announcement," Lady Branscombe explained, excusing the lie by telling herself that it was, in a sense, true. An agreement *had* been made, if not between Tris and Julie, at least between their mothers. "But it will be announced one day soon."

"I see. But until it is, surely another suitor may try to court her, may he not? Isn't that what society agrees is perfectly permissible?" She couldn't argue the truth of that, he told himself. She *had* to say that he was free to try his hand. Believing that he'd struck a wounding, if not mortal, blow, he waited for her capitulation.

But this dragon was not so easily slain. "Whatever society may say, my dear boy," she said so complacently that he realized he'd not even wounded her, "is quite beside the point. Anyone with motherly feelings toward you, as I have, would warn you not to try. Julie *loves* Tris. I, her mother, know this well. I tell this to you in confidence, for your own good. I don't wish to see you waste your efforts on a hopeless venture that would, in the end, only bring you pain. Now, as I was saying, Miss Frobisher there—"

"Yes, ma'am, I do thank you for your advice. But the butler has just announced dinner, and I'm ordered by our host—Tris himself—to escort your daughter to the table. So, if you'll excuse me . . ."

He bowed and walked off, but not before he caught a

glimpse of chagrin in her eyes. Yes, he'd had the last word and made the last point. But he hadn't defeated her. In his first fight with the dragon, he wasn't even sure he'd achieved a tie.

# 15

THE SEATING ARRANGEMENT AT THE DINNER TABLE was as formal as the setting. Lord Canfield, the guest of honor, was placed at his hostess's right. And Tris had made sure that the seat at Peter's other side was occupied by Julie. But not being content to let matters take their natural course, Tris had seen fit to take her aside, just before the viscount had come to claim her arm, to remind her of the instructions he'd given at least twice before: be saucy, and keep laughing.

Julie took her place feeling sick to her stomach. Tris's whispered instructions had completely overset her. She had believed that she and Lord Canfield were getting on very well, but Tris must have disagreed. Otherwise, he wouldn't have found it necessary to remind her of how she should comport herself. She wished he hadn't spoken to her; his deuced reminder did no good at all. She didn't know how to be saucy or how to laugh on cue. All he'd done was destroy her confidence and cause her to become instantly self-conscious and tongue-tied.

Julie glanced over at his lordship, who'd just settled in on her right. He seemed completely at ease. He complimented Lady Phyllis on her table, exchanged pleasantries with the vicar, Mr. Weekes, who sat opposite him and attacked his pickled salmon with cucumber dressing with gusto. Julie, barely able to eat a bite, was occupied with trying, without any success, to think of something saucy to say to him. In desperation, she glanced down to the foot of the table where Tris sat, only to find him watching her.

When their eyes met, he made a motion with his hand urging her on. To do what, though, she had no idea.

Lord Canfield, noticing that she was not eating, looked at her curiously. "Can it be you don't like the salmon? I find it delectable. Had I a poetic bent, I'd write an ode to it."

Julie wondered if Tris would consider the remark witty enough to qualify for a laugh. To be on the safe side, she tried to force one out. The sound that came from her throat rang out more like a high-pitched hiccough than a laugh. Canfield was taken aback by it. "I'm not joking, my dear," he said earnestly. "You really should try it."

Again she had the sensation of wishing she could die to avoid this feeling of humiliation. The smile on her face was so forced, she was sure it looked like a grimace. Her reaction to what was merely an innocuous comment on the food had been ridiculously inappropriate, and the realization made her feel so foolish that she couldn't utter a word. She could only lower her head and play with the fish with her fork.

When she sensed that Lord Canfield had returned his attention to his food, she glanced down the table toward Tris to see if he'd noticed her blunder. He was frowning at her as if he had.

Canfield, meanwhile, was puzzled at Miss Branscombe's sudden awkwardness and withdrawal. A few minutes before, out in the drawing room, she'd been warm and delightful. What had happened to transform a charming girl into this shy, distant creature?

It was then that he noticed Tris and Julie exchanging looks. It struck him that the glances were familiar and significant, the exchanges of two people who were intimately connected. The quality of those looks surprised him. *Did the dragon really tell the truth?* he asked himself. *Does the girl truly love Tris?*

The answer to the question interested him greatly, though he didn't quite know why. After all, it was not really a matter of concern to him. Although he'd permitted Julie's mother to believe he was interested in courting the girl, it was very far from the truth. He'd only said it as a weapon in the battle of wills between himself and Lady Branscombe. True, he'd found her daughter a lovely, taking young woman, and he was sincere in his determination to dance with her at the next opportunity, but that was as far as he intended to go. If and when he should decide to take a wife (and despite what he'd said to the dragon, he was not at all ready for such a change in his life), there were a number of young ladies in London who had prior —and stronger—claims on his attentions. He had not the least interest in courting Miss Juliet Branscombe.

Nevertheless, he had to admit there was something fascinating about the girl. Her character was quirky, unexpected, unique. He couldn't quite fit all the pieces together. She was a riddle he was drawn to solve. That was why he found himself watching her and Tris surreptitiously during the remainder of the meal. By the time the ladies rose from the table, he'd decided that Julie was indeed in love with her childhood companion. The way her eyes kept seeking his, with an expression that seemed to be asking for his approval, put the matter beyond any doubt.

By the time the gentlemen had finished their brandies and joined the ladies in the drawing room, the chairs had been set up in rows facing a long, narrow pianoforte that had been rolled or dragged to the center of the room. Sir William, who was evidently born to act the role of master of the revels, stepped forward, cleared his throat and announced the first selection: the ballad "She Wore a Wreath of Roses," to be snug by Miss Elinor Severn, accompanied on the pianoforte by Miss Juliet Branscombe. The conversation stilled, the two young ladies took their places, Miss Branscombe played a brief introduction, and Miss Severn began to sing. She had a very sweet voice only slightly marred by a tremulous vibrato, but the vibrations gave her performance an emotional quality that perfectly suited the sentimental lyrics. When she finished, she was so loudly applauded that she was obliged to agree to an encore. After a quick consultation with her accompanist, she sang a throbbing rendition of "Cherry Ripe." This too was very well received. Her cheeks glowed pink as the applause accompanied her all the way back to her seat. Miss Branscombe, meanwhile, slipped back into her own seat quite unnoticed—except by Peter, who thought she'd played very well (and incidentally had looked extraordinarily lovely perched on the piano stool with her rose-colored silk skirt spread out about her like flower petals, and the light from the chandelier haloing her hair) and who was irked that her performance had not been properly appreciated.

Sir William next announced that his own son, Ronald Kenting, would sing—a cappella—a sea chanty called " 'Twas in the Good Ship Rover." Ronny clumped to the front, took a deep breath and burst forth with a rousing rendition of the song in a deep baritone that actually rattled the crystal drops in the chandelier. When he took his bow to tumultuous applause (even louder than the ovation that had greeted Miss Severn), he cast a proud glance in Julie's direction, as if to say that if she were now sorry she'd neglected him, she had only herself to blame.

Next on the program of the musicale was a harp solo to be performed by Miss Eugenia Halloway. Two footmen came forward, rolled the long pianoforte to the side and carried in a harp. Miss Halloway, so tall and gaunt that she'd developed a severe stoop, rose from her chair and came modestly forward, her shoulders hunched as if to protect her face from being seen. Just as she took her seat, however, there was a sound from the back of the room. It was Livesey, the butler, clearing his throat. "Edward Lord Smallwood and the Honorable Cleopatra Smallwood," he announced awkwardly.

In swept Cleo Smallwood, head high, bonnet feathers bobbing and a stylish velvet cape fluttering behind her. She was followed by her tight-lipped, red-faced father. But when they saw the room filled with guests, they both stopped in their tracks, eyes widening in amazement. "Oh!" Cleo gasped. "I didn't expect—"

*"Cleo!"* Tris cried, leaping to his feet.

Her outstretched hand flew to her breast, and she took two steps backward. "Good heavens, I didn't know . . . ! Oh, dear! Please . . . excuse us!" She swung about, grasped her father's arm and headed for the door. "Dash it, man," she muttered to the butler as she went by him, "why didn't you tell us a party was in progress?"

Livesey, the butler, stiffened in offense. Not only was he unaccustomed to being spoken to in that tone, but he'd tried his best to tell the visitors that there was a party going on. The girl had demanded to be announced, and when he'd tried to object, she'd ordered him to hold his tongue and do as he was told. Angry as he was by her unjustified scold, however, he was trained not to show his feelings. His furious sense of offense showed itself only in an almost imperceptible spark in his eyes. "Sorry, madam" was all he said.

But Lord Smallwood didn't like his daughter's scold either. "The fellow didn't tell you," he muttered as soon as they'd crossed the threshold, "because you never gave him a chance. I *told* you not to insist on being shown in—"

But at that moment Tris came hurrying out. "Cleo, wait! It's all right. It's only an informal musicale. Do come back."

"No, no, I wouldn't dream of intruding," she said. "It was dreadful of us to barge in on you without warning."

"Yes," her father muttered dryly, "it's about time you realized that."

"No, please!" Tris motioned for Livesey to take her cape. "You're not barging in. I'm delighted to see you . . . both."

"That is kind of you to say, Tris," Cleo said, beginning to regain her equilibrium. "You are a true gentleman, and I am a . . . a virago."

Tris gave a snort of laughter. "Now, Cleo, really—!"

"I suppose I ought to explain," she went on. "Papa and I are on our way to . . . er . . . Scotland, and we stopped at the inn in Amberford—what was the name of it, Papa? The Pheasant, wasn't it?"

"The Peacock?" Tris offered.

She treated him to a brilliant smile. "Yes, of course, the Peacock. It was there we learned that Enders Hall was so very close by, and I remembered that you'd once said that if ever I should be in the neighborhood—"

"Of *course* you should have called on us!" came a new voice. It was Lady Phyllis crossing the threshold. Just then the rippling sounds of the harp commenced from within, and she quickly closed the door behind her. Then she crossed to the newcomers and put out her hand. "Any friends of Tris are always welcome here."

Tris threw her a grateful glance before making the introductions. "Lord Smallwood, Cleo, this is my mother."

Lord Smallwood stepped forward and bowed over her hand. "How do you do, ma'am. You are most kind to welcome us, but it is unforgivable for us to have intruded at such a time."

"Not at all," Lady Phyllis assured him. "I'm delighted to meet Tris's London friends. I hope you intended to spend some time here with us."

"We wouldn't dream of putting you out," the embarrassed gentleman murmured.

"You aren't putting us out at all," Tris said earnestly. "In fact I insist that you spend some time here with us before you proceed on your travels. We both insist, don't we, Mama?"

If Phyllis had any qualms, she hid them well. "Of course we insist. I shall have Livesey go down for your bags and establish you in adjoining guest bedrooms."

"That is most generous of you, my lady," Cleo said, bestowing her dazzling smile on her hostess. "We accept with pleasure, don't we, Papa?"

The white-haired fellow gave a helpless shrug and surrendered his hat and greatcoat to the butler. Lady Phyllis, sensing his reluctance and shrewdly guessing that he'd been coerced into this escapade, felt an immediate rush of sympathy for him. "Please give no further thought to the manner of your arrival," she assured him. "The only matter for concern is to see to your needs. Do you wish to rest after your journey? Or shall I arrange for you to have dinner? Or, if you'd prefer, you can join us for the rest of the musicale. There will be a light supper served afterwards."

"The musicale, of course," Cleo said at once, and then, in an afterthought, added, "if Papa agrees."

The dignified gentleman shrugged his agreement. Lady Phyllis took his arm. "You will stay, I hope," she said warmly as she opened the door. She urged him into the drawing room, where Miss Halloway, her head bent and her tightly curled forelock plastered against her forehead, which was wet from her exertions, was still plucking the strings of the harp with impressive enthusiasm. Tris and Cleo followed his mother in. Tris settled Cleo onto his chair, and Phyllis resumed her own. Two footmen appeared almost at once with chairs for the two men. All this was done so silently that Miss Halloway was not distracted. A few heads did turn to take another peep at the new arrivals, but the musicale continued without further interruption.

After two encores by Miss Halloway, and another sea chanty by Ronny Kenting, Sir William announced that the musicale was over. The guests rose and began to mill about. Lady Phyllis led the two late arrivals round the room and introduced them. Lord Smallwood responded to each greeting with monosyllables, but Cleo was soon completely at home, exchanging banter, laughing, and charming every gentleman in the room.

As the entire party drifted in pairs or groups to the morning room, where a buffet of light delicacies had been set up, the young lady from London was being observed with interest by several pairs of eyes. One of the observers was Julie Branscombe, who—after studying Cleo's carriage, her curly coiffure and the easy way she spoke to everyone she met—found her to be just as Tris had described: graceful, spontaneous and self-assured. *Good for you, Tris,* she thought.

Lord Canfield was another observer. He not only closely examined the new arrival, but he watched Julie watching her. He concluded that Miss Branscombe was in

trouble. Cleo Smallwood was a beautiful, glib sophisti-
cate, talented at flirtation. He'd seen the type before. If
she wanted Tris Enders for herself, she would ride over
the shy Branscombe chit like a trained racehorse over a
kitten. He felt quite sorry for the unobtrusively lovely
Juliet.

But the keenest observer of the new arrival was Lady
Branscombe. As soon as she could, she pulled Phyllis
aside. "Is that young woman Tris's London paramour?"
she asked bluntly.

"Don't be silly," Phyllis whispered. "She's a very proper
sort of girl. Her father's a baron."

"Hummmph!" grunted Madge, frowning. "That makes
matters worse."

"Why do you say that?" Phyllis asked, feeling a sudden
clench in her chest.

"Why do you think?" Madge snapped. "She's a beauty,
and she's very sure of herself. Tris is evidently besotted. If
she's of good family, we can have nothing at all to object
to, should he decide to offer for her."

Phyllis's optimistic nature vied in her chest with a growing feeling of panic. "Yes, she *is* a beauty, I won't deny
that," she said, her voice quavering, "but it's too soon to
conclude that Tris is besotted, isn't it?"

"Is it? Take a look at him. He's been at her elbow ever
since she arrived, positively slavering over her. If he paid
that sort of attention to Julie, I'd be in alt."

"Oh, dear," murmured Phyllis miserably, "whatever
shall we do?"

"Get rid of her," Madge answered without a moment's
hesitation. "Get rid of her at once."

# 16

GETTING RID OF CLEO SMALLWOOD PROVED TO BE no easy task. For one thing, Tris made the girl promise (without much difficulty) to stay at least a week. For another, Lady Phyllis could not think of a way to hasten her departure without causing the sensitive, quiet Lord Smallwood to be humiliated, for he would surely sense—no matter how subtle her hints—that she was trying to push them on their way. "Besides," she said to Madge as she walked with her to the property line after a brief visit, "if Tris is truly besotted, getting rid of the girl will only cause him to follow her to London. We'd then be in a worse case than we are now."

By this time, the Smallwoods were in their third day of what Madge now realized would be an extended stay. "I don't see how matters can possibly be worse," she said glumly.

"I still have hope, as long as Tris is here near Julie," Phyllis said optimistically. "Perhaps, if Miss Smallwood stays long enough, he'll tire of her and discover for himself how superior our Julie is."

"If *I* haven't discovered that Julie is in any way superior to the Smallwood creature," Madge muttered as she took herself off through a much used gap in the hedge, "I don't see how Tris will."

"You are an unnatural mother," Phyllis called after her. "I can think of a dozen ways."

"Then tell them to Tris," Madge flung over her shoulder. "It won't do any good for *me* to hear them."

While the mothers were bandying words, Tris was out

riding with Cleo. At his mother's insistence, he'd invited Julie too. Julie'd accepted the invitation at *her* mother's insistence, but she kept her horse well behind, knowing that she was intruding.

Tris was very grateful for Julie's tact. In the social flurry of the past two days, he hadn't had any opportunity to speak to Cleo in private. He guessed that she'd gone to great lengths of scheming and maneuvering to be here (the trip to Scotland was, he knew, nothing but a ruse), but this was his first chance to ask her why she'd come. "I don't understand you, Cleo," he said when he saw that Julie was too far back to overhear. "After what happened that last night in London, I thought you never wanted to see me again."

"You should've known that I never meant it," she said, throwing him a glinting look from under the brim of her rakish riding cap. "I was jealous, that's all."

"Jealous? Of whom?"

"Of Julie, of course."

"Julie! Good God, woman, how could you have been so foolish? I told you she was like a sister to me."

"You were leaving me to run home to her. A man does not run off from the woman he claims to love at the beck and call of a sister."

"This man does. She needed me. Now that you've met her, I hope you understand."

Cleo glanced back at the girl riding several yards behind. What she saw—a modest creature in a worn habit, shabby gloves and a head of hair that was blowing in dishevelment about a very pretty face that somehow turned no heads—confirmed what she'd felt from the moment of their first meeting: Miss Juliet Branscombe was not serious competition. "Yes, I do understand," she said, her renewed self-confidence making her generous. "I'm sorry for my outburst that night, Tris. Do you forgive me?"

"Forgive you?" He reached out and grasped her horse's reins, drawing the horses so close that he could whisper in her ear. "There is no question of forgiveness, Cleo. I love you and only you."

The horses shied apart. "We should speak of other things," Cleo said, her manner coy but her eyes sparkling happily. "Julie will see us."

But they needn't have worried. All the while they'd been trotting along the path near the river's edge, laughing and flirting and making up their differences, Julie had quite contentedly kept her distance, absorbed in her own thoughts.

The very person she'd been thinking of—Lord Canfield —was at that very moment out for his daily ride. As he came to the rise leading down to the river, he caught a glimpse of the scene. He could see that Tris and Cleo had their heads together, and that Julie was following at a distance. To him she seemed so forlorn that he found himself gritting his teeth. *Damnation,* he thought, *Miss Cleo Smallwood is moving right in, just as I suspected. And Julie is not even putting up a struggle.*

He spurred his horse and galloped down to the river's edge. He returned Tris's warm greeting, tipped his hat to Cleo and rode up to Julie. "Good morning, ma'am," he said, pulling his horse up alongside hers, "may I ride along with you?"

"I wish you would," she answered cheerfully. "Those two have given me no company at all."

"More fools they," he said.

Julie smiled at the compliment but shook her head. "I believe they have more interesting matters to engage them than to spend their time entertaining me."

"Have they, indeed?" He studied her face for a sign of jealousy, but he saw none. "Are you implying that there is an attachment developing between them?"

"It is not my place to say."

"You are very discreet. Though such discretion makes conversation difficult, I must admit it is an admirable quality in a woman."

"I know you mean that as a compliment. But it suggests that you believe most women are *in*discreet. For shame, my lord! If you were fair, you'd admit that indiscretion is a fault in both sexes."

He held his hands up against her attack. "Yes, indeed, you're quite right. Your point, ma'am."

They rode on in silence for a while, both of them watching the couple trotting so closely together in front of them. "I know that what you see there ahead of us must give you pain," Canfield said at last, unable to resist the urge to offer her his sympathy.

She blinked in surprise. "Pain?"

"Forgive me. It's none of my affair. I have no right to interfere. But I pride myself on being a shrewd observer, and it's plain to me that you care a great deal for Tris."

Julie gaped at him in confusion. "*Care* for him?" she echoed, not quite knowing what to say. "Yes, of course I do. I've known him since childhood. But I wouldn't say—"

"No, Miss Discretion, of course you won't say. But I have no qualms about speaking frankly. And frankly, ma'am, you can easily win him for yourself if you would but try."

Julie was so astounded she could only gasp. "Win him for *myself? Tris?*"

"Miss Smallwood is a beauty, I admit. But you, Miss Branscombe, are just as lovely in your own way. In a more subtle, deeper way."

Those lovely words drove everything else from Julie's mind. Her heart began to pound, and a flush of warmth swept up from her throat to her cheeks. "I . . . I . . . don't know what you mean to . . . ," she babbled, ". . . what you wish me to . . . say . . ."

"I've no wish for you to say anything. I didn't intend to embarrass you, my dear. But, you see, I'm very well versed in the ways of London flirts. Miss Smallwood is one of the most talented, but there's nothing in her packet of tricks that you couldn't learn."

"Tricks?"

"Oh, yes. Truly, ma'am, I could teach you everything you need to know."

Julie, suddenly grasping what he was getting at, stared

at him in utter disbelief. "Are you suggesting, my lord, that you want to help me to . . . to . . . ?"

"To win Tris back from Miss Smallwood, yes. With my help, you'll have him at your feet in a fortnight."

Her heart sank in her chest like a stone. She didn't want to believe that she'd understood him properly. He *couldn't* mean what she thought he meant! "At my f-feet?" she managed to mutter.

"Yes. If you're willing to try. There's nothing at all difficult about it. Just a few little strategems, like—"

"I know," she muttered dryly. "Like being saucy and laughing at all his jokes."

This brought a surprised guffaw from him. "Yes, just so," he said, grinning at her admiringly. "I can see already that you're a quick study."

She shook her head, keeping her eyes from meeting his. "No, I'm not. I have no talent for such . . . such games."

"Yes, you do, I'm certain of it. It needs only firmness of purpose. If you tell me you are firm in your resolve, we can start at once."

"At once?" she echoed, hardly hearing him, so deep were her spirits sunk in disappointment and confusion.

"Right now. The first thing we'll do is leave them. We'll ride off without a word, over to the field where we once raced. If they come looking for us—and I hope they will—they'll see us having a delightful time together. Are you game?"

Unable to speak, she merely nodded. He threw her a broad smile, spurred his horse and started off. She followed absently, her mind in a whirl. The situation was just too absurd. First Tris swore he'd have Canfield at her feet, and now Canfield was swearing he'd have Tris at her feet. Each man was dedicating himself to *passing her off to the other!* It was a most ridiculous situation. She would have laughed out loud if she didn't feel so much like weeping.

# 17

THE NOTE FROM TRIS INSTRUCTED JULIE TO MEET him at the summerhouse at five. She knew why he'd selected the hour—it was the time of day when the ladies rested before dressing for dinner—but she had no idea why he wanted the meeting. Nevertheless, she was there at the appointed hour.

Tris was already waiting. He'd come early enough to observe how the two brief weeks since he'd last come here had brought about a change in the appearance of the place. A patina of spring green shimmered over every living thing. The grass was beginning to show new life, the shrubs glimmered at their edges with new growth, and little shoots of fresh green buds were appearing on the climbing vines. Everything surrounding him had a look of hopeful anticipation, as if in reflection of his own optimistic mood.

He was very happy with himself and the world. Even Julie's careless appearance, as she came into view, did not upset him. If Peter did not mind her tousled hair, her faded skirts and worn dull green shawl, then why should he? He jumped down from the platform of the summerhouse and ran to meet her. He greeted her with a shout of triumph. "I *told* you it would all work out. Isn't it splendid?"

She paused in the act of climbing the stile. "I don't know what you mean," she said, puzzled. "What's splendid?"

"Come now, Julie, it's not like you to be coy. I realized yesterday that Peter is taken with you. He's smitten, surely as I breathe. He'll come up to scratch before you know it, and then our troubles will be over!"

Julie gaped at him in astonishment. "You're speaking utter nonsense," she said. "He's not in the least taken with me."

"You are too modest, as usual. Take my word for it, my girl, your Peter is entranced. I watched him all during the party for signs, and I swear he never took his eyes from you. When you played for Elinor, the fellow had eyes only for the pianist, not the singer. And it was you he applauded when you took your seat."

"Good heavens, Tris," she objected, "a little thing like that doesn't mean—"

"And what about yesterday? Did he or did he not ride off with you with never a second thought for Cleo and me?"

"Yes, but—"

"But me no buts. I saw how you two were laughing and joking with each other when we came riding up to find you. Why, the very manner in which he lifted you from your horse was sufficient proof of—"

"But he was only acting that way because . . . because . . ." She paused, wondering suddenly if it would be wise to tell Tris what his lordship's real intentions were. Tris would surely find the information upsetting. And he would only redouble his efforts to make her saucy and flirtatious, all to no purpose. On the other hand, if he kept believing—for a while, anyway—that Lord Canfield was in love with her, he would cease his attempts to change her. That would be a relief!

Besides, if she *had* to be taught to flirt, she much preferred Canfield's tutelage to Tris's. Lord Canfield made her feel less awkward, less artificial. And he himself had undertaken a great part in the scheme: he was pretending to pursue her. Even if his attentions to her were not sincere but only a sham to make an impression on Tris, she nevertheless enjoyed them. It was a lovely pretense, and she wished the game would never have to end. Certainly telling Tris the truth would bring the end much too soon. No, she decided firmly, she would say no more.

"Well?" Tris was prodding curiously. "He was only acting that way because—?"

"Because . . . because . . . Oh, I don't know what I meant to say. But I will tell you, Tris, that if you put too much stock in your foolish theories, you are letting yourself in for a huge disappointment."

Tris glared at her in disgust. "I'm losing all patience with you, Julie! You push modesty too far. Such humility is not an appealing quality in you." He stalked off angrily, looking back over his shoulder only once, to add, "I hope, when you wed him, you will be generous enough *then* to acknowledge how right I was."

Julie sat on the stile, gazing after him with troubled eyes. Tris was still a boy, she realized. One of these days, when it was finally clear that his lordship had no intention of wedding her, Tris would have to admit how wrong he was. And then he'd see that there was no easy solution to his troubles. If he wanted to wed the girl of his dreams, he'd have to face his mama with the truth. *Tris,* she addressed him in her mind, *the only way for you to win is to become a man.*

# 18

A MORNING RIDE BECAME ROUTINE FOR TRIS, CLEO and Julie, and they were invariably joined by Lord Canfield. Even the frequent April showers that dampened their clothing during the ride did not deter them from this enjoyable exercise. One morning, however, after a week of passable weather, the riders suddenly found themselves deluged by a torrential rain. Riding through a shower was fun, but through a deluge was not.

Since they were at that moment closer to Wycklands than the Enders' estate, they spurred their horses to Canfield's stables. Once the horses were comfortably sheltered, the riders ran for the house. Dripping wet, yet laughing good-naturedly at their condition, they gathered round the drawing room fire to dry and warm themselves. His lordship, assuming that the rain would not let up very soon, requested his butler to do what he could to arrange an extemporaneous luncheon for his unexpected guests. The staff rose to the occasion by providing, with this minimal notice, a hot, two-course luncheon of York ham with poivrade sauce, quail stew, river trout, poached eggs, potatoes au gratin, an assortment of greens, gooseberry tarts and a most delectable Highland cream, all served with gracious ease in the smaller of the mansion's two dining rooms.

After the cheerful and leisurely meal, the diners discovered to their chagrin that the rain still poured down too heavily to permit them to resume their ride. But Lord Canfield would not allow his guests to languish in boredom. "There is a fine billiard room upstairs," he suggested. "Shall we go up and play for a while?"

"Oh, what a splendid idea!" Cleo said eagerly.

"Yes, splendid for you," Tris laughed. He turned to explain to Peter that Cleo had a real talent for wielding a cue and would promptly put the men to shame. "But Julie doesn't care much for billiards," he added with a sigh.

Julie recognized a look of slyness in his eyes. He was plotting something, she was certain of it. "I'll be happy to play, if that's what you all wish to do," she assured them.

But that was not what Tris had in mind. He didn't wish for her to play at all. "No need to sacrifice yourself on our account," he said with bland innocence while giving Julie a surreptitious wink. "Perhaps Peter will show you about the house while Cleo and I play."

"That's an excellent suggestion," Peter said at once, his voice so eager that Julie could have no doubt of its sincerity. "Ever since the night of the musicale, I've been most eager to show Miss Branscombe my pianoforte." He turned to her with a smile. "It was made by Zumpe, you see, and it has—"

"Pedals!" Julie cried, clapping her hands excitedly. "Oh, Peter, how wonderful! I've never actually tried a pianoforte with pedals."

"There, then, that's settled," Tris declared, throwing Julie a look of triumph before taking Cleo's arm and steering her toward the stairs. "You two go along to see the pianoforte, and we'll go up to the billiard room. Don't bother showing us up, Peter. I know the way."

Peter and Julie watched them disappear up the stairs. Then Julie glanced at Peter in embarrassment. "Tris maneuvered that on purpose, you know," she said. "To force you to be alone with me."

"I'm glad he did," his lordship said, taking her arm. "I've truly wanted you to try my piano, for one thing. And for another, Tris's machinations actually caused you to call me by my given name."

Julie reddened. "Did I?"

"Yes, you did. 'Oh, Peter, how wonderful.' Those were your very words. Music to my ears, I might add."

"What humbug," she said as they started down the hall toward the music room. "You needn't flirt with me when Tris is out of earshot, you know."

"I'm not flirting at all, you goose. Don't you know the difference between mere cajolery and sincere compliments?"

"Perhaps I don't. Tris says I don't tolerate compliments very well."

"He's apparently right. From now on, Miss Branscombe, please believe that any compliment I give you is utterly honest. Despite your mother's remark when we first met, I'm not the sort to pour buttersauce over a girl. Promise me you'll take my word."

"Very well, I'll promise. But in return you must stop calling me Miss Branscombe. If I've begun to call you Peter, surely you can call me Julie."

They'd arrived at the music room. Julie gasped at the sight of the magnificent instrument they'd come to see. It was longer than the pianos she'd seen before, made of highly polished rosewood, with curved sides inlaid with brass figures of Greek dancers and musicians. Six gracefully carved legs held up the L-shaped body. Julie immediately noted the lute-like appendage that hung down below the keyboard, bearing three brass pedals. Although she'd heard about this thirty-year-old innovation to the pianoforte, which deepened and enriched the tone, she'd never before seen an instrument that actually *had* pedals. The few pianos in Amberford were too old to benefit from the improvement. She took a step into the room and stared, awestruck.

"Go on, Julie, sit down and try it," Peter urged.

"Oh, no, I . . . I couldn't!" she muttered, backing off.

"Nonsense. No one here is capable of playing it, and it needs to be played."

"Don't you play?"

"I?" He shook his head, amused at the thought. "Men of my ilk are taught riding, hunting and fisticuffs, not music, I'm afraid. Please, Julie, do sit down and play something."

"Very well, if you wish it."

She sat down gingerly on the lavishly upholstered seat, turned the wheel at its side to adjust the height and began to play a simple étude. Her first attempts at pedaling made her jump—their effect on the sound was startling. But she soon accustomed herself to the change and, almost forgetting where she was, lost herself for a few moments in the sheer joy of the quality of the sound she could create on this wonderful instrument. It was only when she heard a distant clock chime the hour that she came back to herself. More than a few moments must have gone by, she realized. She must have been playing for more than twenty minutes! She looked round, embarrassed, and opened her mouth to apologize, but she found him gazing at her with such undisguised admiration that words failed her.

"That was lovely," he said softly. "Please go on."

She shook her head and jumped to her feet. "Thank you, but no. I didn't mean to bore you so long. Please forgive me."

"It was anything but boring. I could sit here and listen to you all day."

"Come now, Peter, you swore you'd give me no buttersauce."

"And you promised to accept—and believe—my compliments."

She felt her throat tighten with grateful tears. No one had ever said such kind things to her before. "I think you should show me some more of the house," she suggested hastily, to hide her emotions.

He did not argue but offered his arm. As they strolled along the hallway, looking into the various rooms, he pointed out—as befitted a polite host—some of the noteworthy accoutrements he'd brought with him from his London house: a pair of magnificent Irish crystal chandeliers in the large dining room, an elaborately designed Persian rug in the drawing room and a number of family portraits they passed on the way. His manner was so pleasant and his remarks about his treasures so modestly humorous that she lost all feeling of self-consciousness and timidity. She felt deliciously comfortable and at home.

This sense of ease emboldened her. When they strolled by a pair of closed doors, and he made no mention of what they led to, she, barely hesitating, brazenly asked what was behind them.

"You don't want to see it," he answered. "It's not fit for guests."

"Aha! A Bluebeard!" she taunted saucily. "I knew you were too good to be true. Is that where you keep the heads of your murdered wives?"

He laughed. "Now that you've guessed my secret," he retorted with a mocking, menacing leer, twirling the ends of an imaginary mustachio, "you will soon find yourself among them. Come! I dare you to step over the threshold." He threw open the doors, his leer changing to a rather embarrassed grin. "It's my library, but as you see, hardly in condition for company."

But Julie, stepping over a pile of wrapping litter, looked about her, entranced. Though the state of the room had not much improved from the time Tris had last seen it, with boxes and packing cases still scattered over the floor, books still spilling out of them and dust still covering everything, she could see, nevertheless, what an impressive room it was. She gazed in wide-eyed admiration at the tall windows, the paneled walls and the lovely gallery. "What a wonderful room!" she breathed, clasping her hands to her chest. "Why have you left it in such neglect?"

"I want to arrange my books myself," he explained, "but I've had no time of late to attend to it, having become involved in the affairs of a silly chit who claims to need lessons in flirtation."

Her eyes fell from his face. "That is most selfish of her," she murmured. "You should tell her at once that you have more important things to do with your time."

He came up to her and lifted her chin, forcing her to meet his gaze. "Even if I find time spent with her more enjoyable than sorting through books?"

"M-more enjoyable? Really?"

"Infinitely more enjoyable."

She felt her heart swell up again. "If I had the choice," she admitted in her soft voice, "I would find sorting books more enjoyable than lessons in flirtation." Her eyes looked pleadingly into his. "We have time this afternoon. Tris and Cleo will play for hours. May I not help you with the sorting now?"

"Now? Impossible."

"But why?"

"Because it's filthy work, for one thing. Your clothes would become so grimy they would be beyond recovery. Take my word for it. My valet has already had to discard three of my shirts."

"I don't care a fig for these old riding clothes. Please, Peter. I'd love to see some of your books."

He could not resist. He took off his coat, tossed it over an unopened crate and led her to a packing case resting in the far corner. "I've just started on this batch—my poetry books," he said. "I plan to shelve them here, near the window."

She nodded eagerly. "How shall we proceed? I can sit on the floor, dust off the books one at a time, read off each title and hand the book to you for shelving. Does that sound efficient?"

"Oh, yes, quite. But I can't permit you to sit on the floor with a dustcloth like a housemaid."

"You have not the right to 'permit' me anything," she declared firmly, picking up a cloth and sitting down on the floor before he could say another word. "I may behave as I wish. Besides, I'm not above dusting. I've wielded a dustcloth many a time." She pulled a volume from the box, dusted it and read the words on the spine: "Edmund Spencer, *The Faerie Queen.*"

He hesitated a moment, unwilling to take advantage of her good nature. But after another glance at her determined expression, he shrugged and took the book from her hand. They proceeded with the labor in that way for a long while, going through half the packing case without deviation from the system she'd devised. When she handed him Herrick's *Hesperides,* however, she chanced to remark that it was a favorite of hers. "Of mine too," Peter said with a pleased smile, and he sat down beside her to read his favorite passages. This led to a reading of selections from Dryden's *The Hind and the Panther,* Thomson's *Seasons* and Milton's *Samson Agonistes.* So engrossed were they in the discovery of each other's poetic tastes that they did not notice that two hours had passed, that the rain had stopped and that the late afternoon sun was slanting through the windows and illuminating their bent heads. Peter, reading aloud Andrew Marvell's "A Definition of Love," had arrived at the penultimate stanza:

> As lines, so loves oblique, may well
> Themselves in every angle greet;
> But ours, so truly parallel,
> Though infinite, can never meet.

After reading those words, he looked up and saw that she had tears in her eyes. "Julie!" he exclaimed. "Why—?"

"Is that the definition of love?" she asked, embarrassedly wiping away the tears with her fingers, causing smudges to appear under both her eyes. "Two parallel lines that can never meet?"

"Not necessarily," he said with a smile, taking note not of the smudges but how the sun was haloing her hair. "Marvell is adopting Plato's definition—love as a longing that is never fulfilled. But one needn't accept—"

"I think there may be much truth in it," she said, sighing sadly and lowering her head.

"Come now, my dear," he said gently, "the verse has more poetic charm than truth. You are too lovely to believe that your life will be spent in unfulfilled longing." He reached out and lifted her chin again. "The parallel lines will bend for you, I promise."

Her mouth trembled. "You don't know—! You can't promise . . ."

Something about her—the liquid eyes, the parted lips, the smudged cheeks, the sun-tipped hair . . . he would never know what—aroused in him an irresistible impulse. Almost without thought, he leaned toward her and kissed her mouth. It was a gentle kiss, so soft she did not jump or pull away; she merely made a little sound in her throat, and her hand come up to his cheek. The touch roused him even more. Before he quite realized what he was doing, there in the mote-filled sunshine, he lifted himself up on his knees and pulled her into a tight embrace, his mouth never leaving hers.

It was at that moment that Tris came in search of them. He opened the door of the library and saw them. In the dusty light they appeared to be frozen into immortality, like the figures in a painting by an Italian master, their faces shadowed, their bodies outlined in gold. The sight was almost heavenly, so eloquently did the scene speak of rapture. To interrupt them would have been like interrupting a benediction. His throat constricted, and he silently backed out and closed the door.

But both Peter and Julie heard the sound; they broke apart at the instant of the door's closing. Peter's eyes flew to the door. "It must have been Tris, looking for us," he said.

She, however, was not able to turn her eyes from him. The embrace had been shattering for her. Never had she felt so overwhelmed with emotion. Every drop of blood in her body seemed to be dancing, every cell trembling with a kind of ecstatic agony. "Oh, Peter!" she gasped.

He gazed at her guiltily. "I'm sorry," he muttered. "I don't know what possessed me. The poetry, I suppose. Please, Julie, blame Andrew Marvell if you must place blame."

Her eyes clouded. These words were not what she wanted to hear. "I don't wish to blame—"

"I know," he muttered with a troubled frown. "You are concerned about what Tris must think. But you mustn't be. It will be all to the good. I can almost guarantee that at this moment he is writhing with jealousy."

Julie felt her heart sink in her breast. Peter had completely misunderstood her feelings. She could not care about what Tris was feeling, not after what she'd just experienced. The sad part was that Peter had not had a similar experience. For Peter, the embrace had apparently been nothing more than a careless impulse. For her, however, it had been all-encompassing, a whirlwind that had lifted her heart right out of her. After their lovely compatability during the poetry reading, when their feelings seemed so similar, how could they each react so differently to the kiss? They were indeed a pair of parallel lines that would never meet!

And as for Tris, she thought in despair, he was far from writhing with jealousy. If she knew anything of the matter, he was standing out in the hallway dancing with joy.

But out in the hallway, Tris was leaning against the wall, breathing hard. His mind was in turmoil. He should have felt happy as a lark, for his mission to get Julie wed seemed to be succeeding beyond his most optimistic expectations. Why, then, did he have this peculiar but unmistakable urge to take Peter by the throat and choke the life out of him?

# 19

ALTHOUGH LORD SMALLWOOD'S EYES WERE FIXED on the *Times* in his lap, he was not really reading. He was trying to find the courage to ask his hostess, who'd joined him in the downstairs sitting room and was placidly knitting, a very personal question. He needed to know the answer, but he was reluctant to broach so private a matter with a woman who was, to all intents and purposes, a stranger.

He knew that Lady Phyllis would have been offended to hear herself described as a stranger, for she'd been very companionable toward him since his arrival. She'd accompanied him on daily strolls, joined him for breakfast, engaged him in comfortable conversation in the late afternoons after they'd both napped, and done many other kindly acts to keep him from feeling deserted. But he thought of her as a stranger nevertheless, especially when it came to dealing with intimate matters like this.

Lord Smallwood had come to Amerford with the utmost reluctance, but after a fortnight at Enders Hall, he had to admit that the time was passing very pleasantly. It was not only the companionship of his hostess. It was also that the country air made him feel fit; that the meals Lady Phyllis laid before him were more delectable than any London cook could ever devise; that her ladyship never objected to his napping in an easy chair during the long, quiet afternoons; that the London newspapers were placed at his elbow daily; that his daughter was happily engaged in the rituals of courtship; and that the days were languidly peaceful. He would have been content to remain indefinitely, if he did not feel like a blasted interloper. After all, he and his daughter had imposed themselves on Lady Phyllis without so much as a by-your-leave, and he could not feel completely comfortable in taking continued advantage of her kind hospitality. Every morning, when he managed to see his daughter alone, he asked her to set a date for departure, and every morning she responded, "As soon as Tris makes an offer."

"But when is that to be?" he'd ask querulously.

"Any moment now. I'm sure of it."

But Lord Smallwood could no longer take the answer seriously. A fortnight of moments had come and gone, and Tris had not come up to scratch.

He looked across the room to where Lady Phyllis sat and cleared his throat. She looked up from her work, her eyebrows raised. "Did you say something, Smallwood?"

"I wish to ask you a question, ma'am," he said, hiding his unease by speaking too loudly.

"Yes?" she urged, thrusting the knitting needles into a ball of yarn to give him her full attention. "Go on, I can hear you."

"It is a . . . a rather personal question," he mumbled in a lower voice, "so if you decline to answer, I shall understand."

"Very well," she agreed.

He took a deep breath. "Does your son have any intention of wedding my Cleo?" *There!* he said to himself in triumph. *I've asked it, and I'm glad I did, no matter how she responds.*

Lady Phyllis blinked at him in surprise. "Wedding *Cleo*? Whatever gave you such an outlandish idea?"

"What's outlandish about it?" Smallwood demanded, thrusting aside his newspaper. "The two are courting, are they not?"

"Of course they're not. How can they be? Tris is betrothed to Julie."

"To Julie? You mean the Branscombe chit? How can that be?"

"What do you mean, how can it be? That's a silly question. They've been betrothed since childhood. Everyone knows it."

"Well, ma'am, *I* don't know it. And neither does Cleo."

"Perhaps I exaggerated about 'everyone.' But everyone here in Amberford knows it, even though it won't be officially announced until Julie and Tris are ready to set a date for the nuptials. Lady Branscombe and I are hoping to make the formal announcement very soon."

Lord Smallwood gaped at her, wondering what to make of this news. If Cleo learned of it, he dreaded to think what her reaction might be. There was sure to be a frightful scene, full of tears and noise and emotional excess. But above and beyond all that, Cleo would be heartbroken. She was sincerely attached to the Enders chap, more so than to any man she'd ever met. In truth, Lord Smallwood had grown rather fond of him too. This news was very upsetting. Very upsetting indeed. "Ridiculous," he muttered aloud.

Lady Phyllis stiffened in offense. "What's ridiculous about it?"

"Everything. Your son doesn't seem nearly as interested in Miss Branscombe as Lord Canfield is, for one thing. For another, he appears to be utterly enchanted with Cleo. Hasn't left her side for a moment since we arrived."

"Yes, but all that can be explained."

"How?"

"Well," Phyllis said thoughtfully, "as far as Lord Canfield is concerned, Madge Branscombe and I are convinced that Julie is using him to make Tris jealous and prod him into action."

Lord Smallwood sneered. "So he needs prodding, does he?"

Lady Phyllis looked troubled. "I know that sounds as if the boy's reluctant, but Madge says every man needs a bit of prodding in such situations."

"Hummmmph!" the old fellow snorted. "Tris doesn't seem to need any prodding when it comes to pursuing my Cleo."

Phyllis glared at him. "He's *not* pursuing her, I tell you!"

"Then what would you call his behavior?"

"I'd call it friendship. As a friend, and her host, he's obliged to squire her about, is he not?"

"Friendship, ha! There is no such thing as friendship between a man and a woman."

Phyllis drew herself up in defiance. "What folderol! Of *course* there is such a thing as friendship between the sexes. Why, just look at you and me. We're a perfect example."

"I would not be too sure of that either, ma'am, if I were you," the white-haired fellow muttered, reaching for his discarded newspaper. "You're too good-looking and good-natured to go about assuming that we men—I or any other fellow you know—have nothing on our minds but friendship."

Phyllis gaped at him. "Whatever do you mean by that?" she demanded.

He lifted the paper and hid his face behind it. "I mean nothing, ma'am," he said. "Nothing at all."

She stared in his direction openmouthed, but all she could see was newsprint. After a moment, she shrugged and reached for her knitting, for she knew by instinct that it was useless to pursue this interesting conversation. As far as Lord Smallwood was concerned, there was nothing further to be said.

# 20

THE BIMONTHLY AMBERFORD ASSEMBLY WAS about to be held again. Like most rural assemblies, this one was usually anticipated with more eagerness by the ladies than by the gentlemen. Ladies were always excited by the prospect of dancing, flirtation and gossip, but gentlemen often chafed at the formality of the affair. This time, however, at least two gentlemen were looking forward to it. For very different reasons, both Tris and Peter were expecting this particular session to be a significant event, Peter because he was determined to dance with Julie in defiance of her mother's displeasure, and Tris because he suspected that Peter would use the occasion to offer for Julie.

Tris had completely regained his determination to see Julie married to the viscount of Canfield. The shock and abhorrence he'd experienced when he'd come upon them kissing was, he told himself, a momentary aberration. He couldn't really explain why he'd felt what he'd felt, but it was not a matter of importance. If an explanation had been required, he would probably have excused himself by saying that it had been merely a brotherly reaction, natural and protective.

But whatever the explanation, the feeling had passed. It was Cleo he adored, not Julie. There was no question in his mind that it was Cleo he wanted to wed. Cleo was more than beautiful; she was lively, witty and constantly, delightfully surprising. Julie, on the other hand, was drab, shy and held no surprises for him. So even though the scene in the library—the two embracing figures drenched in golden, mote-spangled light—sometimes recreated itself in his memory, it no longer disturbed him. He merely brushed it aside.

Thus, on the evening of the assembly, the gentlemen of two Amberford households—Enders Hall and Wycklands —prepared for the occasion with unwonted eagerness. And at Enders Hall, another gentleman was becoming interested in the event. Lord Smallwood, who had told his hostess earlier that he had no intention of participating in such "rustic folderol," was dressing himself in his evening clothes. When he later joined Lady Phyllis at the bottom of the stairs, she looked at him in surprise. "I thought, Smallwood, that you didn't want to attend this affair tonight. Didn't you say that this sort of evening would be a great bore for you?"

"Yes, but I changed my mind. I want to observe your son and this Branscombe chit with my own eyes before I take it on myself to inform my daughter that her expectations are hopeless."

"Don't be foolish," Phyllis said flatly. "You won't learn anything of that nature tonight. Tris and Julie are not the sort to make public display of their feelings."

"Don't underestimate my powers of observation, ma'am."

She shrugged. "In any case, whatever your reason, I'm glad you're going. Here, let me adjust your neckcloth. You've got it twisted around somehow."

"Thank you, ma'am," he said, offering himself to her ministrations. "It's a deuced nuisance dressing for a formal evening without a valet. If I'd known how long we would be here, I'd certainly have taken my fellow with me."

Tris came down at that moment. It gave him a gleeful sense of satisfaction to see his mother and the man he hoped would be his father-in-law apparently getting on so well. "Where is your daughter, sir?" he inquired. "It's getting late."

"Here I am," came a voice from the top of the stairs, and Cleo came wafting down in a flutter of copper-red silk chiffon. She was utterly breathtaking. Her short, dark curls framed the perfect oval of her face with a rakish charm, her bare shoulders gleamed in the light of the sconces on the wall behind her, and the diamond studs that glittered in her ears were not any brighter than the glow in her magnificent green eyes. "Oh, I say!" gasped Tris. "You *are* lovely! I'd wager our Amberford Assembly, in all the years of its existence, has never seen your like!"

Cleo paused in the middle of the stairway and gazed down at him. "Praise is even better when coming from someone who himself deserves praise," she said with charming formality. Then she threw him a beaming smile. "You look top-of-the-trees yourself."

His chest swelled with pleasure. He reached up a hand for her and drew her down the remaining steps. "The other fellows will be wild with jealously when they see you on my arm," he murmured in her ear.

She laughed in pleasure, a deep, velvety sound that seemed to go right through him. "Does that mean, you greedy boy," she asked, placing her other hand in his, "that you don't intend to let anyone else dance with me?"

"He'll have no choice about that," Lady Phyllis put in quickly, suddenly alarmed at the effect this coquettish London baggage was having on her son. "Our assemblies require that a gentleman may dance no more than three dances with the same partner."

"There's no rule that will keep us from sitting together through the rest of them," Tris retorted. He drew Cleo's arm through his and led her out to the waiting carriage. Behind the backs of their departing offspring, Lord Smallwood threw Phyllis a look that asked quite plainly, *And what do you make of that little scene, eh?*

Lady Phyllis said nothing, but when they approached the carriage she insisted that Cleo and her father climb into it ahead of her. Then, pulling her son aside, she grasped the lapels of his coat with a desperate urgency. "Be sure you dance with Julie, do you hear me, Tris? The first dance in particular."

Tris rolled his eyes heavenward. "If I must," he muttered in disgust.

This response did nothing to relieve Phyllis's sense of alarm. She climbed into the carriage with a decidedly anxious heart.

Meanwhile, Julie and her mother had already arrived at the hall. The girl's entrance had caused a pleasing stir, for she was in especially good looks. She was wearing, at her mother's insistence, a violet silk gown with a daring décolletage and a deep flounce that she'd not had the courage to wear before, and she'd brushed her hair into a single soft curl that fell over her shoulder. Her color was high, her skin glowed, and her eyes were alight with anticipation. The dowager onlookers put their heads together and agreed that Juliet Branscombe was having her bloom at last. And best of all, Lord Canfield, when he arrived some moments later, smiled across the room at her with unmistakable approval.

When the party from Enders Hall arrived, however, Cleo's entrance caused more than a stir. The reaction might have been called a gasp. While the dowager circle whispered disapprovingly of the daring color of her gown, the men in the room eyed her in awed delight. She was immediately surrounded by a crowd of eligibles who demanded a chance to dance with her. Tris reluctantly surrendered her arm and made his way to Julie, who'd already retreated to her usual seat in the shadow of her mother. "May I have the honor of the first dance?" he asked his childhood friend with a mockingly formal bow.

Julie rose and took his arm. "I should think you'd want to stand up with your Cleo," she whispered as they approached the dance floor, where a number of couples had already taken their places. "She is looking spectacularly beautiful."

"Yes, isn't she? But Mama ordered me to dance with you first. Besides, it will give us time to go over a few final instructions."

They took their place in a set. "What final instructions?" Julie asked with a frown.

"On your behavior tonight. If all goes well, it would not surprise me to learn that tonight is the night Peter will make his offer."

"Don't be a clunch," Julie said in annoyance as the music began. "He has no intention—"

They had to break for the first figure. When they came together again, Tris spoke to her through clenched teeth. "Don't waste time arguing with me, my girl. Just listen. I'm not going to suggest anything daring. You've been doing very well so far. Just remember to laugh at his quips. And to—"

They had to break again. When they came together, Tris tried to continue his instructions, but Julie cut him off. "You needn't go over the same ground again, Tris Enders. I'm quite capable of remembering your blasted instructions. And I don't see why you feel a need to re-mind me of them at all, especially when you've just said you think I've been doing so well."

"I just wanted to suggest one new tack. When he stands up with you tonight, he's bound to tell you how lovely you look—and, by the way, with your hair that way, you *do*—"

"Thank you for bothering to notice," she said dryly.

He ignored her interruption. "When he says it, tell him that praise is even better when coming from someone who himself deserves praise. And then add that he, too, looks very fine."

"Good God!" She peered at him in surprise. "How on earth did you think of *that?* It sounds like a stilted line of dialogue from a particularly bad play! You surely don't think a man like Peter would enjoy such—"

They had to turn away from each other again, but not before Tris threw her an offended glare.

"Cleo said it to me," he snapped when they came to-gether for the final figure, "and I thought it was a particu-larly pleasant compliment."

Julie wanted to retort that she didn't need Cleo to com-pose conversational tidbits for her, but she held her tongue. The dance ended, she and Tris exchanged bows, and she quickly walked off the dance floor, not even waiting for his escort. She'd had more of Tris Enders and his deuced suggestions than she could bear.

She'd just taken her seat again when she looked up to find Peter standing before her. "May I have your hand for this dance?" he asked, smiling broadly at her but glancing sidelong at her mother. "I have it on good authority that it will be a waltz."

"I'd be delighted," Julie said, rising quickly to her feet in an attempt to forestall her mother's inevitable interference.

But Lady Branscombe was not easily forestalled. "I beg your pardon, my lord," she said at once, her voice loud and icy. "My daughter doesn't waltz."

"But of course she does," his lordship contradicted blandly, taking Julie's arm firmly in his. "She told me so herself."

Lady Branscombe's mouth dropped open at this brazen effrontery. She gaped, immobilized for a moment by astonishment.

Peter moved quickly. Before the shocked, white-lipped dragon could rally herself and think of a reply, he'd drawn Julie several steps toward the dance floor. "Don't look back," he muttered to the wide-eyed girl. "There's nothing your mother can do now. She's hardly likely to shout or to jump to her feet and dash after us, not with everyone's eyes on us."

They stepped on to the floor, where several other couples were also gathering for the dance, Tris and Cleo among them. Peter placed his hand on Julie's waist. "You *do* know how to waltz, don't you?"

"Not very well," she admitted in a shaking voice.

But he was not going to lose the battle for so insignificant a reason as that. "Well, don't worry, I do. We'll be fine."

She smiled up at him uncertainly. "Will we?"

"Take my word. Besides, you look so lovely tonight that you'll be the object of admiration no matter how you waltz."

A deep, gurgling laugh escaped her as she realized that

Tris had been right. "Oh, *Peter,*" she breathed, following Tris's instructions in her own way, "so will you!"

He didn't know why she'd laughed, but the sound of it delighted him. For the first time in many years, he found himself actually enjoying being with a girl on the dance floor. As the music began, he tightened his grasp on her waist and smiled down at her with real warmth. "Ready?" he asked.

She nodded.

"Good. Then just take a deep breath and follow me."

He started slowly. She took only a moment to understand how the hand on her waist was guiding her. Soon she was following easily. The waltz was not difficult, she realized, when one's partner was so expert. After a few moments, they were swinging round the floor as if they'd been partners for years. Julie, her feet almost flying and the flounce of her gown whipping about her ankles, was ecstatic. She felt lithe, graceful and utterly free. It was as if she, Peter and the music were all alone in the world and had somehow, miraculously, become one beautiful amalgam of music and motion.

Peter too was finding this dance a remarkable experience. The waltz was nothing new to him, but the girl was. It was not merely that she was light on his arm and completely responsive to his lead, for many of his partners in the past had been equally adept. It was Julie herself. He'd never known a young woman so fresh, so unspoiled, so open and frank in her responses, so unself-conscious. Julie Branscombe was more than beautiful, she was lively, witty and constantly, delightfully surprising. He looked down at her glowing face and found himself wishing that this moment would never end.

The excitement they both were feeling must have communicated itself, at least in part, to the others on the floor, for two by two they stepped aside to watch. But Cleo and Tris, watching with the others, had very different reactions. Cleo was irritated; she did not like watching another young woman take center stage away from her.

She knew the feeling was petty and ungenerous, and she hated herself for it. But she couldn't seem to help it.

She would have felt a great deal worse if she'd guessed what Tris was feeling. For some ridiculous reason that he couldn't understand, he found that he was furious. His emotions churned in his chest in an inexplicable, illogical turmoil. What right, he asked himself, had the damnable Lord Canfield to embroil Julie in such a crass, vulgar display? And why was Julie so lost to the rules of decorum as to smile so beatifically at her partner, looking for all the world as if this indecent exhibition were inspiring her with heavenly joy? If he had his way, he'd give her a tongue lashing she'd never forget! And as for Canfield, he deserved the trouncing of his life!

On the sidelines, watching every move, Lady Branscombe was experiencing emotions as livid as Tris's. How dare Lord Canfield behave in that high-handed way and take her daughter to dance in spite of her declared opposition? Had the fellow no manners, no proper upbringing, no respect for his elders? "I'd like to wring his neck, the impertinent coxcomb!" she muttered to her friend.

But on the other side of Lady Phyllis, Lord Smallwood was interpreting the scene in quite a different way. "I do believe you're right after all," he remarked to Phyllis sadly. "Your Tris is indeed in love with Miss Branscombe. Cleo has been wasting her time."

Phyllis stared at him. "Whatever drew you to that conclusion?" she asked in astonishment. "When Tris and Julie danced the country dance together, they seemed to be squabbling like cat and dog. And now that Julie's waltzing with Lord Canfield, she looks positively in alt!"

"Yes, but take a look at Tris. He's so riddled with jealously I fully expect his face to turn green."

Phyllis looked. It was true! No one could mistake the look on Tris's face. Could it be that Lord Canfield's interest in Julie might be the very factor that would bring her and Madge's dream to fruition? She leaned over to her friend. "Madge," she hissed, "take your eyes from your daughter and look at Tris!"

Madge looked. After a moment, her mouth dropped open. "Heavens!" she whispered back. "Does that mean what I think it means?"

"He's green as grass!"

Madge Branscombe's eyes widened, and a smile slowly suffused her face. "Dare I trust my eyes? Have Canfield's detestable attentions actually shaken Tris up?"

"It certainly seems so," Phyllis breathed, her gaze fixed in awed astonishment on her son's face.

"I can scarcely credit it." Lady Branscombe fell back against her chair and used her fan to cool her overheated cheeks. "Good God! To think that a moment ago I was ready to scratch his lordship's eyes out. Now I only want to take him to my bosom. The dear, *dear* man! Whoever would have thought—? I never dreamed I'd say this, Phyllis, but I do believe I shall live to bless the day when Lord Canfield came among us!"

# 21

THE NEXT EVENING, A HALF HOUR BEFORE DINNER, Lord Smallwood requested his daughter's company on a stroll round the rose garden. Cleo was perfectly aware that her father had no interest in roses (which, incidentally, were not yet in bloom), so she was quite prepared for a fatherly scolding. The April atmosphere, however, did not seem appropriate for scolds. The air was mild, the breeze gentle, the sky a glowing purple, and the setting sun, like a Midas, was tipping everything it touched with gold. But Cleo was too uneasy to enjoy the view. "Well, Papa, let's have it," she said as soon as they set foot on the gravel path.

"Cleo, my love," he began, his tone gentle and full of sympathy, "it's time for us to take our leave."

In spite of having anticipated this, the girl was not ready to face it. "I thought you were enjoying this rustication," she said evasively.

"That is neither here nor there. When you persuaded me to join you in this venture, you had a specific purpose: to determine the extent of Tris Enders's feelings for you. A fortnight has passed, during which you have been daily in his company. If you haven't determined it by this time, you are not the clever girl I take you for."

She cast a quick, guilty glance up at his face. "Perhaps I'm not very clever," she mumbled.

"You know better than that, Cleo. I would say, instead, that perhaps you're letting your wishes cloud your good sense."

She pulled her lace shawl more tightly about her shoul-

118

ders, though there was no chill in the breeze. "You mean that I'm unwilling to face the truth, is that it?"

"I'm afraid so."

She stalked a few steps away from him, but then she paused. "I don't think so, Papa. If I were certain Tris loved Julie, I would depart at once. But until last night, he behaved in so adoring a manner toward me that I could not doubt him. He seemed as much in love with me as I could wish." She sank down on a stone bench, her head lowered. Her voice cracked on her next words. "Until l-last night."

"Are you saying that his behavior last night was an aberration?"

She nodded. "The evening started out so beautifully. You saw that for yourself. Then he watched Julie waltzing with Lord Canfield, and his mood changed. For the remainder of the affair, he was glum . . . and completely unresponsive to every attempt I made to distract him. I don't know what to make of it."

Lord Smallwood leaned on his cane for support while he peered at his daughter speculatively. Then, after a moment, he came to a decision. Seating himself beside her, he took her hand. "Did you know, my dear, that Tris is *betrothed* to Miss Branscombe?"

She swung round to him, her eyes wide with shock. *"No!"*

"Yes, it's quite true. His mother told me."

She gaped at him, her chest heaving. "It *can't* be true!" she cried, pulling her hand from his grasp and pressing it to her mouth. "We've been together every day, all of us. There was never the slightest sign—!"

Her father shrugged. "For some silly reason, they've kept it secret. But it's been in effect for years."

"I can't believe it! He even *told* me he loves me! He declared himself in just those words!"

"Did he? Then why hasn't he offered for you?"

She drew in her breath. "I don't know," she said, her lips trembling. "Do you think that's why? Because he's already . . . already—?" But she couldn't bring the word *betrothed* to her lips.

"Already committed to another? Yes, I do." He spoke quietly but with an unequivocal firmness. "What else is there to think?"

"There could be some other explanation," she said desperately.

"For instance?"

"I don't know . . . I can't *think!*"

"The most reasonable explanation I can find for his behavior," Lord Smallwood suggested in as kindly a tone as he could command, "is that he's chosen you—forgive me, my dear, but it's time to be blunt—as a . . . a . . . sort of last fling before he's launched into wedlock."

His daughter's eyes widened in horror. "A last *fling?*"

He could only nod and drop his eyes from the agonized look in hers.

"Oh, God, I *am* a fool," she muttered, white-lipped. "I, Cleo Smallwood, who had half of London at my feet! To have let myself be used so!"

They sat in silence for a while, she picking with nervous fingers at the fringe of her shawl, and he with his hands clasped on the head of his cane, his chin resting on them. They made a touching picture, with the setting sun behind them framing them in fire. But there was no one watching, no one either to admire or to sympathize. They were completely alone.

At last she lifted her head. Two large tears were making their way down her cheeks. "Oh, Papa, I do love him so!" she murmured. "Give me a few days more. A few days. Just to be sure."

"Of course, my love, if that's what you wish." He watched as she wiped away the tears with the back of her hand. She was so lovely at this moment, with the last rays of the sun playing heavenly magic with her curls, that he could hardly blame Tris Enders for being tempted by her. With a deep sigh, he heaved himself to his feet and pulled her to hers. "Come. We must make an appearance at the dinner table. Do you think you can face them with some semblance of cheerfulness?"

She turned to him with a sudden, completely brilliant smile. No one would dream it was utterly false. "There? Will that do?"

"Admirably," he said, patting her hand. "That's my plucky girl."

They started back up the path arm in arm. "I may be a fool," she said, throwing her shoulders back proudly, "but no man can say that Lord Smallwood's daughter is a coward."

# 22

HEAVY RAINS POURED DOWN FOR TWO DAYS, preventing any outdoor activities. And since no special indoor activities had been planned—no parties, no dinners, no festive teas—there was no intercourse among the three houses—Enders Hall, Larchwood and Wycklands. A kind of pall settled over them all.

At Wycklands, Peter used the time to work in his library, but every so often he found himself slumped down on a packing case with a book in his hand, staring into space. It was Julie he was thinking of, and his thoughts did not please him. He was reluctant to admit something in words that he'd known in his heart for some time: he'd fallen in love with the girl.

He'd been in love before, but lightly. This was different, much too deep and all-pervading, and he didn't like it at all. It was bad enough that the love was unrequited; what made it worse was that these feelings were, in a sense, a betrayal of her trust. He'd promised to help her capture Tris, her foolishly blind childhood sweetheart, not to attempt to win her away from him. But now that he'd become aware of his own feelings, it was becoming very painful to have to do what he'd promised. How could he hand her over to that superficial, self-absorbed Tris Enders, who didn't appreciate his marvelous luck one whit, when he, Canfield, wanted with every fiber of his being to keep her for himself?

He began to rue the day he'd ever encountered Juliet Branscombe and, even more, the impulse that had led him to promise to deliver Tris to her on a platter. But

Julie had given him to believe that she loved the deuced coxcomb—*that* was the rock on which the wave of his emotions broke. She loved Tris; there was no getting round it. And if she loved him, she would have him. That was his pledge, and he was honor-bound to keep it, no matter how it hurt him to do it.                                    .

But he had no intention of enduring this painful situation any longer than absolutely necessary. He had to get away, and the sooner the better. The only way, in honor, that he could do so was to bring Tris to his knees as soon as possible. If he was any judge of the signs, the poor fellow was already reeling. During the assembly, Tris had shown unmistakable signs of jealousy. He'd looked as if he would have liked to throttle Julie's waltzing partner with his bare hands. One more such experience and, Peter surmised, the battle would be won. And then he, Peter, could run away to London with a clear conscience and begin the arduous task of forgetting all about the lovely, dreamy-eyed Juliet.

At Larchwood, Lady Branscombe too was eager for Tris to endure another such experience as the one he'd encountered at the assembly. She was convinced that Julie's dance with Lord Canfield had shaken Tris up and brought him to realize how much he cared for her. Another such occasion might be the turning point that Madge and Phyllis had been waiting for.

Madge Branscombe wracked her brain to concoct some sort of plan—an outing or a gala of some kind—to bring the young people together again. She mulled it over in her mind at breakfast, continued throughout the morning, all during luncheon and even at tea. But it was not until Horsham, her butler, was removing the tea things that the solution came to her. Julie had already gone up to her room, and Lady Branscombe was on her way out when the butler chanced to ask if he might permit the maids and some of the footmen to take the next afternoon off. "The fair starts tomorrow," he explained.

Lady Branscombe paused in the doorway. "Fair?" she inquired.

"The Amberford Spring Fair. You do remember, don't you, ma'am? It's an annual event. I know it's not so important or grand as the Whitmonday Country Fair, but I do like to let the staff have a bit of a frolic whenever there's any sort of fair in town."

Lady Branscombe's eyes lit up. "The spring fair, you say? Isn't it a little early?"

"No, ma'am. It's usually held near the end of April."

"I must have forgotten. I haven't gone for years. Is it still as it always was, with booths and games and entertainments?"

"Oh, yes indeed, your ladyship. Mainly there's the cattle sale and the horse auction, but there's many other things going on. Games and sports and all kinds of shops, like cheese stalls and wine merchants and fruit sellers. And all sorts of delicacies you can buy. The men like the skittle alley, and the maids do enjoy the smockraces, for sure, and everyone likes to lose a penny or two on the games of chance. There's no balloon ascension like there is at St. George's field in London, but sometimes there's a magic show, and there's always a gypsy telling fortunes. The staff do love it, for certain."

"Tell me, Horsham, do any of the gentry still attend?"

"Oh, yes, ma'am, they surely do. Not on the first day, of course, when they mostly let the hired help have the day to theirselves, but every day after that you'll see the gentry hobnobbing with everyone else."

"I see. Well, thank you for the information, Horsham." She crossed the room to her writing desk, adding in as pleasant a tone as the butler had ever heard her use, "And you may certainly permit the staff to take the afternoon."

She smiled to herself as she pulled out a sheet of note paper. The spring fair, she thought, would not make the most exciting diversion one would wish for, but it would do well enough. She cut a nib, dipped it into the inkwell and dashed off a quick note to Lady Phyllis, informing her that she was arranging an outing to the fair for the day after tomorrow, weather permitting, and that she hoped (nay, *expected*) that Phyllis herself, her son, and her guests would attend. *I am also,* she added, *sending a note to Lord Canfield informing him of the affair and requesting his company.*

The weather continued to be depressing until mid-morning of the appointed day, when, to Lady Branscombe's intense delight, the sun broke through the over-hanging clouds. The entire party, including Lord Canfield, gathered at Larchwood just after luncheon. It was a very frolicsome, excited group that set off on foot to the town square, for after two days of enforced boredom, the prospect of a fair was a tonic to their spirits. With the eagerness of children let out of school, they romped, frisked and skipped down the hill and over the stone bridge to the town square, where the fair was taking place on the green.

A gaudily brilliant sight met their eyes. Dozens of tents and booths had been set up in two rows along the sandstone walkways that edged the green, each trying to outdo the other in the loudness of its colors. Yellows and oranges vied with reds and purples, as gaily garish as the penants and flags that floated over them in the breeze. A hundred or more villagers milled about the green, laughing and cavorting and bargaining with the merchants in loud voices. A great deal of shouting emanated from a tent where a wild cockfight was going on. A large group of children were surrounding a booth where a Punch-and-Judy show was stirring them to shrieks of laughter. Delicious aromas of roasting pig and frying pies rose in the air. Madge Branscombe was immediately heartened by the holiday atmosphere. "It's better than I dared hope," she whispered to her friend.

Unable to agree on which attraction to visit first, the group split up to indulge in their different likings. Lord Smallwood went off to wager on the cockfight. Phyllis made for the stall where a particularly famous local cheddar cheese was being sold, while Madge began immediately to haggle with a wine seller. Tris, who was interested in adding a horse to his stable, excused himself to attend the horse auction. And Peter laughingly challenged Julie and Cleo to a game of ringtoss. Cleo, who had been at considerable pains to hide her depressed mood, made up her mind to concentrate on the game, and she not only surpassed Peter in her score but bested every other participant who competed. By the time the proprietor of the booth awarded Cleo a prize for her skill—a huge doll with a painted porcelain face—she was ready to agree with everyone else that she was having a marvelous time.

The afternoon passed quickly. Tris, not having seen a horse to his liking, soon rejoined his friends and spirited Cleo off to see the magic show. On the way to the magician's tent, Cleo, delighted at his renewed attention, almost pranced as they made their way across the green. "I'm so glad you didn't spend all afternoon at the auction," she said.

"So am I. I'd much rather be with you." Tris glanced over at her and noticed for the first time that something was tucked under her arm. "What is that you're carrying?" he asked.

"A doll. Look at it, Tris. Hasn't it a charming face?" She peeped up at him with a grin. "I won it with my tossing skill."

Tris gazed down at her in admiration. "You, Cleo Smallwood, are amazing in your talents. Riding and billiards and now this! Top-of-the-trees, that's what you are."

It was a very happy young woman who took his arm.

Meanwhile, Julie and Peter strolled along the sandstone paths, stopping here to taste a plum pastry and there to watch a wrestling match. The sun was almost setting when Julie spied the gypsy tent, set off by itself a little way behind the row of booths and stalls. It was a shabby structure, its green-and-pink striped fabric so faded it almost looked gray. Julie was surprised she'd even noticed it, for it was almost hidden by a brightly painted booth bearing a sign reading "HOT BRANDY BALLS, TUPPENCE." "Look, Peter, a gypsy fortune-teller!" she cried.

"Where?" he asked, looking about.

"There, behind the brandy ball booth." She looked

down at the ground, feeling a bit shamefaced. "Excuse me, Peter, but I must go in. I know it's all foolishness, but I've always wanted to have my palm read."

"Then by all means do," he urged, pressing a gold coin into her hand.

She thanked him, walked quickly round to the shabby tent, hesitated for a moment and finally lifted the tent flap and stepped inside. The interior was very dark. It took a moment for her eyes to adjust to the dimness. When they did, she saw a wrinkled old woman sitting at a table covered with a long, colorful cloth that hung down to the floor. The woman was colorful too, with a striped bandanna covering her head and more than a dozen strands of beads hanging from her neck. "You wish fortune?" the woman asked in an exotic accent.

"Yes," Julie said timidly.

"Sit, then," the gypsy ordered. "Sit an' give me right hand."

Julie did as she was bid, her hand trembling slightly in the gypsy's tight grip.

"This," the woman said, feeling her palm with a knobby forefinger topped by a long, cracked nail, "is life line. Nice, long. Is good. But this . . . love line . . . is strange. Broken off."

"Broken off?" Julie asked, puzzled and somewhat frightened.

"Yah. Broken 'ere. But starts up again 'ere, see?"

"No, I'm afraid I don't—"

The gypsy shook her head impatiently. "Better we look at crystal ball, eh?"

"Crystal ball?"

"Yah. There." And she pointed to a large globe on the table before her.

Julie had not noticed it before, but now it began to glow with an eerie, flickering light. "Oh!" she exclaimed, staring at it in fascination. "Can you read my fortune in there?"

"Per'aps. For two silver coins."

"This guinea is all I have," Julie said, handing her the coin Peter had given her.

The gypsy's eyes brightened at the sight of the gold coin. She snatched it with her knobby, ring-bedecked fingers and tested it with her teeth. Satisfied, she cocked her head. "Ain't got no change," she muttered, pocketing it.

"That's all right," Julie assured her.

The gypsy smiled. "You good sort lady. I tell you good fortune," she said, leaning forward.

"How do you know it will be good if you haven't read it yet?" Julie asked.

The gypsy was not thrown by the question. "Good because true," she answered promptly.

The light in the crystal ball brightened, and as the gypsy woman passed her hands over it, the light seemed to move with the motion of the hands. Then clouds of smoke filled the globe, floating and shifting into formless shapes. "I see man . . . no, two men . . . ," the gypsy said in a low monotone.

"Where?" Julie asked, peering into the glowing orb but seeing nothing. "There in the ball?"

The gypsy ignored the interruption. "Men both dark. One tall."

"Yes?" Julie urged eagerly, nevertheless feeling quite foolish.

"They argue."

"Argue?"

The old woman peered closer into the light. "Then they fight. Terrible fight. I see blood." She looked up at Julie with a glittering, piercing gleam. "They fight for you."

"Oh, no, I hardly think—"

"Yes. They fight for you. Terrible fight."

"Not with . . . pistols!" Despite her skepticism Julie was completely caught up in the tale.

"No, no. With fists. Terrible fight. I see big crowd watching. Oh! The tall one down. Not get up."

"Oh, dear!"

The gypsy looked at her closely. "You wish other man to win? Tall one?"

"Yes! No! I mean, this is silly." She tried to think sensibly in a situation that made no sense. "I don't even know what men you're speaking of. You're the one who sees them, not I."

"Ah, that is so. I see, you not see. But tall man will not win, not ever, unless . . ."

She could not help herself. She had to ask. She had to know. "Unless . . . ?"

"Unless . . . unless . . ." The gypsy peered closer into the ball, but the light was quickly fading. "Oh . . . is going . . . is gone." She looked up at Julie and shrugged. "Sorry. Is all."

"All? Is it over? So soon?"

"Sorry. Crystal ball is ruler, not me."

"Oh." Julie rose from the chair, unmistakably disappointed, but ashamed of herself for feeling so. The silly tale was scarcely worth a gold guinea. "Well, good-bye," she said, turning to the flap of the tent. "That was . . . interesting. Thank you."

*"Au 'voir,"* the gypsy said.

But as Julie reached out to lift the flap, another voice echoed through the tent. *"Unless you untie the knot you knit yourself."*

She whirled about. "What?" she asked, staring at the gypsy suspiciously. But the voice she'd heard was different from the old woman's and had had no trace of a foreign accent. Nevertheless she peered at the old woman accusingly. "What did you say?"

Again another voice, speaking in perfect English, reverberated through the tent. *"The tall man will not win unless you untie the knot you knit yourself."*

The gypsy woman had not spoken. When the strange voice faded, the old woman fixed her glittering eyes on Julie with an expression that was completely unreadable. *"Au 'voir,"* she said again.

It was an unmistakeable dismissal. Julie knew that those were the last words she'd hear from her.

# 23

MEANWHILE, OUTSIDE ON THE GREEN, PETER WAS passing the time watching the Punch-and-Judy show. The laughter of the children and the slapstick on the small stage so thoroughly amused him that when a hand grasped his shoulder and pulled him round, the smile still remained on his face. But there was no answering smile on Tris's face. Something about Peter bothered Tris of late. He'd truly liked the fellow when they first met, but now, inexplicably, the very sight of Canfield raised his ire. "Where's Julie?" he demanded rudely. "Don't tell me you were so buffleheaded as to let her go off by herself!"

"Cut line, man, she's perfectly safe," Peter assured him. "She's gone to have her palm read, there in that green-and-pink tent behind the brandy ball booth."

"You sent her to the *gypsies?* Alone? You must be mad."

"Don't be foolish, Tris," Cleo put in. "Gypsy fortune-tellers aren't a bit dangerous."

"Nevertheless," Tris said stubbornly, feeling a sudden prick of annoyance with her for interfering, "I'd better go and fetch her."

Peter realized that, in Tris's present mood, the time was ripe for the act that would propel him into Julie's arms. "No, you wait here with Cleo," he said, grasping Tris's arm to stop him from walking off. "I'll go." And before Tris could object, he ran off round the brandy ball booth to the gypsy tent.

"Wait, damn you!" Tris shouted and started to follow him. This time, Cleo caught his arm and held him back.

"Peter can find her easily enough," she said, taking his arm. "You needn't go chasing after him."

The little prick of annoyance Tris had felt toward her swelled up and became a tidal wave of irritation. "I don't need a managing female to tell me what to do," he snapped, abruptly shaking off her hold on him. This caused her to drop her doll. It fell to the ground, its porcelain face striking the sandstone slab with a clunk. The sound was enough to indicate that the porcelain had smashed. "I'm . . . sorry," Tris muttered in shamed reluctance.

"The doll needn't make you sorry," Cleo said quietly, glancing from the ruined plaything to his face. "It was an accident. But what you just said to me was no accident, and therefore more deserving of apology."

His expression hardened. "I'm concerned for Julie's safety. That needs no apology."

"I think it does. Am I a 'managing female' because I don't believe Julie's in danger? And because I pointed out that if she were, Peter was capable of seeing to the matter?"

"I don't agree. And I don't think this is the time to discuss it. I must go. If you'll excuse me for a moment—"

She felt a strange tremble at her knees. "If you leave me now, Tris," she said in a voice she herself did not recognize, "you will not find me waiting when you come back."

"It seems to me, ma'am," Tris retorted as conflicting paroxysms of rage, shame and impotence clashed in his breast, "that you gave me a similar ultimatum in London a few weeks ago. It was as unwarranted then as it is now." He turned on his heel and stalked off in the direction Peter had taken, leaving Cleo staring after him, aghast, her broken doll lying sprawled at her feet.

When Peter arrived at the gypsy tent, Julie was just emerging, looking distracted. But there was no time for him to investigate the cause. "Julie, listen," he said quickly, grasping her arms at the shoulder. "Tris is about to come storming round that booth. He's on the verge of falling into your arms. All he needs is a push over the edge. If he'd catch a glimpse of us kissing, I believe that would be enough to do it. So, please, don't struggle when I—"

Julie, blinking in the light and taken utterly by surprise, took a backward step. She only knew that Peter was completely mistaken in Tris's motives. "No, Peter, you don't understand," she said, deeply troubled. "Tris doesn't—"

"There's no time to talk," he cut in urgently. "He may come at any moment. He must find us embracing, or the moment will be lost." Without giving her time to respond, he pulled her close. His arms tightened about her, and he put his mouth to hers.

She didn't struggle. Her mind was too full of confusing impressions to think clearly. She'd not yet recovered from the shock of the mysterious voice in the gypsy tent when Peter had come upon her with this urgent demand. It was all too much to sort out now. She simply melted into his embrace and let herself enjoy the sensation. There would be time later, she thought, to figure things out.

Tris did not immediately appear, but Peter did not let her go. He was certain that Tris would follow him momentarily. Meanwhile, he too surrendered to the pleasure of the embrace. This would be the last time he'd hold this beloved girl in his arms, and he had no difficulty in convincing himself that he might as well savor every sensation while he could. He could not concern himself now about the difficulties he would encounter later, when he'd be trying to forget her. Yes, this would be a difficult memory to erase, but for now it was a taste of heaven to hold her like this. He would take what he could from the present; there would be plenty of time later, when the future was upon him, to pay the price.

In the pure joy of the embrace, Peter almost forgot why he'd done this thing. But as he'd predicted, Tris did appear. And, in Peter's view, much too soon.

Tris came striding round the brandy ball booth like an avenging knight. When he saw Julie and the dastardly Canfield locked in each other's arms, he exploded. "Good

God!" he swore in fury. "You damnable makebait, unhand that woman!" And he savagely pulled Peter around.

Julie tottered backward and almost fell. "Tris, what's the *matter* with you?" she cried, startled at his vehemence.

Tris ignored her. "Just *what* do you think you're *doing?*" he shouted at Peter.

"That's obvious, isn't it?" Peter replied coolly, determined to goad the fellow into action. "And what business is it of yours?"

"I'll show you what business it is of mine," Tris said through clenched teeth. And he swung his fist like a madman into Peter's jaw.

Peter went down like a stone. Julie screamed. A crowd began to gather, their eyes wide with curiosity and ribald delight. "A mill!" someone shouted. "There's gonna be a mill!"

"Why, it's young Enders," said a female voice.

"And that's the viscount from Wycklands," cried another in salacious pleasure.

"Get up, you blasted gudgeon," Tris shouted at the fallen man. "Get up and let me give you another!"

"Right," yelled a man in the crowd. "Get up, yer lordship, an' give 'im yer fives!"

Peter lifted himself on one elbow. A trickle of blood leaked from a split in his underlip. With a cry of alarm, Julie knelt beside him, agitatedly mopping up his blood with her handkerchief.

"Get away from him, Julie," Tris ordered. "I'm not finished with him yet."

"I'm not getting up," Peter said in rueful amusement. "I have no intention of engaging in fisticuffs with you."

"Get up, I say, or you're a damned poltroon," Tris insisted furiously.

But it was Julie who rose. She ran to Tris's side and clutched his arm. "What on earth's gotten into you, Tris?" she muttered into his ear in utter perturbation. "Isn't that kiss just what you *wanted* to happen?"

Tris gaped at her, arrested. What she'd said was true! He blinked at her for a moment like a man just awakening from a dream. Of *course* that was what he'd wanted. What *had* gotten into him? In his struggle to find an answer, the madness that had enveloped him during the last few minutes dissipated. His fists relaxed, his arms dropped to his side, and he shut his eyes in a kind of agony. Then, dazed and confused, he turned away from Julie's bewildered gaze and saw the mob. *Confound it, what have I done?* he asked himself. Awash in humiliation, he blundered his way through the crowd, ran round the intervening booth and disappeared.

The crowd, realizing that the fun was over, began to disperse. Julie helped Peter to his feet. "What was all that about, Peter?" she asked. "Did you *plan* to let yourself be knocked down?"

He licked his bloody underlip. "Well, I didn't expect to get a swollen jaw and a split lip, but, yes, I suppose I did. It was the only way I could think of to make him recognize his feelings for you. I think the young idiot knows them now. Go to him, Julie, and let him tell you himself."

Julie shook her head. "I think you *both* are idiots. But never mind that now. Let's go back to Larchwood and get your lip tended to."

"No, thank you, Julie. My wound is trivial. Your purpose now is to find your Tris. As for me, now that our goal has been accomplished, I think I'll take myself home and rest on my laurels." He looked down at her with a small smile, bowed briefly and set off for his home.

Julie's throat tightened in pain. "But Peter," she called after him, "you don't—! There's something I ought—"

He wheeled about. "Don't say anything, please! If there's anything I don't want from you, it's thanks." He took three quick strides back to her and lifted her hand to his lips. "Good-bye, my dear. I wish you happy." That said, he hastily walked away, leaving her staring after him in despair.

Just a few steps away, hidden by the brandy ball booth, Cleo stood leaning against its side, her cheeks white. It was there her father found her a few moments later.

"Cleo, my love," he exclaimed at the sight of her deathly pallor, "what is it?"

She lifted her head and peered at him as if at a stranger. Then she fell against his shoulder, as limp as a doll. "Oh, Papa!" she murmured miserably.

He stiffened in alarm. "Good God, girl, what's *happened* to you?"

She was silent for a moment. Then, with a slight shudder, she stood erect and straightened her shoulders. "Papa," she said in a muted voice, "let's go home."

# 24

AT ENDERS HALL THAT NIGHT, DINNER WAS NOT served. No one wanted to eat it. Lord Smallwood had announced that he and his daughter were departing for London immediately and would not stay for dinner; Tris had not been seen since the fair had closed at dark; and Lady Phyllis, the only one left, had no appetite. So dinner was canceled.

The staff did not mind. They had quite enough to do, readying the guests for departure. On strict orders from Lord Smallwood himself, the maids and footmen had only one hour in which to ready their coach and bring it to the door, help Lord Smallwood and Cleo to dress, pack their bags and bandboxes, carry them down and load them atop the carriage. Why there should be such a great hurry all of a sudden, when the Smallwoods had been dallying in complete ease at the hall for more than a fortnight, was a question no one on the staff could answer.

Lady Phyllis, who had by this time completely forgotten that when the pair had first arrived she'd longed for their quick departure, was now quite upset by this abrupt decision to leave. It did not help in the least to hear Lord Smallwood's inadequate answer when she'd asked if anything was wrong. He'd only said that it was urgent they return to London at once.

Phyllis stood helplessly in the entryway watching the footmen rush in and out. Neither Smallwood nor Cleo made an appearance until the coach was ready to depart. They came down the stairs together, dressed for travel and looking strained. "I wish you will sit down and take a light repast before leaving," Phyllis begged.

"Thank you, ma'am," Smallwood said brusquely, "but we must be off."

"Can you not even wait for Tris to come home? I have no idea where the boy has gone for so long, but he's certain to come home at any moment. He'll be so dismayed at having missed seeing you off."

"He'll get over it," Lord Smallwood muttered.

Cleo threw him a quick, disapproving look. Then she threw her arms about Phyllis's neck and held her tight. "I shall never forget your generous hospitality," she said in a shaking voice. "Thank you from my heart, ma'am." And she ran out the door.

Lord Smallwood, using his cane to help the limp that had suddenly become very pronounced, hobbled across the floor to his hostess and took her hand. "I too will never forget your many kindnesses, ma'am," he said.

"Come now, Smallwood," Phyllis demurred, "we've surely become good enough friends to skip these formal thank-yous."

He smiled sadly. "Yes, I suppose we have. I only wish . . ."

"Yes?" she prodded eagerly.

He shook his head, dismissing the unspoken thought. "Well, no point in dwelling on wishes," he muttered as he limped to the door. "My mother used to say, 'If wishes were buttercakes, beggers would be fat.'"

She followed him out to the carriage and watched as a footman helped him climb up. Then the steps were lifted, the door was shut, and the coachman cracked his whip. Lord Smallwood lowered the window and poked out his head. "Good-bye, m'dear," he shouted against the noise of the horses' hooves.

"Good-bye," she answered sadly. "I also wish . . ." But the carriage was already moving down the drive. He probably hadn't even heard her.

# 25

TRIS CAME HOME REELING. HE TEETERED TOWARD the stairway, trying not to make any noise, for it was past midnight. But his mother, who'd been waiting in the sitting room, heard him. She hurried out to the hallway, took one look and gasped. "Tris! You're *drunk!*"

"Yes, ma'am. As a lord."

She glared at him, aghast. "How *could* you? Tonight of all nights, when I have such important matters to discuss with you!"

He blinked at her woozily. "Wha' important matters?"

"I can't tell you now. Not when you're in this indecent condition."

"Yes, y'can. I'm a bit mizzled bu' not yet seeing by twos."

"A bit *mizzled?* You can barely stand! I'm surprised you're not walking on your knees."

"Dalderbash!" He threw back his shoulders and tried to stride past her into the sitting room, but he stumbled and would have fallen if she hadn't caught him.

He shook her off, tottered into the room and dropped down on the nearest easy chair. "There, now. Wha'dye want t'say t'me?"

She shrugged and sat down on the sofa opposite him. "For one thing, your guests have departed for London."

He blinked at her, openmouthed. "Cleo? Gone?"

"Yes, with her father."

"Gone, eh? Hmmmmm." He thought the matter over for a moment. "I'm not . . . surprised."

His mother shook her head. "You look surprised."

"Well, in a way I am surprised. An' then again I'm not."

"That's a logical answer," Phyllis said sardonically. "For a drunkard."

"Cleo did indi . . . indicate t'me that she might leave," he managed.

"When did she do that?"

He wrinkled his brow in thought. "T'day, I think. This after . . . noon."

"Did you quarrel?"

"Yes. No." He put up a hand to steady his swimming head. "I dunno."

Phyllis eyed him in disgust. "Really, Tris, this is getting us nowhere. You should go to bed."

"Quarreled wi' Canfield, though. Remember that right enough. Gave 'im a facer. Knocked 'im off 'is pins."

"Tris!" She rose from her seat in concern. "Are you saying you actually engaged in fisticuffs? With *Peter?*"

"Knocked 'im right off 'is pins."

"But why?"

"Th' bounder wuz kissing Julie. Had no right t'kiss Julie."

Phyllis's eyes widened, and her heart gave a jump in her chest. Suddenly, in this useless and depressing exchange, she heard something to delight her. "Oh, *Tris,*" she cried, dropping to her knees before his chair and taking his nerveless hand in hers, "do you know what that means?"

"It don't mean anything. On'y means I floored 'im wi' my fives. Nothing at all nigsifigant . . . fignisigant . . . significant in that."

"But it *is* significant. It means you were jealous! And jealousy, my dear boy, is a sign of love."

He fixed his eyes on her blankly. "Is it?"

"It means you love Julie! Just as we've always wished!" She got to her feet and gazed at him fondly, her anger gone. "But never mind now, dearest. You need to sleep away your inebriation. We'll talk about this tomorrow. I'll ring for Livesey to put you to bed." She went to the bell-pull, her step almost dancing. "You dear, dear boy!" she chirped excitedly. "You've made me the happiest of mothers!"

Those words were the first Tris remembered when he awoke the next morning. Something in his head hammered painfully, preventing him from understanding the words' significance. It was a long while before he was able to think clearly, but when he could, he began to understand what it was that had made his mother so happy: she'd concluded that he loved Julie after all.

Perhaps it was true. He'd certainly been acting like Julie's lover these past few days. Ever since he'd seen Peter kissing her in the dappled sunlight of his library, he'd been like a man possessed. After plotting and scheming to encourage Peter to fall in love with her, he'd made a complete about-face. Now he seemed to be scheming, instead, to tear Julie from Canfield's arms. What did that mean? It was jealousy, certainly. But was jealousy the result of love?

What did he really know about love, after all? he asked himself. He'd truly believed he loved Cleo, but these last few days he'd barely noticed her, so blinded had he been with jealousy. And when she'd tried to interfere with him, he'd felt nothing but irritation. Had his love for her simply died away? Passed like a spring rain? Or had it never existed at all?

Perhaps love was a will-o'-the-wisp, like happiness, always floating just beyond one's grasp. Or perhaps it was a quiet, slowly developing emotion, made up of affection and loyalty and undramatic steadiness, like his feeling for Julie—a sleeping beast only roused to passion when driven to extremes of jealousy or lust. He wished he could discuss the problem with someone older, wiser and more experienced than he . . . someone like Peter. But passion had made him punch Peter in the jaw, thus precluding any possibility of engaging in friendly conversation with the man again. Passion had its price.

After another hour of head-hammering contemplation, he was still without a single answer to the dozens of questions his conduct and his muddled feelings had aroused.

There was nothing for it, he decided, but to go down and face the consequences.

His mother, who'd been eagerly awaiting his descent all morning, greeted him warmly. "Do you remember what we talked about last night?" she asked as soon as he sat down at the morning room table for a late breakfast.

"Yes, every word," he assured her.

"Then I think we should run over to Larchwood as soon as you've eaten, and tell Madge. And Julie, of course."

Tris paused in the act of bringing a muffin to his mouth. "Tell them what?"

"Tell them to set a wedding date, of course."

He set the muffin down on his plate unbitten. "Of course," he said at last. "What else could I have been thinking of?"

*What else indeed?* he asked himself as he slowly sipped his tea. His feelings for Julie were obviously very deep, much deeper than he'd dreamed, or else why would he have behaved like such a crazed buffoon these past few days? He would marry Julie, with whom he was always completely comfortable. They would live together in the blessed familiarity and fond affection that had been a constant condition of their lives. It was evidently meant to be. Their mothers had always known it. It was only childish rebellion that had made them oppose the idea all these years. Well, he'd grown up at last. It was about time.

# 26

JULIE HAD NO QUESTIONS IN HER MIND ABOUT THE nature of love. She knew what love was; she'd recognized it almost at once. Perhaps she hadn't quite admitted it when she'd first laid eyes on Peter at the assembly, but it hadn't taken her long afterward to acknowledge the truth. Though she'd never come face-to-face with that sort of love before, it was not in the least unfamiliar. Love was, to her, an instantly recognizable emotion.

As she lay sleepless on her bed the night after the disastrous fair, she was pondering a problem of another sort—how to win the object of that love. And that was a problem she had no idea how to solve. She'd gone to see the gypsy in the desperate hope of getting a clue, but the experience in the gypsy tent had been too confusing. Besides, it was ridiculous to take fortune-telling to heart. Crystal balls . . . mysterious voices . . . lines on the palm . . . they were all nonsense. Anyone who took such things seriously was a dupe, and she was no dupe. She knew perfectly well that someone had been under the table, holding a candle under the globe and blowing smoke into it. Perhaps that same hidden swindler was the one who'd said those confusing words. There was nothing supernatural about any of it.

And yet . . . and yet . . . Hadn't the gypsy said there were two men, one tall? Julie had known instantly that they were Tris and Peter. How could the gypsy woman have known that? And hadn't the old crone predicted the fight? The mill hadn't been as terrible as she'd said it would be, but there *had* been blood. And a crowd. And Peter had gone down and would not get up. That was a great deal to explain away by calling it coincidence. Perhaps there *was* something supernatural in the midst of all that flim-flam.

But of all she'd heard in the gypsy tent, the words at the conclusion troubled her most. *The tall man will not win unless you untie the knot you knit yourself.* What did it mean? What knot had she knit herself?

If she were honest with herself, she would admit that there was indeed a knot in the threads of her life. She could easily identify it. She'd foolishly admitted to Tris that she was attracted to Canfield, and she'd been a willing participant in Tris's scheme to capture him. If she'd never told Tris how she felt, and if she'd been brave enough to admit to Peter that she was not in love with Tris, the threads would never have tangled. She herself was the one to blame for "knitting" the plot. And that was the knot she had to untie.

But how?

There was only one possible solution: Peter would have to be told the truth. Once he knew that it was not Tris but Peter himself that she loved, the tangled threads would fall apart. The knot would not even exist. But she could not do it. Such a confession would take more courage than the shy Miss Juliet Branscombe possessed.

Besides, even if the knot were untied, there was no reason to suppose that anything would change. No substantial improvement would come of it. Peter didn't love her. If he did, wouldn't she have seen a sign of it? Of course, he *had* kissed her once, that afternoon in his library, but that had been because they'd both been drunk with poetry. Though it had been an unforgettable moment for her, it had not meant anything to him. There was, therefore, no reason to put her courage to the test. She would make no confession. There was no point in it.

The next morning, hoping that life would go on as it had before the altercation at the fair, she took out her horse as she usually did when the weather permitted. To her surprise, there was no sign of Cleo or Tris at their usual meeting place. She trotted along the river to the place where Peter generally joined them, but there was no sign of him either. She circled around for a while, hoping he might eventually appear, but he did not. She wondered if, now that he believed his goal for her had been accomplished, he no longer wished for her companionship. She was crushed with disappointment. Though they might never be lovers, she'd hoped they would still be friends.

Deeply depressed, she returned home. When she came in the door, Horsham informed her that her mother, Lady Phyllis and Sir Tristram awaited her in the upstairs sitting room. Without pausing to change her riding clothes, she hurried up the stairs to them.

The warmth of their greetings surprised her. Her mother was smiling broadly, and Phyllis too looked as if she were bursting with good news. But it was Tris who spoke. "Sit down, Julie, for we have something to tell you."

"Really?" She glanced from one to the other in puzzlement as she sank down in an armchair. "You all look as if you've a surprise present to give me. But it isn't my birthday."

"It's better than a birthday present," Phyllis said, giggling.

"Tell her, Tris," her mother ordered. "The suspense is becoming too much for me."

Tris perched on the arm and took her hand. "We're going to be married," he said, smiling down at her fondly. "I've made up my mind. We need only to set the date."

"Oh, Tris!" Julie exclaimed, her eyes brightening. "So Cleo has accepted you at last!"

"*Cleo?*" The shocked cry came from her mother, but everyone's face fell.

"No, you goose," Tris said quickly. "I meant you."

"Me?" The gladness faded from her face. "You want to marry *me?* Have you lost your mind?"

"What a thing to say!" her mother exclaimed, shocked. "Of course he hasn't lost his mind. He's regained it!"

Julie leaped from the chair, almost knocking him over. "No, he hasn't. He's mad!"

Her mother reddened in enraged disappointment. "You're the one who's mad!" she cried. "Oh, what have I done to deserve such a contrary daughter?"

But, Julie, who'd heard all that before, took no notice of her. It was Tris who troubled her. "What's gotten into you, Tris?" she demanded, glaring down at him. "Have you forgotten all about Cleo? And about all the machinations to get me wed to someone else just to clear the way for you?"

"I haven't forgotten," he muttered, abashed. "I just grew up is all."

"What on earth does that mean?"

"I grew up. I suddenly realized that our years of knowing each other, of closeness and friendship, made a sound basis for marriage. We've always been good together, haven't we? Then why wouldn't a marriage between us be good?"

Her brows knit suspiciously. "Cleo turned you down, is that it?"

"Not at all. Just the opposite."

"The Smallwoods have gone back to London," Phyllis put in gently. "You see, when Tris became insanely jealous of Lord Canfield, it became clear to everyone, including Tris, that he loved you."

Julie peered at Lady Phyllis in disbelief. "Are you saying that Tris—on his own, without coercion—decided to offer for *me* instead of for Cleo?"

"Yes. That's exactly what she's saying," Tris declared.

"So stop all this foolishness," her mother ordered, "and help us to plan the wedding we've been dreaming of all these years."

"No, I will not!" Julie cried, wheeling about to her mother, an uncontrollable fury overwhelming her usual cowardice in the face of her mother's imperiousness. Angry tears filled her eyes and began to roll down her cheeks. "I don't *care* about your dreams! Have you, or

Tris, or even Phyllis ever given one thought to *my* dreams?"

*"Julie!"* her mother exclaimed, appalled at this out-burst.

"Oh, my dearest girl!" Phyllis clutched her hands to her bosom in anguish. "Don't you *want* to marry Tris? Are you trying to tell us you don't love him?"

"Tris knows *exactly* how I feel," the girl replied, wiping at her cheeks uselessly, for the tears continued to pour from her eyes. "And to th-think that he, who knows me so well, could possibly b-believe that I would accept this complete about-face without so much as a by-your-leave and agree to w-wed him is . . . is . . . the outside of enough!"

All three gaped at her, aghast. She looked from one to the other, hoping for a flicker of sympathy, but she saw only utter astonishment. Why, she asked herself furiously, were they so astonished at what she felt was a perfectly reasonable reaction to their high-handed assumption that she would jump as soon as Tris snapped his fingers? It was the last straw. She did the only thing she could—she fled from the room.

Out in the hallway, she came to a stop and leaned against the stair bannister, her chest heaving. Her mind was in a turmoil, but above the anguish and chagrin and all the other disturbing emotions, she felt a touch of pride. Never before had she been valiant enough to face her mother down, but she'd done it now. She'd spoken her mind, and in no uncertain terms. Where had that burst of bravery come from?

As she stood motionless, trying to catch her breath, a new thought came to her. Perhaps, while this heady infusion of courage still raced through her veins, she could do the other thing that required courage—courage that until this moment she didn't know she possessed: she could go to Wycklands and make her admission to Peter. *Yes,* she told herself firmly, *now is the time to untie the knot I made. With this feeling of pluck inside me, I can do anything!*

She brushed back the strands of wild hair that fell over her face, took another swipe at her eyes and started down the stairs. She would go now, this very minute, before anything would happen to change her mind. But she'd taken only three steps down when Horsham came round the turn of the landing. "I was just coming to find you, Miss Julie," he said, holding out a note. "There's four draymen downstairs carrying in a pianoforte. From Wycklands."

"What?" She stared at him in bewilderment. "A *piano?*"

"Yes, ma'am. So big they could barely get it in the doorway. I told them to put it in the drawing room, between the windows, which they're doing right now, but they'll hang about to see if you wish to move it somewhere else."

She still didn't understand. "What are you saying, Horsham? The piano is for me?"

"Yes, miss. P'rhaps the note will explain."

She took it from his hand and broke the seal. There were only a few lines written in a neat, firm hand. *Dear Julie,* she read. *By the time you read this, I will be gone and my house closed, so don't try to return my gift to sender. I realize that it is a bit early to send you and Tris a wedding gift, but since I'm not likely to be available at the time of your wedding, this seemed the best time to send it. An instrument like this needs playing. I hope that playing it will bring you many happy hours, and that married life with Tris will be everything you dreamed. Please accept the sincere best wishes of your humble servant, Canfield.*

By the time she finished reading, her hands were trembling. After a frozen moment, during which she stared at the butler with unseeing eyes, she came to herself, brushed passed him and ran down to the drawing room. The four draymen were placing the beautiful rosewood pianoforte at an angle between the windows so that the light would fall over the player's shoulder onto the music page. But Julie didn't care about that. "What does he mean, the house is closed?" she demanded of one of the draymen.

He knuckled his forehead. "Wycklands, ye mean? 'Tis closed, miss," he said. "The master an' staff's gone off t' Lunnon."

"To London? For a visit? When will they be back?"

"Dunno, miss. Not fer a long while, seems t'me."

"How long a while? A week? A month?"

The man shrugged. But another, who'd been kneeling to adjust the wheel at the bottom of one of the piano legs, stood up and wiped his hands on his apron. "I 'eard from 'is lordship's cook that they didn' think they'd be back fer a year'r more."

"A *year?*" Julie sank down on the piano bench, the color draining from her cheeks as all the energy drained from her body. *I'm too late!* she told herself in despair. *My courage came too late!*

"Is this place for the piano t'yer likin', miss?" the first man asked.

She didn't respond. It was as if she wasn't even there.

Horsham, peering at her worriedly, motioned for the men to go. Then, throwing her a last look of concern, he quietly followed them and closed the door.

She turned slowly on the seat, absently brushed back the strands of hair that had fallen over her face and ran her hand lightly over the piano keys. It was a lovely instrument, a magnificent gift. But it was all she would ever have of Peter Granard, Lord Canfield. She gasped in the agony of that realization. It was terribly painful to discover that no gift, however magnificent, could keep a heart from breaking in two.

She did not know how long she sat staring, unseeing, at the piano keys, but the sound of the door being opened broke into her revery. She looked up to discover her mother, Phyllis and Tris standing in the doorway, eyeing her—and the piano—with concerned bewilderment. "It's from Lord Canfield," she explained. "A wedding gift."

"A wedding gift?" Tris asked, amazed. "Good God!"

"At least *he* believes there's to be a wedding," Lady Branscombe muttered dryly.

"I must believe it too," Julie said with a small, sad smile, "for apparently I've accepted the gift. I suppose that means, Tris, that I've decided to marry you after all."

# 27

JULIE GAVE HERSELF A GOOD TALKING-TO. WITH her mother blissful, Phyllis walking on air and Tris declaring himself in love with her (though that was still very hard to believe), it would be ill-natured and mean to be unhappy. She could not, in good conscience, spoil the happiness of those around her by permitting herself to indulge in bad moods and crotchets. Whatever pain she felt in her heart had to be hidden. More than that, it had to be overcome. She was going to marry Tris, who was as dear to her as anyone in the world, and she was determined to make a good job of that marriage. True, she could never love him in that special way she'd loved Peter, but perhaps Tris was right when he said that friendship and loyalty and long years of familiarity were a better basis for wedlock than romance.

So she smiled at everyone, everywhere, whenever she felt anyone was looking. She smiled at the dinner party the vicar and Mrs. Weekes held in honor of the betrothed couple. She smiled at the assembly, when Tris stood up with her for three dances. She smiled when the banns were read at church, when she rode with Tris in the mornings, when Mama and Phyllis met with her to discuss wedding plans, when Mama's modiste came for the first fitting of her wedding gown. She sometimes believed that the contrived smile would be forever frozen on her face.

A month went by. The time had passed pleasantly enough, Julie told herself, what with everyone finding ways to celebrate the coming event and making her the center of attention. With the wedding set for the second week in June, only one more social event was looming up before it—Lady Phyllis's prenuptial ball. Other than the wedding banquet itself (which, if Lady Branscombe's plan came to fruition, would be the grandest ever held in the vicinity of Amberford), the ball was to be the most splendid affair of the prenuptial festivities. Phyllis had sent to London for champagne, three maids had been hired to assist in the kitchen, and no fewer than nine musicians had been engaged to provide dance music.

On the eve of the ball, it was not only Enders Hall that was the scene of excited activity. At Larchwood too, the servants were scurrying about madly. Lady Branscombe had found a crease in the sash of Julie's gown, a bead was missing from the trim on the neckline of her own dress, and the hairdresser who'd been specially hired to cut Julie's hair had not yet arrived. Her ladyship was beside herself. "We'll never make it on time!" she shouted at anyone who came near her.

The matter of the hair was troubling Julie. Tris had made a special request that she cut her hair short. "It's always getting in your face," he'd said bluntly, "and never looking as it ought. Why don't you just cut it off and wear it curled?"

*Like Cleo?* she'd almost asked, but on second thought she'd held her tongue. She'd agreed to the request because she'd made up her mind to be a generous, obedient girl and agree to everything. But in the matter of her hair she could not keep from feeling reluctant. She liked her long, unruly hair. It was a significant part of her. She knew that her habits of tossing it back, of twisting it round her finger when absorbed in thought, of letting it hang in a careless plait when she wanted it out of the way, were irritations to Tris, but she herself would miss all that when the hair was gone. It was a sacrifice she was making on the altar of wedlock. She hoped she would not live to regret it.

The hairdresser, who was Lady Kenting's abigail and had been recommended as a genius with a scissors, arrived an hour before the ladies were due to leave. "We 'as plenty o' time," she assured the nervous Lady Branscombe. "Time t'cut Miss Julie's 'air an' curl it too."

But when she lifted the scissors to the first strand, Julie cried out a resounding "No!" She was not prepared to sacrifice as much as that.

After considerable discussion, the hairdresser surrendered to the girl's insistence that she find some way to put the hair up without cutting it. A Grecian style, with the long hair bound into a tight chignon at the back of the head and a few strands hanging in curled freedom at the sides, was finally agreed upon. Lady Branscombe, who was waiting at the bottom of the stairs in nervous suspense, sighed in relief at the sight of her daughter. "It's very becoming," she assured the uneasy girl. "I'm glad you didn't cut it off."

"Tris won't be," Julie muttered as she covered her head with the hood of her cape.

"Yes, he will. You look too lovely for him to object."

Lady Branscombe proved to be right. Tris said very flattering things about her appearance when he greeted her. And so did everyone else. Julie was so relieved that she began to believe she was having a very good time.

When Tris presented himself to her for the last dance of the evening, Julie suggested that they go out on the terrace for a breath of air instead. It was a perfect night for a ball, with a clear, moon-bright sky and the mildest of spring breezes. "Everything was perfect tonight," she said, gazing up at the stars. "Your mother must be pleased."

Tris perched on the balustrade beside her. "Yes, she is. Did I tell you she's arranged for us to stay with the Contessa Dimanti when we get to Venice on our honeymoon trip? She's a distant relative, and has a house right on the canal."

"That will be lovely." She lifted her hand to one of the strands of hair hanging loose at the side of her face and twisted it round her finger. "Speaking of honeymoons, Tris, there's . . . er . . . something I've been wondering about."

"What's that?"

"I hope you won't mind my asking. It's rather . . . personal."

"Good God, Julie, don't be a clunch. You've known me forever. What can you possibly ask that would be too personal?"

"Very well, then, here it is. Did you ever kiss Cleo?"

There was a moment of shocked silence. Then Tris slid off the balustrade. "What sort of question is that?" he muttered in annoyance. "Why do you want to know?"

She dropped her eyes from his face. "I just do, that's all."

He remained silent for another moment. Then he threw up his hands in a gesture of disgust. "If you must know, I did. Of course I did. I kissed her. Several times."

"I see."

"It's nothing to be bothered about," he said in quick self-defense. "Kissing is just something that a man and a woman *do* when they go about together."

"We don't."

"What?"

"You and I. We don't kiss. We've *never* kissed."

He gaped at her, nonplussed. "Damnation," he muttered, taken aback by what she'd just said, "stop twisting your damned hair." He strode away a few paces, then swung about and stormed back. "We have *so* kissed."

"Have we? When?"

"Lots of times. Birthdays and . . . and special occasions."

She snorted. "Cheek kisses. They don't count."

"Why don't they?"

She tossed him a sneering look. "The kisses you gave Cleo weren't cheek kisses, I'd wager."

He rubbed his chin. "No, they weren't."

"That's what I thought."

"What are you saying, Julie? What's the point?"

"I don't know. Is there . . . something wrong with us?"

"Because we haven't kissed? There was a perfectly acceptable reason for that. We were like brother and sister. Brothers and sisters don't kiss."

She gave him a long look. "But we're not brother and sister any more. We've been betrothed for weeks now."

His brow knit as he considered the problem, but since the solution was obvious, his expression cleared almost at once. "Very well, you idiot, come here. I'll kiss you right now."

She held up a restraining hand. "No, not now. It doesn't feel appropriate right now."

"Yes, it does," he insisted, and he pulled her into his arms.

"Tris, no!" She turned her face aside. "I don't *want* you to kiss me now."

"Why not? Now is as good a time as any." He forced her face up and kissed her mouth. She struggled against him for a moment and then remained still. But there was no answering pressure from her lips, and after a moment he let her go. "I'm sorry," he muttered, deflated. "I shouldn't have forced you. It will be better next time."

"Will it?" She gazed at him quizzically.

"Of course it will."

"What if it won't?"

His eyes clouded over, but he didn't answer. With a slight, discouraged sigh, Julie turned to go inside. But she paused with her hand on the doorknob and looked back at him. "Perhaps, Tris," she said quietly, "it's something we ought to think about."

# 28

JULIE LET TRIS THINK ABOUT IT FOR A WEEK. During that week he kissed her twice, once when he helped her down from her horse, and once when he brought her home after an evening musicale at the Kentings'. The first time, the surprise of it made the embrace seems a wee bit exciting, but the second time was as meaningless as the kiss on the terrace. It was quite depressing to realize that she felt no physical attraction toward her betrothed, but what was even more worrisome was her distinct impression that Tris was as unhappy as she was. He too seemed to be forever forcing a smile. Something about this betrothal was decidedly amiss.

When the week was over, she sent him a note asking him to meet her the next morning at the summerhouse. It was time to talk the problem over frankly and in private.

Tris was there first, as usual. She found him sitting inside on a bench, his shoulders stooped, his head lowered. He was taking no notice of the lush greenery and the vines bursting into bloom all around him. She went up the steps and dropped down beside him on the bench. "For a prospective bridegroom," she said quietly, "you don't look very happy."

He lifted his head and grimaced at her. "Happy? I've forgotten what the word means."

"Oh, dear," she murmured.

He took her hand. "It isn't working, is it?"

"No, it isn't."

He signed in despair. "I don't understand why."

155

"Yes, you do. You've said it often enough in the past. We just know each other too well. There are no—"

"No surprises," he finished. "But what have surprises to do with marriage?"

"I don't know. But I do know that we've been like brother and sister for too long. I, for one, cannot easily make the change from sister to lover. I can't even manage to kiss you properly."

"I know. Neither can I."

"Tell me the truth, Tris. Do you still love Cleo?"

He rubbed his forehead wearily. "I'm not sure. Sometimes I miss her so much that there's an ache right here in my chest. But if I love *her,* why was I so insanely jealous of Canfield when he kissed *you?*"

"I've given that some thought, Tris. It seems to me that you were reacting like a brother who didn't wish to see his sister being manhandled by an outsider."

"No, I don't think it's as simple as that. I've been giving it a great deal of thought as well. I think it's worse than that. I'm convinced that I'd become accustomed to your little-girl adoration of me, and I just didn't want to lose it."

"Even when you had Cleo to love you?"

"Yes," he said, shamefaced, "isn't it dreadful? I can't believe how selfish my feelings were. I wanted to be free to love anyone else I wished, but I wanted you to remain caring for no one but me."

"Like a child," she said, nodding understandingly.

"Yes, like a spoiled child."

"Well, if true, it's a sign of maturity that you recognize it now."

He shrugged. "For all the good that does. What shall we do, my dear? I, for one, am at wit's end."

"We must break the engagement, for one thing," she said firmly. "The longer we pretend, the harder it will be to come forward with the truth."

"Yes," he said, looking closely at her face, "but only if you're sure you really don't wish to wed me."

She lifted a hand to his cheek and patted it kindly. "I

would not wish to wed you even if you truly loved me above all others. You see, Tris dear, I too am in love with someone else."

He could not meet her eye. "I know. Canfield. I mucked that up for you too, didn't I?"

"Not at all. There was nothing to muck up. He never really cared for me."

"I don't believe that. I saw him kissing you!"

"He only did that to make you jealous."

"Nonsense. When he kissed you in his library, he had no idea that I was watching."

"Heavens!" she exclaimed, blushing. "Were you there?" The thought was disturbing. That Tris had been an observer poisoned a precious memory.

"Yes," he admitted ruefully, "I'd just stepped into the doorway and saw you embracing. You were drenched in sunlight, looking like a Dutch painting. It was the first time I ever in my life experienced jealousy. I wanted to grind Peter to dust under my heel."

She shut her eyes, as if the act would somehow block the memory of the scene from her mind. She didn't want to remember. But shutting her eyes did no good. She opened them and fixed them on Tris. "It was an insignificant event, you know," she told him firmly. "The kiss, I mean. A whim of the moment."

"It didn't look that way to me."

"You must take my word for it," she insisted. "I know better."

"Very well," he agreed, sensing her pain. "No point arguing."

"None at all. Besides, we have more pressing matters to discuss than my nonexistent romance." She stood up and paced about the wooden floor of the summerhouse. "If we're to break the engagement, we must gird our loins to tell our mothers."

Tris groaned. "The very thing I most dread."

"I more than you, for my mother is a growling bear compared to yours. But when it's over, we shall finally be free. And that, may I remind you, is what we've wanted from the first."

"Yes, to be free." He stood up and stretched out his arms. "Free to follow our own destinies, not a future decreed by our mothers. Let's do it! Today!"

"Yes, today!" She smiled at him as they pledged by shaking hands. "Won't it be grand? We'll be free to marry whom we please. Cleo for you, who-knows for me." But as second thoughts assailed her, her smile abruptly died. "Of course, what is most likely," she mused as they started down the steps, "is that I shall remain an old maid."

"Probably I shall never marry either," he said glumly, "for Cleo won't have me now. She'll never forgive me for what I've done."

"You won't know that until you try." She squeezed his hand in farewell and set off toward the stile.

"Oh, I'll try right enough," he replied as he marched off in the opposite direction, "but I probably won't succeed." Suddenly he paused and laughed ruefully. "Wouldn't it be poetic justice if we both remained single for the rest of our days?" he called to her over his shoulder.

"Justice for whom?"

"For our mothers, of course. What an ironic punishment for them *that* would be!"

# 29

*IF IT WERE DONE WHEN 'TIS DONE,
then 'twere well It were done quickly . . .*

Julie quoted those lines of Shakespeare to herself as she walked home. She would take Mr. Shakespeare's advice and do the deed quickly. Telling her mother the truth would be difficult, to say the least, but she'd pledged to do it today. It would be better to get it over with this very morning than to have the prospect of that dreadful confrontation hanging over her like the sword of Damocles.

She found her mother in the sewing room with her modiste, both of them laboriously stitching seed pearls onto the bodice of Julie's elaborate wedding gown. The sight of that gown increased Julie's already unbearable tension. In spite of all the labor and expense that had gone into its creation, she was now about to inform her mother that she had no intention of wearing it. Her mother would be *livid.* "Mama," she asked in a trembling voice, not daring even to step over the threshold, "may I speak to you for a moment?"

"Now?" Lady Branscombe peered at her daughter over her tiny, square spectacles. "We're in the midst of—"

"Yes, now, please, Mama. It's very important."

Lady Branscombe bit off a thread, thrust the needle into a pincushion and pulled herself to her feet. "I'll return shortly," she promised the modiste as she stepped out into the corridor. "What is it, Julie?" she demanded impatiently. "I haven't time to stand about gossiping. You know how much there is to do before the wedding."

"It's not gossip. Let's go into the sitting room." The girl

was so nervous her voice shook, but her purpose remained firm. "I think you should be seated when you hear what I have to say."

Her ladyship's eyebrows rose. She opened her mouth to object, but something she saw in her daughter's face stilled her tongue. Without another word, she turned and led the way down the hall. In the sitting room, she lowered herself upon the sofa, removed and pocketed her spectacles, folded her hands in her lap and looked up at her daughter. "Well, here I am, seated just as you asked. What is it you want to say?"

Julie, standing before her mother like a guilty child, clenched her fingers together and took a deep breath. "I'll say it right off, Mama. Tris and I have decided not to marry after all. I know this news will pain you. I'm very sorry."

Lady Branscombe stared up at her, agape. "What are you saying? I don't understand."

A flame of irritation flared up in Julie's chest. She'd had no expectation that this chore would be easy, but if her mother was going to resist even facing the bare facts, it would be impossible. "It's not hard to understand," she said with precise clarity. "The words are perfectly simple: *Tris and I are not going to marry.*"

"But—"

Julie burst out with "I know what you're about to say, Mama, so you needn't bother." Anticipating her mother's anger, she worked up an anger of her own to combat it. She turned away from Lady Branscombe's anxious eyes and paced about the room. "You will say I can't be serious," she said, continuing to storm. "That we've announced the nuptials to all the world. That I've been feted and congratulated by everyone in town. That Phyllis has given me the grandest ball ever held in these environs. That you are already preparing the wedding feast. That my blasted wedding dress is being made right down the hall. Well, I don't want to hear all that! I know it well enough. It can't be helped."

"I was not g-going to s-say any of that," came her

mother's voice, a voice so shaken with tearful regret that Julie could scarcely recognize it.

The girl wheeled about. Her mother—the stalwart, unbending, implacable, strong-minded Lady Branscombe—was weeping into her hands. *"Mama!"* Julie cried out, startled out of countenance.

"I knew it," the older woman sobbed, "I knew it. I just couldn't f-face it."

Julie had never seen her mother cry. Her anger seeped out of her like the air from a punctured soufflé. Nevertheless, she could not quite believe what was happening. It was not beyond possibility that her mother would use tears as a ruse. She crossed back to her mother's side. "Knew what, Mama?" she asked suspiciously.

Lady Branscombe wiped her cheeks and, taking hold of herself with an effort, gazed up into her daughter's face. "I'm your *mother,* Julie. Did you think I wouldn't notice your unhappiness? Did you think I'd be fooled by that pitifully false smile you showed the world? I knew something was wrong, but I didn't know what to do about it."

Her sincerity was evident. Julie, shamed to the bottom of her heart by her earlier suspicions, knelt down and took one of her mother's hands. "I shouldn't have snapped at you, Mama. Blame it on sheer terror. I was afraid of telling you the truth, knowing how much you desired this wedding. But, you see, the truth is that Tris and I don't love each other. Not in the way that's right for man and wife. We're fond of each other, like brother and sister, but we would be miserable if we were wed."

Lady Branscombe winced painfully. "Yes, I do see. I think I've always seen it. I just haven't wanted to admit it until now."

"I'm sorry."

"No, it's I who should apologize," her mother said miserably. "You were right when you said I indulged my own dreams, without thinking of yours. I've spent years dreaming the wrong dreams for you." Her tears began to fall again as she dropped her face in her hands. "I d-don't even know how to make amends. I hope, Julie, my love, that you can f-forgive me."

Julie, dumfounded by her mother's unexpected and complete collapse, cast herself on the sofa beside her mother and threw her arms about her. "Oh, Mama, don't cry! A mother can be forgiven for having dreams for her child."

They remained in the embrace for a long time, drawing solace from this unwonted display of affection. At last Julie spoke. "I know how hard it will be for you to let everyone know the wedding plans have been canceled."

"I shall manage it," her mother assured her. "It will be worth the effort, and even the disappointment, if it means I've won my daughter's affection back." She brushed aside a strand of her daughter's hair fondly. Then she rose from the sofa with a sigh. "Thank goodness the wedding gifts have not yet begun to arrive," she said as she prepared to return to the sewing room. The wedding gown came to her ladyship's mind as she walked slowly to the door. She would finish it anyway, she told herself, for it was unlikely that it would go to waste. *This* wedding would not take place, but her lovely daughter would certainly be married sooner or later.

"Wedding gifts?" Julie asked, not having thought of them before.

"They would have had to be returned, of course," her mother explained, "but I shan't be put to that trouble because none have yet arrived." Having been forced to give up her dreams of this wedding, she was ready to dream of the next. She glanced over at her daughter with a calculating look. "Except for that beautiful pianoforte. You'll have to return it, I suppose. It's really too bad. I know how much you've enjoyed playing it. Unless . . ."

Julie stiffened. Her mother's eyes had taken on a familiar gleam. It was the look she always had when she wanted to manipulate fate by manipulating the people under her influence. It alerted Julie's defenses. "Unless?" she prodded cautiously.

"Unless there is a reason for you to keep it." Lady

Branscombe cocked her head and asked innocently, "Wasn't there something going on between you and Lord Canfield?"

Julie jumped angrily to her feet. Her mother, it seemed, had very quickly recovered from her momentary show of affection. Peace with that woman, Julie realized with a pang, would probably never be more than short-lived. "You're dreaming again, Mama. There was nothing at all 'going on' between his lordship and me."

"It's not a bad dream, you know," Lady Branscombe went on, quite as if Julie hadn't spoken. "If you're not going to have Tris, then I'm willing to grant that Lord Canfield has much to be said for him: good looks, brains, charm, wealth. Not a bad dream at all."

"Really, Mama," Julie snapped in disgust, "have done! I don't want to hear another word on this head. There's to be no more dreaming on my behalf, do you hear? I hereby declare a ban on dreaming. Your last was enough for a lifetime."

# 30

PEACE BETWEEN TRIS AND HIS MOTHER CAME about more easily, although the scene was equally tearful. When it was over, Lady Phyllis regretfully accepted Tris's decision to call off the wedding and acquiesced in his determination to return to London. By the next morning, he was gone.

As soon as she'd waved good-bye to her son, Phyllis walked across the fields to Larchwood, hoping to console her friend for what she knew was an overwhelming disappointment. To her surprise and relief she found Madge in moderately good spirits. "Since a wedding between them is not to be," Madge said placidly as she poured her friend a cup of tea, "we may as well make the best of it."

Phyllis eyed her suspiciously. "I don't like the sound of that, Madge. You are being too sanguine. Have you some plot up your sleeve?"

"Of course not," Lady Branscombe said, dropping a generous spoonful of sugar into her cup. "A good general knows when to retreat."

"This is more than a retreat, my dear. It's a complete surrender." Phyllis lowered her eyes to her teacup as she added fearfully, "Tris has gone off to London to offer for Cleo Smallwood."

Madge Branscombe did not even wince. "Yes, I supposed as much," she said calmly. "I hope he will be successful."

This was too much for Phyllis to accept. "You can't mean it! Are you saying you *want* him to wed her?"

"Under these circumstances, I do. Since I am now convinced that he and Julie don't suit, I think Miss Smallwood is the next best choice."

Phyllis expelled a breath of real relief. "So do I," she admitted. Then, after sipping her tea thoughtfully, she broached the other subject that was on her mind. "Now if we can only see Julie happy with someone, I shall rest content."

Madge glanced at her from the corner of an eye. "What do you think of Canfield as a possibility?" she asked, nonchalantly stirring her tea.

"*Canfield?*" Phyllis brightened at once. "Yes! Of course! I should have thought of him myself. He's *perfect* for her."

"Exactly."

"But . . . isn't it too late? I hear that he doesn't intend to return to Wycklands for a long while. He's gone back to London, dash it all!"

Madge merely smiled. "London isn't the end of the world. In fact, my dear, I've been thinking that London is the very place for you to hold Tris's betrothal ball. As soon as he sends word that he's betrothed, we should all go down and join him in town to make the preparations."

Phyllis's eyes took on a sparkle of excitement. "By 'we' you mean—?"

"Yes, the three of us," Madge said, her smile widening to a mischievous grin. "You, of course, with Julie and me to help. It should take weeks. A month at least. Don't you think it possible that a great deal might happen to Julie in a month?"

Phyllis grinned back at her. "A very great deal. Madge, my love, I've said it before and I'll say it again. You are a genius!"

With that satisfying remark hovering in the air, Madge refilled their cups and the two of them contentedly drank their tea. But neither lady realized they had little cause for contentment, for Madge Branscombe's plan had a crucial weakness. It depended on Tris becoming betrothed to Cleo, and Tris was at that moment discovering that such a betrothal would apparently never come to pass.

# 31

TRIS ARRIVED IN LONDON IN THE LATE AFTERNOON. After arranging for rooms at the Fenton Hotel, he immediately went to call on Cleo at the Smallwood townhouse. He was bursting with eagerness to get down on his knees and apologize for his strange behavior on her last day at Amberford. But the butler would not admit him. He was coldly informed by that high-in-the-instep personage that neither Lord Smallwood nor Miss Smallwood would agree to see him.

He spent that night lying awake in his dreary hotel room trying to think of a plan of action to overcome this first obstacle. It had to be overcome, for if she would not even see him, how could he convince her of the sincerity of his contrition? The next afternoon he purchased the entire contents of a street vendor's flower wagon and, tottering under the load, again appeared on her doorstep. Again the supercilious butler told him he would not be admitted. "Hold these for a moment," Tris begged the fellow. "I want to get something from my pocket for you."

The butler, no fool, guessed that Tris intended to bribe him. Not being opposed to bribes, he took the huge pile of blooms in his arms. Tris fished out a gold sovereign from his pocket. "Here, this is for you, if you will only bring the flowers up to her and come down and tell me what she says."

The butler did not take long to agree, a gold sovereign being worth almost three pounds and therefore only slightly less than a month's wages. "Wait there, sir," he said, backing into the hallway with his load and closing the door with his foot.

Tris paced about on the doorstep for several minutes. Then, to his delight, he heard a window being opened somewhere above him. He looked up eagerly to discover a cloud of flowers being flung down at him. They fell like a shower of arrows about his head and shoulders, one almost piercing an eye, and finally lay strewn on the doorstep, ankle-deep. In utter discouragement, he waded through them and went back to his hotel.

By the next day, he was furious. What right had she to treat him in this shabby way? he asked himself. He hadn't done anything to her that was so unforgiveable, had he? He'd only broken a silly doll and left her alone on the green. Was that so very dreadful? Did he deserve to be so callously spurned? In a rage, he stormed up to her door, brushed by the butler as soon as the fellow opened it, and demanded loudly to see Miss Smallwood at once.

"She won't see you," the butler said, not unsympathetically. After all, he'd been enriched by a sovereign, and with any luck some other bribes might be forthcoming. "I'd like to help you, sir, really I would. But I have my orders. I'm not to let you in."

"Well, I *am* in. So go and tell the lady I'm waiting."

"I can't, sir. You don't want me to get sacked, do you?"

"She won't sack you," Tris said, throwing him another coin. "Hop to it, man. *Now!*"

The butler pocketed the coin, shrugged and went up the stairs. In a moment he returned, followed by two footmen. Without a word, the footmen grasped Tris, one at each arm, and lifted him off the ground. "I'm very sorry, sir," the butler said as the footmen carried the protesting caller across the hall to the door.

"Then get Lord Smallwood," Tris shouted desperately, bracing his feet against the door frame to keep the footmen from ejecting him.

"His lordship knows you're here," the butler said, rather enjoying this opportunity to ride roughshod over one of the "swells." "He won't see you either." Then, with a grin, he nodded at the footmen to indicate that they were to get on with the job. Obediently, the footmen wrenched Tris away from the door frame, lifted him over the threshold, carried him out the door and deposited him unceremoniously on the pavement.

That night Tris wrote a note to Lord Smallwood, pleading for an interview. *I am at wit's end,* he wrote. *If you have an ounce of human kindness in your heart, meet me at White's at one tomorrow. I will be eternally grateful if you grant this request.*

At one the next afternoon, Tris was standing in the bow window of White's club, watching for Lord Smallwood. When a quarter hour had passed with no sign of him, Tris felt so discouraged he was ready to give up the entire matter. But at twenty past one, the Smallwood carriage drew up in front of him. It was with an overwhelming sense of relief that Tris watched his lordship climb down from the coach.

A few moments later they were ensconced in easy chairs in the club lounge, drinks in hand. Tris did not speak until Lord Smallwood had downed half his whiskey. Only then did he feel ready to broach the subject. "Thank you for coming, my lord," he began. "I'm exceedingly grateful."

"Yes, so you said in your letter," Smallwood said brusquely. "But I must be frank, my boy. I did not come to talk about Cleo. I only came to inquire after your mother."

"My mother?" Tris echoed, surprised.

"Yes. She's a fine woman. How does she get on?"

"She's very well, thank you. I'll tell her in my next letter that you asked for her."

"Good, send her my best regards. A very fine woman, your mother."

"Yes," Tris agreed. But discussing his mother's character was not the subject that interested him. He took a sip of his drink and plunged in. "I asked you to meet me, Lord Smallwood, to beg you to do a great favor for me."

"I know what it is, young man, so don't bother to ask. I

cannot intercede on your behalf because my daughter won't even let me mention your name to her. And, to be frank, I wouldn't even if I could."

Tris felt as if he'd been struck in the chest by a hard fist. "Why wouldn't you?" he asked desperately.

"Because I didn't care for your treatment of her, that's why. You won't get any help from me because you don't deserve it."

"I made a mistake, I admit, but surely it was not so dreadful as to be beyond forgiveness."

Smallwood threw him a look of disgust. "If you don't think your actions were dreadful, then you're a worse case than I thought. Any man who pursues one woman while being betrothed to any other is a cad."

"I was *not* betrothed to another," Tris declared so loudly that some gentlemen in chairs nearby turned to look.

"Then as near betrothed as makes no difference," Smallwood retorted. "And keep your voice down. I don't want my daughter's affairs bandied about in clubs."

"I'm sorry," Tris said sheepishly, lowering his voice, "but this matter is very important to me. I love your daughter. I want to marry her."

"You do, do you? Then what about Miss Branscombe, eh?" He leaned forward and jabbed at the air with a finger. "What would *she* think of this interview we're having?"

"She wishes me well in my suit, I swear it! She told me she'd like nothing better than to see me betrothed to Cleo."

"Hummmph!" his lordship snorted. "It didn't seem that way to me when I last saw you. You were so jealous of Miss Branscombe's admirer you wanted to slay him."

Tris looked down at his shoes. "I know. It was a mental aberration of some sort, too hard to explain."

"Then don't bother. Explanations won't help your cause with me in any case. Or with Cleo either."

"Are you sure of that, my lord? If she understands that my feelings for Julie were merely brotherly, and that I love her and no one else, couldn't she find it in her heart to forgive me?"

"No, she couldn't," Smallwood said flatly, putting down his glass. "She no longer has any interest in you." He used his cane to help him to his feet. "Do yourself a kindness, my boy," he said, frowning down at Tris, "and go back to Devon. Forget about my daughter. She wants nothing to do with you."

Stricken into discouraged silence, Tris watched Lord Smallwood make his limping way to the exit. "I won't give up, no matter what you say," he muttered under his breath.

At the doorway, Lord Smallwood looked back at him. "Don't forget to give my regards to your mother," he said. "A very fine woman, that. Don't know how she bore such a cad for a son."

# 32

THE MESSAGE JULIE RECEIVED FROM TRIS COULD not be ignored. *Cleo won't have anything to do with me,* he wrote. *I need your help, even more than you once needed mine. I know how you hate the idea of coming to town, but this is most urgent. I am at the end of my tether. Come at once. Please! Tris.*

With the note clutched in her hand, Julie went to her mother. "I must go to London at once," she said firmly, handing over the missive for her mother to see. "Today, in fact."

To her astonishment, her mother gave her no argument. "Of course you must," she said. "It wouldn't be right to ignore such a forlorn request. However, my love, I cannot permit you to go without chaperonage. London is not Amberford. A young woman cannot dash about town unescorted."

"I'll take one of the maids," Julie said promptly.

But that was not what Lady Branscombe had in mind. "I'll go with you, and so will Phyllis," she said with brisk finality. "We've wanted to take you to London for years. This will be our chance."

"But, Mama," Julie objected, "I'd prefer—"

"If you want to go to London, my girl, you will go with our escort. Like it or not."

Like it or not, that was how Julie went. And that was how, the very next day, she found herself standing in the lobby of the Fenton Hotel surrounded by the great number of bandboxes, trunks and portmanteaus that her mother and Phyllis had packed for the occasion. While

171

the two older ladies made arrangements with the desk clerk for their accomodations, Julie looked about her with the fascination that a country girl feels in a large city. There were more people rushing in and out of the hotel lobby than she would see in the Amberford square in a week. And they were of many more varied styles, styles that seemed to typify London. Moving about among the potted palms were several elegantly clad ladies, with curled plumes on their bonnets and gold tassels hanging from the tips of their pelisses, details of adornment quite unknown in Amberford. Some of the ladies were accompanied by gentlemen so well dressed they would have won approval from Beau Brummel himself. But not all the women milling about were refined ladies, nor all the men nonpareils: there were overdressed dandies whose high-pointed shirts and tight-fitting coats were too ornamental to be comfortable; harried footmen whose uniforms bore more gold braid than a general's; housemaids and abigails in black bombazine dresses and white, frilled caps; draymen whose dark work clothes were covered with striped aprons; women of the "muslin company" whose loud, revealing gowns gave garish evidence of their trade; businessmen from the city in neat, conventional blue coats; and tradesmen whose ill-fitting coats were more practical than dandyish. Such color and variety, Julie thought, wide-eyed, could be found nowhere but in London.

She found herself looking more than once at a lady pacing about impatiently near the outer doors. The lady stopped after every dozen or so paces and peered out the windows that flanked the doorway, obviously watching for someone who'd not arrived on time. The woman was young—Julie estimated her age to be about twenty-two—and very beautiful. It was no wonder, for her eyes were green and framed by thick, black lashes, her hair was coppery-red and topped with a straw bonnet tied fetchingly under her ear with wide green ribbons, and her green jaconet gown, cut low across the bosom, revealed a figure both slim and seductive. What struck Julie as remarkable was that although everything the young woman wore seemed to call attention to itself, none of it could be called vulgar or lacking in taste. The gentleman for whom the lady was waiting so anxiously (for Julie was certain that only a gentleman could cause such impatience in a woman's step) must be, she thought, a very lucky fellow.

Julie's attention was distracted by a hotel footman who asked permission to begin carrying up the luggage. When she looked over at the doorway again, she was just in time to see the young woman cast herself into the arms of the newly arrived gentleman. Julie couldn't see the gentleman's face, for his back was to her, but the lady's face expressed an enviable joy. The sight of the happy embrace made Julie smile. She watched as the gentleman took the young lady's arm and led her out the door. Though she was not usually given to idle curiosity, this time she couldn't help watching for the pair to pass the window, just to glimpse the gentleman's face. When she did, however, her heart lurched in her chest. It was Peter! The man was none other than Peter Granard, Lord Canfield!

She felt a stab of pain so sharp it made her stagger. To avoid falling, she sank down upon one of the boxes and tried to catch her breath. Her mother and Phyllis approached her at that moment. "It took some doing," her mother was saying, "but we managed to cajole the manager into finding three adjoining rooms for—" She stopped short when she saw Julie's white face. "Julie? What's amiss? Good God, you look as if you've seen a ghost!"

"No, it's nothing, Mama," she said, forcing a smile and jumping to her feet. "Nothing at all."

Lady Branscome knew her daughter well enough to realize that *something* had occurred to upset her, but she also knew that Julie could not be coaxed to explain when she wanted to keep silent. Therefore, after exchanging a speaking look with Phyllis, she proceeded as if nothing had happened, directing an army of footmen in the disposition of the baggage and herding her friend and her daughter toward the stairs. "We must all lie down for a nap," she commanded them, pretending not to notice how shaken her daughter still was, "before we meet Tris for dinner."

After an hour alone in her room, Julie managed to recover her equilibrium, if not her spirits. She'd given herself a good scolding for her unwarranted reaction to what she'd seen. It was excessively foolish, she told herself, to be shocked at the sight of Lord Canfield with a beautiful woman. It would be shocking if he were not. Handsome and desirable as he was, he was probably never without a woman on his arm. The only thing that should have astonished her was to see him here, at this very hotel, on the very day of her arrival. *That* was a shocking coincidence, but nothing else she'd seen should trouble her. There was nothing between her and Canfield that would justify these feelings, so she had no choice but to rid herself of them. She had to try to forget the incident, and to forget him.

When Tris tapped at her door before dinner, in the hope of exchanging a few words with her alone before meeting with their mothers, she was able to face him with the appearance of normality. He perched on the window seat and gave her a brief account of what had passed—or, rather, not passed—between Cleo and himself. As he spoke, she studied his face. It was lined with sleeplessness and despair, and her heart went out to him. She gave the circumstances several minutes of serious consideration before suggesting that perhaps she herself should try to talk to Cleo. "Perhaps your defense will be more convincing coming from me," she said. The mere suggestion so filled him with hope that his spirits rose. As a result, he was able to be a charming host to the ladies at dinner.

The next afternoon, he drove Julie to the Smallwood townhouse himself. "I'll wait right here for you," he said, almost breathless with tension, "but talk to her as long as she'll let you. Don't worry about keeping me waiting. The longer it takes, the more hopeful I'll feel."

Julie mounted the steps and tapped at the door. When the butler invited her in, she threw Tris a smile of encouragement before stepping inside. After sending up her

name, she was kept waiting an interminably long time
before she heard Cleo's footsteps on the stairs. She
looked up and almost gasped. Cleo, who'd always been a
veritable fashion plate, was now pale and unkempt. Her
once-bouncy curls lay flat, her eyes looked red-rimmed
and without sparkle, and, though it was late afternoon,
she was still wrapped in a wrinkled morning robe. "Forgive me for not being dressed," she muttered as she
greeted Julie with a weak handshake. "I've not been feeling quite the thing today and decided to stay abed."

"I'm sorry," Julie said hurriedly. "If you'd rather not
see me now, I'd be happy to come back at a more conve-
nient time."

"No, now that you're here, you may as well stay and tell
me what you've come to say. Let's go to the sitting room
where we can be private."

Julie followed her down the hall. When they passed the
open door of the drawing room, Julie caught a glimpse of
Lord Smallwood looking up in surprise from the pages of
the *Times*. But since Cleo did not pause to let her visitor
and her father exchange greetings, Julie had no choice but
to proceed without a word. She could only hope that Lord
Smallwood would not think her rude.

When they were seated opposite each other on easy
chairs in the sitting room, Julie looked about her. It was a
small room with two tall windows that faced the street.
The easy chairs faced a fireplace topped by a huge mirror.
In it, she could see Cleo studying her with a penetrating
stare. "You do not look like the blooming bride I expected
to see," Cleo remarked bluntly. "In fact, you're almost as
Friday-faced as I am."

"If you think that my 'Friday face' is caused by my not
being Tris's bride, Cleo, you're fair and far off," Julie said,
turning her eyes from the mirror and facing the other
young woman bravely. "Tris and I have never wanted to
marry. That's what I came to tell you."

Cleo crossed her arms and sat back in her easy chair,
her posture clearly indicating her intention to reject anything she heard. "I didn't ever believe you wanted to

marry Tris. It was plain as day to me whom you wanted to wed. But you cannot say the same for Tris. Not after what happened at the fair."

"Yes, I can. It took us—Tris and me—a long while to understand ourselves, but I think we do now. We were raised like brother and sister, you see, but we were never taught the difference between the brother-sister feelings and lovers' feelings. I believe it was our mothers' fault. Their hearts were set on our marrying. But Tris and I always knew that was something we didn't intend to do."

"Always? Even as children?"

"Always. And when he fell in love with you, that was the final proof. It was you he wished to wed, not me. That was why he tried so hard to get me married off to Lord Canfield. The trouble was that Lord Canfield, just like our mothers, decided that I loved Tris and ought to wed him."

"Peter?" Cleo's brows knit in disbelief. "Are you telling me that Peter was trying to marry you off to *Tris?*"

"Exactly. You don't believe me, do you? Tris never could believe it either. He convinced himself that Peter cared for me. It's hard to blame him, for Peter decided— not with my consent, I may add—to pretend to make love to me to make Tris jealous."

"Let me understand you," Cleo said, leaning forward with sudden interest. "Do you mean to say that while Tris was urging you toward Peter, Peter was urging you toward Tris?"

"Yes, just so! Do you know, Cleo, that I sometimes think men are quite idiotic?"

Cleo gave a hiccoughing laugh. "I've known *that* for years!" For the first time since she came down the stairs, her eyes took on a sparkle, and her voice was warm. "But, please, Julie, do go on. This is quite fascinating."

"There isn't much more to tell. When Tris saw Peter kissing me, he felt an unexpected and unexplainable anger. He and all the rest of us interpreted that anger as jealousy. If he was jealous, we all reasoned, he must be in love with me. That seemed a logical explanation, affecting everyone's judgment, even mine. We actually became be-trothed."

Cleo's eyes fell. "Yes, I . . . I heard."

"But I knew almost at once it was a mistake."

"Of course it was a mistake," Cleo muttered. "You were in love with Peter. What's become of him, by the way?"

Julie was tempted to reveal what she'd seen that after-noon, knowing it would be soothing to share her pain with another woman, especially one who'd also suffered. But she'd come here to discuss Tris's problems, not her own. Dropping her eyes from Cleo's face, she fixed them on her folded hands. "Peter never cared for me in that way, you know," she said quietly. "His whole pursuit of me was a sham for Tris's benefit."

"So *that's* why you're looking so peaked," Cleo said with sincere sympathy. "I'm sorry, Julie. Truly."

"Thank you," Julie muttered, looking up again. "But I didn't come here to talk about me. May we return to the subject of Tris?"

"Yes, of course. I've already admitted being fascinated. You were saying that you knew the betrothal was a mis-take. How did you know?"

"It's simple. You see, through all the days of the en-gagement Tris never kissed me. Even Peter, who doesn't care for me at all, once kissed me in a moment of sponta-neous affection. But Tris never did."

Cleo gasped at that. "Never?"

"Not once. We both realized that was strange. So we talked it all out. Tris believes, and I agree with him, that it wasn't love but a kind of brotherly protectiveness that made him so angry with Peter. A strange man was maul-ing his sister, you see. That's all it was."

"Brotherly protectiveness?" Cleo frowned doubtfully. "That hardly seems an adequate explanation."

"Tris has a somewhat darker one. He thinks he *was* jealous, in a way. I'd always been his adoring little play-mate, you see, and suddenly he was losing that adoration. He felt an unreasonable resentment toward Peter for stealing away that adoration. In some dark corner of his mind, he says, he quite selfishly expected me to go on adoring him and no one else, while he, on the other hand, could be quite free to love wherever he chose. He realizes now how childish those feelings were."

Cleo's eyes stared into hers, wide with astonishment. "I see," she said in a small voice. Shaken, she tucked her legs up under her and curled up in her chair, arms wrapped tightly about her as if she were protecting herself from the impact of this new information.

"He never stopped loving you, you know," Julie said gently. "The time of our betrothal was the worst of his life. I hope you believe that."

Cleo peeped over at her, tears filling her eyes. "I w-want to believe you," she said with a sob.

"You do love him, then?"

"Love him? I'm b-besotted!" She buried her face in her arms. "I haven't been able to get back to my old life since the day I left Enders Hall. I do nothing but m-mope about, whining and feeling s-sorry for myself, like the foolish heroines of silly romances. Yes, I'd say I love him! More than I want to. And much more than he d-deserves, the idiot!"

"Oh, Cleo, I'm so glad! He's waiting right outside, you know. With his heart in his mouth." Julie stood up and smiled at the tearful girl huddled in her chair. "Shall I tell him to come in?"

Cleo raised her head, her eyes flying up to Julie's face in sheer terror. "Now? No, I can't! Look at me, Julie! I'm a sight!"

"He will think you the most beautiful creature he ever laid eyes on, I promise. I'm like a sister to him, and I know."

Cleo got slowly to her feet, ran her fingers through her curls and gave a timid nod. Julie didn't wait for more but ran down the hall and out the door. Tris, whose eyes had been glued to the doorway all this time, leaped from the carriage and grabbed her shoulders. "Well?" he asked tensely.

"Go to her, Tris," Julie said with a tremulous smile.

The light of pure joy transformed Tris's face. He glowed like a just-lit candle. With a gulp, he took time only to press Julie's shoulders with intense gratitude before dashing into the house.

Julie climbed up into the carriage, wondering if she should wait for him or go back to the hotel by herself. It was getting late. The sun had set, and the street was darkening. She looked over at the Smallwood house as if she might find an answer in its facade. What she saw was the window of the sitting room. Inside Cleo was lighting a lamp. Julie could see her reflected in the mirror over the fireplace. As she looked, another figure appeared in the mirror. Tris had burst into the room. He said something brief. Was it her name, or the words I love you? Julie couldn't tell. But she saw Cleo lift her arms in response. Immediately, Tris took her into a fervent embrace. They held each other tearfully for a long time before he actually kissed her.

Julie turned her eyes away. Not only was it improper to watch, but it hurt too much. It wasn't jealousy, exactly. It was envy . . . the pain of realizing that she would never have the good fortune to experience just that sort of embrace.

After a quarter hour, Tris came out and opened the carriage door. His eyes were shining. "I'll never forget what you did, Julie. You're the best sister I never had."

"Am I?" she smiled.

"In every way. So, like the good sister you are, go on home without me. My lovely, forgiving, adorable Cleo would like me to stay here a while longer."

"I'm so glad for you, Tris. Go back to her. I don't mind waiting, really I don't."

"But I mind. I'll enjoy myself more fully if I don't have to think about you sitting out here in the dark."

"Very well, I'll go. But how will you get back to the hotel?"

He grinned as he shut the carriage door. "Don't worry about me," he chortled. "I'll float."

# 33

THAT EVENING, SINCE THE LADIES HAD NO MALE companions or social engagements, they dined modestly at the hotel and retired early. Though it was not yet nine, Lady Phyllis began to prepare for bed. She removed her shoes and took down her long gray hair, after which she brushed and plaited it. Just after her abigail finished unbuttoning the back of her gown, there was a tap at her door. The abigail answered. A hotel footman informed the girl that there was a gentleman down in the lobby who was insisting on seeing her ladyship. Phyllis, clutching her gown together at the back, pattered in stockinged feet to the door. "A gentleman? Is it my son?"

"No, ma'am."

"Then it must be a mistake."

"I don't believe so, ma'am. He asked for Lady Phyllis Enders."

"Well, whoever it is, tell him to go away. It's too late for me to see callers."

"He was very insistent, ma'am. In a high state of perturbation, I'd say."

"Oh, you would, would you? And did this gentleman in a high state of perturbation give you his name?"

"Yes, ma'am. Lord Smallwood, he said."

Phyllis started. "Smallwood? Why didn't you say so at once? Go and tell him I'll be down in five—no, ten minutes."

She put on her shoes and fidgeted nervously while the abigail did up her dress again. It was not a dress she would have chosen to wear when meeting Smallwood again, for the color was drab and the white tucker that reached up to her chin made her look like a governess, but since there was nothing to be done at this late hour, it would have to do. Her hair was a more serious problem. It hung down her back in a loose plait, fit only for sleeping. To dress it properly would require undoing the plait, brushing it again and pinning it into some sort of knot. Even the simplest style would require more time than she had. She and the abigail tried hastily to pin the braid up into a knot, but it was too heavy and kept falling down. With a helpless shrug, she decided to let it hang.

When she came down to the lobby, a mere fifteen minutes from the time she'd sent the message, she did not immediately see him. She walked about, peering round chairs and potted plants with no success. Suddenly, behind her, an angry voice said, "So there you are, ma'am! You've kept me waiting long enough, I must say!"

She swung about, her temper snapping. "Blast it, Smallwood, I should have kept you waiting longer. I was undressed!"

"Ridiculous," he snapped back. "It's only nine."

"Yes. Much too late an hour for civilized people to make calls."

"You are in London now," he pointed out icily. "We do not keep country hours here."

"Hummph!" Not able to think of a better retort, she merely glared at him. But as her eyes darted over him, she noticed that the hand clutching his cane was trembling. Her anger melted away at once. "Are we going to argue this way all night," she asked, letting a smile peep out, "or would you rather get to the point of this call?"

"You're right, ma'am. We are wasting precious time. Is there a private room where we may chat, or must we discuss personal matters right here where any passerby might hear?"

"I'm sure that an inquiry at the desk is all that will be needed to provide us with a private parlor," she said, and with a toss of her head that caused her long braid to flip, she marched off to make the arrangement. In a few moments they were ushered into a small, beautifully furnished room off the lobby. When the door was closed, she sat down on a red-and-gold striped sofa and looked up at him. "Won't you sit down, your lordship?"

"I will not sit down," he barked. "I have come to ask a question, ma'am. Do you know where your son is at this moment?"

The question surprised her. "I have no idea. The boy is of age, you know. He doesn't have to report to his mama on his comings and goings."

"Is that so? Well, then, let *me* tell you the answer. At this very moment he is at my house, in my sitting room, on my own leather chair, with my own daughter in his lap. When I left, they were kissing. It was a long kiss. I have no doubt it is still going on."

Her face took on a beaming smile. "Really? How *wonderful!* I was so afraid your daughter might not be willing to forgive him. I'm so happy for them both!"

"Happy for them, ma'am? *Happy* for them? I do not agree. It is a tragedy. You must take him away from London at once!"

Her eyebrows rose in bafflement. "Good God, why?"

"Because he will make her miserable, that's why."

"What utter nonsense! What makes you think so?"

"I think so because he's already done so. *Twice!*"

"I know that. But I don't see it as a portent of the future. He was muddled before, largely because of me, but he's seeing much more clearly now."

"He sees nothing clearly. He is a spoilt, headstrong, self-centered *cad* who—"

"Cad?" She jumped to her feet, furious, her braid slapping against her back in an angry reflection of her mood. "Tris? A cad? How *dare* you, Smallwood! That's my *son* you're maligning! He is most certainly *not* a cad. There's nothing he's done—nothing!—that warrants such unkind judgments!"

"Nothing, eh?" He came up to her until they were almost nose to nose. "From what I've seen of him, he's nothing if not scheming, manipulating, cocky and . . .

and . . . " He seemed to freeze for a moment before going on in almost the same voice, "And you are the most beautiful woman I've ever seen."

"What?" She was sure she hadn't heard properly, for the words did not suit the tone at all.

"I said you are beautiful." He looked at her belligerently, as if he would defend the statement with his life.

She took a step backward, agape. "Are you *mad?*"

He shrugged as if madness were of no concern to him. "You must know how beautiful you are."

She shook her head at his insanity. "Smallwood, you poor, crazed fellow, I'm fifty-eight years old."

He nodded. "Yes, a lovely age for a woman."

"Oh, yes, quite." She had to laugh, for she was suddenly beginning to enjoy herself. "A lovely age indeed. I shall be fifty-nine in three months, and *sixty* shortly after that. Are those lovely ages too?"

"For you, yes. And so will sixty-eight, and seventy-eight and on and on."

Since he was not smiling, she had to assume he was serious. She sank down upon the sofa in bewilderment. "Surely you didn't come here to give me foolish compliments. Try to be sensible, man! What is it you really want of me?"

"I thought I *was* being sensible," he muttered, limping to the nearest chair, sinking down on it and putting a shaking hand to his forehead. "I left my house for the purpose of enlisting your aid in an attempt to separate our offspring. But the sight of your face has completely undermined me. It now occurs to me that perhaps my aim in coming here had more to do with seeing you again than with separating Cleo and Tris. I have ached to see you again, you know."

"Have you really? How lovely of you to tell me." She gazed across at him tenderly. "I've missed you too."

He smiled. It was only a small, rather wan smile, but it was the first one since his arrival. "How lovely of *you* to tell *me.*"

"Perhaps so," she said, "but that does not mean I can

ignore your insulting comments about my son. Are you serious about wishing to wreck his affair with your daughter?"

He thought about it for a moment and then sighed. "No, to tell the truth, I'm not. Hang your son and my daughter! Let them take care of their own lives. Let's you and I get married."

Her mouth dropped open, but only for a moment. Then she snapped it shut and got to her feet. "I've had just about enough of your foolishness, Smallwood. I'm going to bed."

"Don't you *want* to marry me?" he asked plaintively.

She tossed her head. "I've never given the question a moment's thought."

"Then think about it now. We get on well, don't we? We spent every day for a fortnight in each other's company, and enjoyed every moment, didn't we? Without ever disagreeing or arguing?"

"There were several disagreements, as I recall," she reminded him, but even as she spoke she was remembering their days together quite fondly.

"All right, yes, we had disagreements," he granted, "but they were more in the nature of spirited fun than real arguments."

"Yes, I suppose they were."

Sensing his advantage, he leaned forward eagerly. "And we miss each other when we're apart; you just admitted that. And we are neither of us in the flush of youth, which means we haven't so very many years to waste in fiddling about making up our minds. Of course there is *one* problem . . ."

"Oh? And what, pray, is that?"

"I cannot spend the rest of my life hearing you call me Smallwood. My intimates call me Harry."

"Do they, indeed?" She gazed down at him speculatively, head cocked. "It doesn't suit you. You should have a dignified name, like Gerard, or Cuthbert or Sebastian. But I suppose I could call you Henry, if you like."

"I like Harry."

She put up her chin. "It's Henry or Smallwood, take your pick."

He rose from the chair and came toward her, his spirit so much revived that he barely used his cane. "Except for Cuthbert, you may call me anything you like. Now that that's settled, will you marry me?"

"My dear Henry," she said, both amused and bemused, "the leap from the first use of your given name right into the bonds of wedlock is a very large leap to make all at once."

"I know. Loving you has made me agile. No, more than agile. It's made me daring. I've always been a timid, pedantic sort of fellow, but suddenly I'm ready and eager to make this very large leap. I know it's true for you too. I can see it in your eyes."

She lowered them at once. "Can you, indeed?"

"There's a man at my club whose brother is a bishop. He can get me a special license. We can be wed tomorrow morning."

She lifted her hand to his head and brushed back a lock of white hair from his forehead. "You *are* mad, you know. As Tris would say, upper works completely askew."

Ignoring her remark, he reached for her hand, lifted it to his lips and kissed the palm. "Are you heeding me, ma'am? Tomorrow morning. It's an order. I'd like you to wear your hair just as it is now, but if you must wear it up, I'll forgive you. There's a bonnet I've seen you wear— yellow straw with roses along the brim—that will look bridal, I think. I'll bring yellow roses for you to carry. I shall call for you at ten-thirty. Be ready."

She stared at the palm he'd kissed. "Henry, you fool," she murmured in a choked voice, "I can't be ready for a wedding overnight." Then she lifted her eyes to his face. "Give me one day more."

# 34

LADY BRANSCOMBE COULDN'T HELP BUT WONDER why her friend Phyllis was behaving so strangely. For one thing, she had forgotten their plans to shop at the Pantheon Bazaar and had disappeared for an entire day. Then, when they met at dinner, Phyllis didn't make any explanation. Madge had too much pride to press her, but she fully expected that Phyllis would offer one freely. To her disappointment, however, none was forthcoming. Furthermore, Phyllis excused herself after dinner and left the hotel under the escort of Lord Smallwood. Madge surmised that they wanted to discuss plans for a betrothal fete for Cleo and Tris, but she didn't quite understand why she herself was not included. Helping Phyllis plan the fete was one of the reasons Madge had come to London in the first place.

She intended to say as much to Phyllis when they met in Madge's room for breakfast the next morning. But when Phyllis arrived looking particularly pink-cheeked and bright-eyed in spite of it being a rather rainy morning, Madge decided that a scold would not be in order. "You look very pleased with yourself," she said instead. "You and Smallwood must have come to a happy agreement about the betrothal party."

"As a matter of fact, we did," Phyllis chirped. "We're going to hold a small champagne breakfast right here in the hotel on Saturday, for us and the Smallwoods and a few of our London acquaintances. Probably no more than twenty."

This was too much for Madge. She would have to speak

out even if it drove the pink bloom from her friend's cheek. "Good heavens, Phyllis, have you forgotten all our plans?" she cried. "We were to hold a ball, and invite a crowd! How else can we manage to inveigle Canfield? In your excitement over *Tris's* good fortune, have you forgotten all about *Julie?*"

Phyllis reached across the table and grasped her friend's hand. "Of course I haven't. Julie's situation hasn't been out of my mind for a moment. We'll simply invite Canfield to the breakfast. The chances of their being thrown together are much greater at a small party than at a ball."

Madge's brows knit. "Perhaps you're right. But must the breakfast be held so soon? I was hoping Julie and Canfield might meet at the theater or at some evening gala *before* the betrothal celebration, to give that meeting a little momentum."

Phyllis smiled complacently. "I've arranged for that too. You see, Smallwood's friend, Lord Chalmondeley, is hosting a ball for the prince, and Smallwood's arranged for the three of us to attend under his escort. He says it will be a dreadful squeeze, but for one thing, it will give Julie a chance to meet Prinny!"

"Yes, she will certainly enjoy that," Madge muttered, "but what has that to do with—?"

"Wait! I haven't told you the best part." Phyllis looked across the table with a triumphant grin. *"Canfield will be there!"*

Madge gasped in pure ecstasy. "He *will?* Are you sure?"

"Positive. Chalmondeley said so."

"Oh, my goodness! Tomorrow?" She clasped her hands to her bosom in dismay. "How can we possibly—? I haven't yet had time to order a new gown for her! And she hasn't a decent pair of gloves! We can't possibly be ready!"

"Yes, we can," Phyllis said serenely, rising and gliding to the door. "She can wear the lilac gown she wore to the last assembly. Canfield himself admired it, remember? And as for gloves, she can have mine."

Thus, on the following evening, Julie, dressed in her lilac silk and wearing Phyllis's gloves, found herself making her way up the crowded stairway to the Chalmondeley ballroom, her mother ahead of her and Phyllis and Smallwood following. She'd been told that the prince was expected to attend, but no other name had been mentioned. Although the prospect of meeting the prince face-to-face was certainly exciting, she was otherwise not looking forward to this evening. She knew no one in the huge crowd, and she wondered if any young man at all would ask to stand up with her. It would probably turn out to be an affair not unlike the Amberford Assembly, only larger. She would be a wallflower in London just as she was at home.

She took a seat in her mother's shadow, as usual, and sat miserably through three dances. She glanced into the corner where a large clock bonged quietly to mark every passing quarter hour. Forty-five minutes had still to pass before Prinny was to make his appearance at midnight. To Julie, convinced she'd never been so miserable, it was an eternity. Suddenly, however, Lord Smallwood appeared with a young man in tow. "Miss Branscombe, may I present the Honorable Horace Chalmondeley, who earnestly desires to stand up with you?"

The fellow was probably not more than twenty years old, but he was quite good-looking and marvelously dressed. Julie jumped up and took his arm without even glancing at her mother for permission, so grateful was she to escape her role as wallflower for a little while.

The Honorable Horace did not say anything as they walked to the dance floor, but once they took their places in the set, he began to speak. "I've been watching you all evening," he said with an assurance beyond his years, "and I can't determine why you've been hiding away back there. Girls as pretty as you usually station themselves where they can be seen."

"Yet you managed to see me, didn't you?" she answered flippantly, thinking that Tris would find that retort saucy. He'd be proud of her.

"Only because I'm more observant than most," the cocky young fellow said. "You weren't hiding away because you're spoken for, are you?"

She was about to give him another saucy retort, but the music started. It was a lively selection called "Mutual Promises." She very much enjoyed the opportunity to expend some of her pent-up energy. She laughed at the Honorable Horace's every quip, swung on his arm with spirit and was almost sorry when the music stopped. Just as they left the floor, however, she was accosted by two other young men, each requesting her company for the next dance. As she hesitated, not knowing how to choose between them, a third man came up. "Sorry, gentlemen," he said, "but this dance is mine."

"Pete— Lord Canfield!" she gasped, the blood freezing in her veins.

He smiled down at her. "You can't refuse me, my dear. The next dance is a waltz."

"N-No, I couldn't refuse that," she said breathlessly, managing to smile up at him.

He took her arm, and they started back to the dance floor. "It's good to see you, Julie," he said warmly. "What are you doing so far from home?"

"Tris sent for m—" she began and then realized that the words might give him the wrong impression. All she wanted him to know was that Tris was betrothed, and *not* to her. However, she couldn't just blurt it out. "I mean . . . ," she began again, blushing, "that Mama and Phyllis decided to . . . to . . ."

He sensed her embarrassment, though he couldn't explain it. "Where *is* the lucky dog, anyway?" he asked. "I haven't seen him here."

She sighed in relief. Now that he'd asked, it would be perfectly proper for her to tell him that Tris was just where he ought to be, with this betrothed, Cleo Smallwood. "He's not here," she said eagerly. "He's spending the evening with—"

The music began at that moment. Peter placed his arm round her waist, causing her voice to fail her completely. *I'll tell him after the dance,* she promised herself. *There's plenty of time.*

They quickly got into position and started to dance. They'd taken no more than three steps, however, when the music stopped abruptly. After a brief pause, the musicians struck up the "Rule, Britannia." Peter looked down at her, his face showing real chagrin. "Dash it," he muttered, "that means the prince has arrived. We shall have to—"

He was cut short by the arrival of a young woman who'd run across the floor to him in a flurry of jade-green flounces and who now grasped his arm. Julie recognized her as the same young lady he'd met at the Fenton. She now looked even more spectacularly beautiful. "Peter, he's here!" the lady cried excitedly. "You promised you'd introduce me! Come quickly!"

Peter's look of chagrin deepened. "Julie, this is Miss Catherine Marquard. Kat, I'd like you to meet Miss Juliet Branscombe. The Branscombes are my neighbors in—"

"A pleasure, Miss Branscombe," Kat Marquard said in breathless and uninterested dismissal, not even giving Julie a second glance. "Peter, please!" She pulled at his arm urgently. "If we don't hurry, he'll be surrounded by a crowd and we won't get his attention!"

Peter looked down at Julie miserably. "Excuse me, Julie, I must go."

"Yes, of course," Julie said numbly. "Good-bye."

With one backward look, he let the girl hurry him away. Julie was left standing alone on the now-deserted dance floor. Her knees shook as she started back to where her mother had been seated. But her mother was on her feet and approaching her, looking white-faced and agitated. "Were you just conversing with Lord Canfield?" she asked Julie tightly.

"Yes. Why do you ask?"

"Why? *Why?*" Her face reddened in agitation. "Because he doesn't deserve your attention, that's why!" She looked about her to make certain no one was close enough to overhear, but the area where they stood was completely deserted. Everyone who hadn't managed to squeeze out to the reception area to greet the prince was crowded round the door. "Canfield is an unprincipled scoundrel and shall henceforth be beneath our notice."

"How can you say that, Mama? He is a neighbor of ours, is he not? And a friend."

"He is no friend of mine! And not of yours, either."

Julie was baffled. "I don't understand you, Mama. Not more than a fortnight ago you said that he was handsome and wealthy and charming—a gentleman a girl could dream about."

Lady Branscombe waved her hand dismissively. "You must have misunderstood me."

"Come now, Mama, your words were perfectly unambiguous. You sounded as if you would have liked him to *offer* for me. And now you say he's unprincipled. How can you make such a complete about-face? And how, may I ask, can you say he's unprincipled?"

"He *is* unprincipled. He told me in Amberford that he was a suitor for your hand. Now I'm reliably informed that he's about to be betrothed to someone else."

This caught Julie off guard. "B-Betrothed?" she stammered, her chest contracting as if from a blow.

"Yes, betrothed to a Miss Marquard. If that isn't unprincipled, I know not what is!"

Julie, shaken as she was, nevertheless felt impelled to defend him. "He was never a suitor for my hand, Mama," she said, trying to speak calmly despite the fact that her throat burned and the floor seemed unsteady under her feet. "It was all a pretense to entrap Tris. Lord Canfield has every right to attach himself to Miss Marquard . . . or to anyone else who suits him."

"Well, if he's not to attach himself to you, there's no point in giving him any further thought. Besides, if he's foolish enough to leg-shackle himself to that flibbertigibbet, I'm glad to be rid of him! Did you *see* the girl in that vulgar jade-green costume? I'd wager she damped the underdress, the ostentatious creature! I would have thought the man had better sense."

"Please, Mama," Julie begged, her emotions stretched to the breaking point, "have done. She seems to me to be a lovely young woman." Her knees gave way, and she sank down on the nearest chair. "He c-calls her Kat," she added miserably.

Her mother peered down at her, taken aback by those pathetic words. Only now did it occur to her that her daughter was truly smitten with the fellow. Her heart was stricken with sympathetic pain. But she knew that if she showed it, they would both dissolve in tears. In this public place, that would not do. They had no choice but to be strong. She squared her shoulders. "Come, my love, I think we should go home . . . that is, back to the hotel."

"I wish we could go home," Julie muttered under her breath as she got to her feet. Home in Devon was where she wanted to be. Home was the best place for nursing wounds. But this was not the time for self-pity, she reminded herself. They'd come to London for Tris's sake, and here they would stay until their duties were over. She too squared her shoulders. "What about Phyllis and Lord Smallwood?" she asked her mother. "I can't see them in that crowd, can you?"

"Let them stay. We can go home in a hack."

She glanced at her mother curiously. "But don't you want to see the prince? I thought that was why we came."

"It's not why *I* came. But I'll stay if you wish. He's the reason *you* came, after all."

"I suppose he is," Julie said dully, "but I find I'm not as eager as I was earlier. You're quite right, Mama. Let's go home."

# 35

MADGE BRANSCOMBE WAS ALMOST ASHAMED TO admit to herself that she had little stomach for the wedding breakfast that Saturday morning. After learning that Lord Canfield was to be betrothed, her enthusiasm for London and everything in it had considerably waned. Although she was glad that Tris was embarking on what would undoubtedly be a happy marital voyage, he was leaving her Julie behind, alone on the shore of spinsterhood. It was enough to dishearten any mother.

Nevertheless, Tris was like a son to her and Phyllis her closest friend. She had to put a good face on it for their sakes. That being the case, she dressed herself that morning in a new tiffany-silk gown in imperial purple and topped it with a silver turban bearing half-a-dozen plumes in a color that matched perfectly. When Julie saw her, her eyes lit with admiration. "I say, Mama, you look positively regal."

"Thank you, my love. And you are looking very fine as well. I might not have chosen sprigged muslin for so important an occasion, but it does look charming on you. And it is almost summer, so I suppose you may be forgiven." With that motherly compliment Julie had to be content.

The betrothal breakfast was already in progress when Lady Branscombe and Julie joined the party in a private room on the hotel's main floor. The room was bright with sunshine and so massed with greenery it looked like a conservatory, its white walls and green-and-white painted chairs adding to the cheery atmosphere. A long buffet table had been set up along one of the walls, and a few of the guests were already partaking of the hot cheese buns, smoked salmon, lobster au gratin, scrambled eggs with truffles, tiny apple soufflés, tomatoes hollandaise and all sorts of pastries, jellies and creams. In the center of the table a large fountain gave forth a steady stream of champagne. It was a sparkling sight, but not nearly as sparkling as Cleo, who stood near it. Her curls bounced, her cheeks glowed, and her gown—a soft, filmy rose-colored creation twinkling with gold threads and tied just below the bosom with a wide gold band—set off her figure and her eyes to perfection. Tris, standing beside her, beamed with pride. "I think, Mama," Julie whispered, "that I've never seen Tris looking happier."

Phyllis came up to greet them as they entered. "Julie, my love," she said as she embraced the girl, "how very lovely you look. That sprigged muslin couldn't be more perfect for the occasion."

Julie threw her mother a taunting grimace before going off to greet those guests she knew and to meet those she didn't. Two hours passed with much eating, drinking and merriment. Finally, however, Lord Smallwood tapped on his wineglass for order. "I believe it behooves me at this time to make a toast," he said in his precise, scholarly way. "I shall save my wittiest bon mots for their forthcoming nuptials, but for now it will suffice for me to say: here's to my beautiful, foolish and headstrong daughter and the charming scoundrel she loves. May they always be as happy as they are today, and may they present their devoted parents with many bouncing grandbabies!"

"Hear, hear!" his friend Lord Chalmondeley shouted, and as Tris kissed his blushing betrothed, everyone cheered, applauded and downed more champagne.

Lord Smallwood tapped his glass again. "May I have your indulgence for another announcement? It is only a small bit of news, but a very happy one. I think it will surprise you all. Two days ago, a very lovely lady and I were married quietly by special license. Therefore I would be obliged if you would lift your glasses to my wife, the erstwhile Lady Phyllis Enders." While everyone gasped in astonishment, he crossed the room to where Phyllis stood smiling at him and raised his glass. "Phyllis, my love, to you!"

Shock had frozen everyone into immobility. The room was absolutely silent. Suddenly there came a sound between a groan and a gasp, followed by that of a glass crashing to the floor, and Lady Branscombe, her purple plumes waving madly, took a step forward, declaring, "This is . . . too much!" in a strangulated voice. Then, with everyone's eyes fixed on her in horror, she stalked across the room and out the door.

"Mama!" Julie cried, appalled, and started to run after her.

But Phyllis stopped her. "No, dearest, let me," she said quietly. "Please, everyone, go on with the party."

Phyllis found Madge in the lobby, leaning on the back of a chair, breathing heavily. She came up behind her and laid a soft hand on her shoulder. "Forgive me, Madge, dearest. It's all my fault. I should have told you. Prepared you."

Madge threw her an angry look over her shoulder. "Yes, you should have. I thought we were friends. I never had an *inkling* of something like this going on between you and Smallwood."

"I wanted it to be a surprise. I thought it would be a happy one. I should have realized how difficult the news would be for you."

"Difficult is hardly the word," Madge said, turning her back on her friend. "I am flabbergasted."

"I know. I've said I'm sorry. But when the shock is over, you will be happy for me, won't you?"

Madge wheeled about furiously. "Happy for you? How can I be?"

Phyllis looked stricken. "But, Madge, you *must* be. Henry and I love each other, you see, although we didn't admit it until just a few days ago."

"Why didn't you tell me?"

"I don't know." Phyllis, troubled by the realization that

there was some justification for Madge's anger, sank down upon the chair Madge had been using to support her. "It was all so ridiculously sudden," she admitted, half to herself. "I thought . . . I suppose I was afraid you would disapprove."

"I *would* have disapproved," Madge retorted sullenly. "I *do* disapprove!"

Phyllis turned in the chair. "But why, Madge? Do you think Henry and I won't suit?"

There was a silence. "I have to think about that," Madge said slowly, her mind switching from consideration of her own offended feelings to those of her friend. "I suppose, on consideration, that there's no reason you and Smallwood shouldn't get on together," she admitted reluctantly.

"Then can't you forgive me, and be happy for me?"

"How can I?" She walked round the chair and looked down at Phyllis more calmly. "Even though, now that I've had time to think about it, I can see that Smallwood may be right for you, the fact remains that I'll be losing you."

"Losing me?" It was Phyllis's turn to be surprised. "Why on earth do you think that?"

"You'll be living here in London, won't you? In Smallwood's town house?"

"Heavens, no! Henry loved living in Amberford. He'll be moving into Enders Hall as soon as we return from our wedding trip. Tris and Cleo may be intending to settle in London, but Henry and I are not."

An expression of real relief brightened Madge's face. "Is that true, Phyllis? You're not just offering a sweet to a bawling baby, are you?"

"Madge, you idiot," Phyllis scolded fondly, jumping up and taking her friend into a warm embrace, "after all these years, how can you think I could ever move far away from you?"

Madge returned the embrace, surrendering to the necessity of accepting and adjusting to those changes with which life is ever surprising us. The two women sat down together, and Phyllis told her dearest friend every detail of her husband's astounding five-minute courtship. "And now," she concluded, "we are off for a honeymoon in Scotland, where we will come to know each other while admiring the lochs."

"And I," Madge sighed, "will return at once to Amberford, where I will try to find some way to mend my daughter's broken heart."

"Why don't you remain here for a fortnight?" Phyllis suggested. "You've always wanted to give the girl a little town bronze. Now is the perfect time. You can take her to parties and routs and theatricals and all that London has to offer. I'm certain the Chalmondeleys will see that you are invited everywhere. Who knows what may transpire in a fortnight? And by then, I shall be back, and we can all return to Amberford together."

Madge considered the idea but then shook her head. "I don't think Julie will agree. She wants to go home."

"Since when have you ever let Julie make such decisions?" Phyllis teased. "Don't tell me, Madge Branscombe, that you are growing soft!"

"Everyone else around me seems to be changing," Madge sighed as she pulled herself to her feet, "so why shouldn't I?"

# 36

MADGE BRANSCOMBE DID NOT CHANGE NEARLY AS much as Phyllis had thought, for she remained as firm with her daughter as she always had, hardening herself against Julie's heartfelt desire to go home. "We *must* stay, for a little while at least," she told her daughter. "With Phyllis and Smallwood gone off to Scotland, Tris and Cleo have no one left to help them with their wedding plans but us."

"But Mama," Julie objected, "the wedding will not be held until fall. Phyllis will be back in plenty of time to make arrangements."

"You don't understand, my love. These matters cannot wait. Weddings, especially fashionable ones of this sort, must be planned months in advance. I promised to help Cleo choose a pattern for her gown. And Phyllis has asked me to make the decisions regarding the date, the guest list, the menu, the wines and all sorts of details. Don't look so stricken, dearest. I promise we won't remain in town one day longer than necessary."

Julie, as usual, surrendered to her mother's pressure with as good grace as her depressed spirits permitted. She did everything her mother suggested without argument. She shopped for gloves and bonnets at the Pantheon Bazaar. She allowed herself to be fitted for two new gowns. She went to the opera at Covent Garden, to the theater at the Haymarket, to a dinner-dance at the home of Lord and Lady Hertford and an excursion to Vauxhall Gardens under the escort of the cocky young Horace Chalmondeley, all in one week. She was sampling all the delights of London social life and feeling absolutely miserable.

Tris and Cleo, on the other hand, were enjoying themselves immensely. Besides being feted by all their acquaintances every evening, they spent every day together in pleasurable activities. They rode in the park, drove to the country for picnics, visited the Elgin marbles, went to the races and shopped for the dozens of items—such as china and linen and plate—that a betrothed couple would need in their new lives. Tris had never before realized that London offered so many delightful things to do.

It was on one of these shopping expeditions that Tris ran into Lord Canfield. He and Cleo had gone to a linen-draper's to choose fabric for the bed hangings in their bridal bedchamber, but Tris, bored with this feminine chore, had excused himself to go outside and stretch his legs. He was strolling down the street, whistling cheerfully, when he saw Canfield coming toward him. He had not seen him since he'd landed the fellow a facer at the fair. "I say, Peter, old man," he shouted in excited greeting, "what a piece of luck! I've been hoping I'd run into you."

"Have you?" Peter asked, shaking his hand. "Why is that?"

"To apologize, of course."

"Apologize? Whatever for?"

Tris made a rueful face. "You know what for. For making a deuced cake of myself that day at the fair."

"There's no need for apologies," Peter assured him. "I goaded you into it, you know. Besides, the whole incident is ancient history . . . of no importance now."

"You're right, of course," Tris said, falling into step beside him, "especially since everything's turned out so well. Have you heard the news? We're betrothed at last."

"I supposed as much." Peter offered his hand again. "Congratulations, Tris. You're a damned lucky fellow."

"I know it very well. I say, Peter, would you care to come and give your best to the bride-to-be? At this very moment she's choosing fabric at the draper's, right there up the street."

Peter, tempted to catch a glimpse of Julie again, hesitated for a moment. But then he thought better of it and shook his head. "No, I'd better be getting along. Besides, I gave her my good wishes when I saw her at the Chalmondeleys' the other night."

"At the Chalmondeleys'?" Tris blinked at him, puzzled. "But she didn't attend—"

At that moment, however, Cleo came running up to him, a fabric sample in her hand. "Tris, wait," she said a bit breathlessly. "What do you think of this pattern for the—?" Then she looked up. "Goodness!" she exclaimed. *"Peter?"*

Peter tipped his hat and bowed over the smiling girl's hand. "Cleo, my dear, how very nice to see you! Are you helping the happy couple choose their trousseau?"

"Couple?" Now, Cleo too was puzzled. "What couple?"

"Why, Tris and—" All at once Peter stiffened and stared from one to the other. "Good God! Can I have been so mistaken? Are *you* the bride-to-be?"

"Yes, of course she is," Tris said, laughing at Peter's discomfiture. "Didn't I say so?"

"No, confound it, you didn't," Peter said, a pulse beginning to throb in his temples. "I simply assumed . . ."

"That it was Julie?" Cleo asked, her smile broadening.

"Yes." His brow furrowed as he tried to adjust to this startling revelation. "I should have known better than to make assumptions."

"Well, now that you know," Tris grinned, "don't you think you should offer my betrothed your good wishes?"

"Yes, of course," Peter said somewhat absently. "You know you *both* have my best wishes." Forcing himself to concentrate on the present moment instead of the confusion in his mind, he bent down and kissed Cleo's cheek. "I am truly happy for you, Cleo. Truly."

"Thank you," the glowing girl said. "I know you are."

Tris slapped him on the shoulder. "Come and join us

for a luncheon at Gunther's. We can reveal all the lurid details of our rocky courtship over one of their chocolate pastries."

"No, thank you, Tris. Much as I'd like to hear the tale, let's make it another time. I must be off." With another tip of his hat and another murmur of congratulations, he started down the street. The betrothed couple, looking after him, saw him pause at the corner as if uncertain of his direction.

"She's still in town, you know," Cleo called after him, a smiling glint in her eyes.

Peter stopped and turned. "Is she?"

Cleo nodded. "At the Fenton."

A slow grin suffused his face. "Cleo, you're a peach!" he said. "Thank you. I'm on my way."

# 37

PETER'S HIGH SPIRITS DID NOT LAST LONG. WHEN HE arrived at the Fenton, he learned that the Branscombe ladies were out. He had to wait for them. This delay gave him time to think. As he sat in the lobby impatiently tapping a foot, he began to realize that there was less reason for rejoicing than he'd first believed. True, Julie was not betrothed; that was the news that had sent his spirits aloft. But whatever made him conclude that she would be happy about it? If she truly loved Tris—and he'd long ago convinced himself that she did—she would now be heartbroken. She might, of course, turn to him for consolation, but was that the sort of reaction he wanted? Could he accept being second choice?

He was mulling over the answer to that question when the ladies walked in. They were carrying parcels, so they'd evidently been shopping. They both looked tired. Peter, whose cogitations had left him feeling decidedly ill at ease, rose and approached them. "Good afternoon," he said, removing his hat. "Lady Branscombe, how do you do?"

Madge quickly recovered from her initial surprise. "Well enough," she said coldly. "You aren't here to call on *us*, are you?"

"On your daughter, yes," he said, smiling down at Julie, who was regarding him, white-faced.

"My daughter has nothing to say to you, my lord," the protective mother declared. "Please excuse us."

Lady Branscombe was acting the dragon again, Peter thought in irritation. How many times would he have to

202

fight her before he could win the girl? "I hope you won't find me rude, ma'am, but I'd rather learn from Julie herself whether or not she'll speak to me."

"Julie will do as I say," Madge Branscombe snapped. "Come along, girl. I'm much too weary to be standing about."

"Then go upstairs, please, Mama," Julie said with quiet decision. "I'd like to visit with Lord Canfield. He's given me no reason to refuse to speak to him."

The dragon reddened in chagrin. "See here, Julie—!"

Julie faced her mother firmly. "Mama, do go along. I'll be up shortly."

Madge glared at her daughter in a fury. Julie met her eyes in a speechless battle of wills. Then Madge's eyes fell. "Very well, do as you wish," she muttered in defeat and marched off to the stairs.

Peter grinned down at Julie. "Good for you," he cheered. "You've learned how to battle the dragon yourself, I see."

She returned his smile with a small, rueful one of her own. "One has to grow up sometime, I suppose," she said.

"No, that's not so. Not everyone manages to do it. I'm very proud of you." He took her elbow and guided her to a sofa. "Shall we sit here? That potted plant will shield us from view."

She nodded and seated herself nervously on the edge of the sofa. He took a place beside her. "I had to see you, Julie. I just learned, this very afternoon, that you and Tris are not betrothed after all. Needless to say, I'm astounded."

She looked down at her hands. "I tried to tell you at the ball the other evening . . ."

"Yes, I realize that now. I'm sorry I had to be so abrupt that night."

"Not at all. You had a promise to keep. I completely understood."

"But that's beside the point. What troubles me, Julie, is *your* situation. I can't help wondering what happened to our plans. I thought that Tris would surely offer for you. I still have a stiff jaw to prove it."

She tried to laugh but couldn't. "Nothing untoward happened," she explained dispiritedly. "We discovered we didn't suit, that's all."

"I see." But he didn't see at all. He tried to look at her face, but with her head bent, the brim of her bonnet hid it from him. "I'm truly sorry. I thought you suited very well."

"Yes, everyone did. We were all mistaken."

"I hope . . ." He hesitated briefly and then plunged on. "I hope you're . . . er . . . reconciled to the outcome."

"To Tris's betrothal, you mean?" She turned her head and looked up at him with convincing sincerity. "Of course I am. I'm very happy for him. For both of them."

He was more than eager to believe her. With a wave of hope surging through him, he took her hands in his. "Are you sure, Julie?" he asked earnestly. "You've had only a very short time to recover from what must have been a painful experience."

She pulled her hands from his grasp and turned her face away again. "Please believe me, Peter, there was *nothing* to recover *from.*"

Nothing to recover from? What did she mean? He stared at her, taking in her bent head with its shrouding bonnet, the graceful line of her neck and shoulders turned away from him, the clenched hands in her lap. Everything in her posture seemed to indicate withdrawal from him. He did not know what to make of her. She seemed to be telling him she hadn't cared for Tris at all, but if she was, why was she so distant, so detached? He wished he could find some way to penetrate these defenses she seemed to have erected between them. "In that case, Julie," he said, forcing himself to sound cheerful, "perhaps you'd agree to come driving with me tomorrow. We could ride up north toward Isling—" He stopped abruptly, for she'd thrown him such a startled, offended look that his tongue was stilled by it.

"The . . . the two of us, you mean?" she asked awkwardly.

"Well, yes," he answered, baffled. "Unless you'd like to take your mother along."

She didn't smile at the quip. Instead, she rose slowly and looked down at him. "Lord Canfield," she said in a kind of trembling formality, "you've been a good friend to me, and I hope you will continue to be. But you surely must understand that it would be improper for me to accept any such invitations from you."

He got to his feet, more bemused than ever. "But I *don't* understand. In what way improper?"

She shook her head, unable or unwilling to reply. "I'm very tired," she said, turning away, "so let me wish you good day. It was kind of you to come, but now please excuse me."

He followed her and grasped her hand. "Just a minute, Julie, please! May I call on you tomorrow? I'd like to speak to you again. There seems to be a great deal I don't understand."

Again she removed her hand from his grasp. "I think it would be best," she said, not meeting his eyes, "if we don't meet again like this. Good-bye, my lord." And she hurried off to the stairs.

He stared after her, dumfounded. Something about her remarks had seemed strangely askew, but he couldn't put his finger on what it was. But one thing was glaringly clear. Though she'd suggested that she no longer loved Tris—and perhaps never had—she certainly didn't care for Peter Granard, Viscount Canfield. She wanted him to remain her *friend!* Remembering those words of hers, he gave a derisive, self-deprecating laugh. For the first time in his life, he'd been soundly rejected by a woman. *I hope you'll always remain my friend.* Weren't those the words every woman used to rid herself of a suitor she didn't want?

Julie, meanwhile, ran up the stairs, brushing away the tears that she'd managed to hold back during the interview. How could he have behaved in that intimate way,

she asked herself, when he knew he would soon be betrothed to his "Kat"? She would have liked to fling that
question in his face, but she'd been too reticent. Besides,
if a betrothal had not yet been officially announced, did it
officially exist? One couldn't even mention it except in
whispered gossip. Perhaps that's why he felt justified in
seeking her company—because the betrothal was not yet
official. But from her point of view it was quite wrong of
him. To show attentions to one woman when you are betrothed to another is the act of a . . . a cad.

Already in pain from the fact of his attachment to that
beautiful red-headed creature, Julie now found herself in
greater pain because of his thoughtlessness. And the only
way she could think of to ease the terrible ache inside her
was to throw herself across her bed and sob her heart out.

But even that sad solace was denied her. Her mother
was sitting on her bed waiting for her. "What did he
want?" she asked, still angry at Julie's disobedience. And
then she saw her daughter's tearstained face. "Julie!" she
cried in alarm.

"I'm all right, Mama, you needn't worry," Julie said,
dashing the wetness from her cheeks with the back of her
hand and speaking as resolutely as she could. "But I do
have something to say to you. You may stay here in London and help Tris and Cleo as long as you like. But as for
me, I'm going h-home. Today!"

# 38

THE FIRST THING JULIE SAW ON HER RETURN HOME was the pianoforte. His pianoforte. The very sight of it troubled her. He'd given it to her as a wedding gift, but she was not going to have a wedding. On the other hand, he was. Hadn't her mother learned, on good authority, that he was going to marry Miss Catherine "Kat" Marquard? His deuced Kat was the one who should have the instrument. Julie had possession on false grounds.

Besides, she, Julie Branscombe, no longer wanted it. Every time she saw it, her heart constricted achingly in her chest. When she sat down to play, she sooner or later found herself crying. The pianoforte, magnificent as it was, had become a symbol of rejection and grief. She had to rid herself of it.

After dwelling on the matter for several days, she decided that as soon as his engagement was announced in the *Times,* she would send the piano back to Wycklands and, in a congratulatory letter to him, inform him of it. Every day, for the next three weeks, she pored over the announcements in the newspaper, searching in vain for his name. She wondered why, if the betrothal was as certain to come to pass as her mother had said, it was taking so long to make it public.

She even wondered if she should write to the brash young Horace Chalmondeley to ask if he'd had any news of the betrothal. Ever since she'd danced with him at the ball, the silly young fellow had been besieging her with love letters. She'd never answered a single one, but her curiosity and suspense regarding Peter's impending nup-

207

tials were so great that she was tempted to contact the boy. But of course she did not.

After three weeks, however, her mother came home in a state of considerable excitement. She'd been visiting Phyllis and Smallwood at Enders Hall, as she'd done every day since their return, and had heard some news. "He's back," she said to her daughter as if announcing a catastrophe.

"Who's back?" Julie asked, not particularly curious.

"Canfield. He's come to pack up his library. Evidently he's decided to sell the property." Unmindful of Julie's immediate stiffening, she babbled on. "I, for one, am delighted he's giving it up. Perhaps now we'll get a new bachelor at Wycklands, someone with better sense, who'd appreciate a true gem when he saw her."

"And perhaps," Julie said as she fled from her mother's diatribe, "it will be bought by a huge family with a drunkard of a father, a whining mother and seven noisy children all under the age of ten."

"Really, Julie," her mother shouted after her, "I don't know what's come over you lately. You are becoming a positive hoyden."

The "hoyden" ran up to her bedroom and shut the door. She had to think about this new development. If Peter had truly returned to Wycklands, perhaps this would be the proper time to send back the piano. Why not? she asked herself. He himself would be there to receive it. What better time would there be?

She sat down at her writing table to pen a note. She started and discarded three before she wrote one she considered acceptable. *To His Lordship, the Viscount Canfield,* she finally wrote. *I have never felt deserving of the magnificent pianoforte you were generous enough to bestow upon me on the occasion of what you believed was my imminent marriage. Since that marriage never came to pass, I feel that my continued possession of it is under false pretenses. You, on the other hand, being yourself anticipating an imminent marriage, will no doubt wish to present it to your bride. I am therefore sending it back with my best wishes for your happiness. Yours most sincerely, Juliet Branscombe.*

That done, she went back downstairs and asked Horsham to arrange for four men and a cart to transport the instrument (and her note) to Wycklands that very afternoon. She hoped she could handle the matter quietly on her own, but when the men came to remove the piano, her mother heard the commotion. She came running down from the upstairs sitting room where she'd been reading, demanding to know what was going on.

"I am returning the pianoforte to Canfield," Julie explained. "You yourself told me that any wedding gifts I'd received had to be returned."

To her relief, her mother made no objection. "It's the right thing to do," she sighed as she went back upstairs, "though it's a lovely thing to have to part with."

Julie watched the carters carry it away with a strange feeling in her innards. It was relief, she told herself. Decided relief. She was truly glad to see it go. Truly. Then why, she was forced to ask herself, were these tears coursing down her face?

Self-pity was a quality she scorned, so she tried to shake away the doldrums that this business with the piano had brought upon her. A vigorous ride along the river might be, she decided, the very thing to lift her spirit. She ran upstairs to change into riding clothes. As she started down again, in her old, shabby skirt and with her hair loose, she was startled to discover that an angry Lord Canfield was brushing past the butler and storming in. *"Peter!"* she gasped, freezing into place halfway down the stairs. What rotten luck, she thought, that he should see her looking so deucedly unkempt.

But he was too out of temper to take any notice of her appearance. "What, ma'am, is the meaning of this?" he shouted, waving a crushed piece of notepaper at her.

"Is that my note?" she inquired, her knees a-tremble.

"If this gibberish can be called a note, then I suppose it is. It has your name on it."

"I don't see why you call it gibberish. I thought I'd

written it in plain English and, if I may be a bit immodest, that it was rather felicitously phrased."

"Felicitously phrased? Are you completely *shatter-brained?*" He took several angry paces about the entry hall to gain control of himself before turning back and looking up at her again. "In the first place, ma'am, you know perfectly well that I wanted to give you the instrument before there was any talk of marrying Tris. So this business of possessing it on false pretenses is utter nonsense."

"Well, you did write in your note that it was a wedding gift."

"A mere excuse, as well you know! And what is this idiotic jibber-jabber about *my* imminent marriage and giving the piano to my bride?"

Her legs were so unsteady she had to cling to the bannister. "Well, I know you haven't officially announced it as yet," she explained uneasily, "so perhaps it was not in the best of taste to mention it, but—"

"Mention *what?*" he roared. "I don't know what you're babbling about."

She drew herself up angrily. "Dash it, my lord, I don't babble! And I don't like being shouted at, either. I am speaking of your . . . your almost-intended, Miss Marquard."

"Who?" He gaped at her, befuddled. "Do you mean my cousin Kat?"

"Your c-cousin?" Julie stammered, taken aback.

"Catherine Marquard is my nuisance of a cousin whom my aunt in Yorkshire insists I must escort about town on her once-a-year visit. *Why* would I want to give her a *piano?* She doesn't even play!"

"But . . ." Julie took a gulping breath, almost afraid to go on. ". . . Are you not intending to . . . to marry her?"

"Marry *Kat?*" Peter gave a snorting laugh. "I'd sooner wed one of those whirling dervishes from the east! I can't abide the chit more than half an hour at a time." Then, with a quick, gasping intake of breath, he gazed up at her, a light of comprehension dawning in his eyes. Suddenly a number of pieces of the puzzle of Julie Branscombe were beginning to fall into place. "Is *that* why you behaved so strangely at the Fenton? Because you thought I was getting *married?*"

She felt her heart jump right up into her throat. "Aren't you?" she asked, choked. "Have we perhaps . . . gotten it wrong? That is . . . can we have heard the wrong name?"

He didn't answer for what seemed an eternity. He merely continued to gaze up at her with a look of intense speculation. Then, when she thought she could not bear the silence a moment longer, he spoke. "Julie, come down here," he said quietly. "Please!"

She started down, slowly and unsteadily, as he came round to the foot of the stairway. When she reached the third step from the bottom, he held out his arms. Without knowing quite what she did, she leaped into them. He held her in a crushing embrace, her feet high off the ground, and kissed her, long and hard, with the intensity that comes from passion long restrained. When they had no breath left, he set her down. "I love you, Julie," he whispered in her ear. "Almost from the first moment I laid eyes on you. I could *never* wed anyone else. I want to marry you even if it means taking second place to Tris in your heart."

*"Second place?"* She broke from his hold and stamped her foot. "Dash it, Peter, I could wring your *neck.* I've been trying to tell you from the moment you started to push me into Tris's arms that it's *you* I love, not Tris."

Even now he couldn't quite believe it. "That can't be so," he said, peering at her suspiciously. "You and he were so . . . so close. It seemed to me you could almost read each other's minds."

"Balderdash. Neither of you could read my mind. He was trying to teach me how to win you, just as you were trying to teach me how to win him. And I, fool that I was, tried to follow the advice of both of you. I was like a marionette, with two idiotic puppet masters pulling the strings."

"My poor darling," he exclaimed, appalled. "And when in the course of this farce did you decide you loved me and not him?"

Somehow the question infuriated her. He still didn't understand her feelings. But as usual, it was hard for her to express them, especially with his eyes fixed so lovingly on her face. "Peter, you . . . you buffleheaded fool," she said, turning and addressing the newel post, "why won't you *listen* to me? I've never loved anyone but you. Not anyone. Not Tris, not Ronny Kenting, not even the Honorable Horace Chalmondeley, who's been importuning me by post to marry him ever since I danced with him at the Chalmondeley ball."

Peter snorted. "Good God, *Chalmondeley?* I should hope not, indeed. The fellow's a looby."

She laughed and turned back to him. "The truth is, my lord," she said shyly to the buttons of his coat, "that you took hold of my heart the night you sauntered into the assembly and I got my first glimpse of you. I've tried to tell you so many times in every way I could think of— except to say the words."

He pulled her into his arms again and brushed back her wild strands of hair. "My sweet, beautiful Julie, you *should* have said them. A buffleheaded fool like me needs to have things said plainly, I'm afraid."

"I was . . . shy."

He lifted her chin and made her look up at him. "I hope, my girl, that you'll never be shy with me again."

"I think I'm much improved in that regard. In fact, I'm almost growing bold. Almost bold enough to ask . . . but perhaps I'd better not . . ."

"Go ahead, girl, be bold and ask it," he insisted.

"Well, then, my lord," she said, tossing him a daring grin, "how long is it going to be before you kiss me again?"

It took no time at all for him to comply. They were in the midst of a shockingly close embrace when Lady Branscombe's voice came to them from somewhere close by. "Julie, where on earth are you?" she was calling. "Horsham tells me that that clunch Canfield has sent the pianoforte *back again!*" Her step came closer and then stopped altogether. She'd caught sight of the embrace. "Oh, good *heavens! Canfield,* you cad, release that girl at once! Or . . . perhaps not. If someone doesn't tell me what has passed, I shall positively *swoon!*"

Julie lifted her head but didn't take her eyes from the face of the man who still held her in a crushing grip. "Don't be so silly, Mama. You never swoon. And as for you, my lord"—she held him off and, with eyes full of laughter, regarded him with head cocked—*"did* you do something so quixotically idiotic as to bring the piano *back?"*

He shrugged sheepishly. "Well, how was I to know the altercation I'd embarked on this afternoon would conclude with you in my arms? And since we're going to be wed anyway—and very soon too if I have my way—what difference does it make where the blasted piano stays?"

*If you enjoyed this book, take advantage of this special offer. Subscribe now and...*

# Get a Historical

## No Obligation

If you enjoy reading the very best in historical romantic fiction...romances that set back the hands of time to those bygone days with strong virile heros and passionate heroines ...then you'll want to subscribe to the True Value Historical Romance Home Subscription Service. Now that you have read one of the best historical romances around today, we're sure you'll want more of the same fiery passion, intimate romance and historical settings that set these books apart from all others.

Each month the editors of True Value select the four *very best* novels from America's leading publishers of romantic fiction. We have made arrangements for you to preview them in your home *Free* for 10 days. And with the first four books you

receive, we'll send you a FREE book as our introductory gift. No Obligation!

**FREE HOME DELIVERY**

We will send you the four best and newest historical romances as soon as they are published to preview FREE for 10 days (in many cases you may even get them before they arrive in the book stores). If for any reason you decide not to keep them, just return them and owe nothing. But if you like them as much as we think you will, you'll pay just $4.00 each and save at *least* $.50 each off the cover price. (Your savings are *guaranteed* to be at least $2.00 each month.) There is NO postage and handling—or other hidden charges. There are no minimum number of books to buy and you may cancel at any time.

# FREE

# Romance

## (a $4.50 value)

### Send in the Coupon Below

To get your FREE historical romance and start saving, fill out the coupon below and mail it today. As soon as we receive it we'll send you your FREE Book along with your first month's selections.

---

Mail To: **True Value Home Subscription Services, Inc. P.O. Box 5235 120 Brighton Road, Clifton, New Jersey 07015-5235**

YES! I want to start previewing the very best historical romances being published today. Send me my FREE book along with the first month's selections. I understand that I may look them over FREE for 10 days. If I'm not absolutely delighted I may return them and owe nothing. Otherwise I will pay the low price of just $4.00 each: a total $16.00 (at *least* an $18.00 value) and save at least $2.00. Then each month I will receive four brand new novels to preview as soon as they are published for the same low price. I can always return a shipment and I may cancel this subscription at any time with no obligation to buy even a single book. In any event the FREE book is mine to keep regardless.

Name _____

Street Address _____ Apt. No. _____

City _____ State _____ Zip Code _____

Telephone _____

Signature _____
(if under 18 parent or guardian must sign)

Terms and prices subject to change. Orders subject
to acceptance by True Value Home Subscription
Services, Inc.

11785-4